I0537019

The
Wrong War

An action adventure novel by

James A. Graves, Jr.

The Wrong War © James A. Graves, Jr.

ALL RIGHTS RESERVED
All names, characters and incidents, depicted in this book are totally the products of the author's imagination. Any resemblance to actual events, locales, organizations, or persons, living or dead, is entirely coincidental.

No part of this book may be produced in any form, by photocopying or by any electronic or mechanical means, including information storage or retrieval systems, without permission in writing from both the copyright owner and the publisher of this book, except for the minimum words needed for review.

ISBN: 978-0-9861109-3-1
Library of Congress Control Number: 2018957501
Published by Global Authors Publications

Filling the GAP in publishing

Edited by Kathy Barnett
Interior Design by KathleenWalls
Cover Design by Vin Libassi

MAYDAY!

Zeke felt the thud and heard the explosion as the right engine separated from the fuselage. The fasten seatbelt sign came on, but he was already buckled. Smoke began to seep into the cabin as he tightened his belt and looked around to see if he could see any visible fire that he might be able to fight with the cabin fire extinguisher.

Then the captain came on the intercom and said, *"We've lost number two, literally, and we're going down. When I say, 'brace, brace, brace', assume the position."*

Zeke watched through the window as the earth rushed up to meet the doomed Citation. Then the aircrew managed to control the descent and level the aircraft out slightly.

"You're looking good." The copilot said to the pilot. "That high plateau straight ahead is your best bet. The chart shows 6000 feet elevation. Looks like mostly grassland with scattered shrubs."

"Let's hope they're friendly shrubs." The pilot replied.

Then the copilot called over the radio. *"Mayday! Mayday! Mayday! Omaha four one foxtrot. Mayday! Mayday! Mayday! We're going down twenty-five miles northwest of St. Johns, Arizona. I repeat, Mayday! Mayday! Mayday! Omaha four one foxtrot is going down twenty-five miles northwest of St. Johns."*

Then the pilot called over the intercom, *"Brace! Brace! Brace!"*

Zeke leaned forward, put his head between his knees, wrapped his arms over his head and stretched his legs forward. Seconds later the Citation hit the ground…

AKNOWLEDGEMENT

Special thanks to Robert "Bob" Collins for his idea for this story

Many thanks to my friend, Vin Libassi, graphic artist extraordinaire, for yet another awesome cover. Sir, you are the master.

OTHER BOOKS BY JAMES A. GRAVES, Jr.

Aftermath I: The Fight For Survival
Aftermath II: The Deadly Game
Assembly Line Justice: The American War On Drugs
Assembly Line Justice: How The American War On Drugs Has
Failed (2nd edition)

Chapter One
Welcome to the Sonoran Desert

Zeke Sikes leaned back from his spotter scope, rubbed his eyes and sighed. He pulled a red bandana from his back pocket and wiped the sweat from his forehead, grabbed a bottle of water from the ice chest sitting beside him, opened it and drank half the bottle. Then he poured the remainder onto his bandana and pressed it over his face and tired eyes.

"My ass is numb," he mumbled from underneath the wet bandana, then removed it and draped it over a nearby brittle bush, blooming with yellow flowers.

He stared at the bandana for a moment, then commented sarcastically, "It'll probably be dry in five minutes." He then shifted his body slightly before pressing his right eye onto the scope's eye piece once again.

A few feet away, U.S. Border Patrol Agent Luís Gonzales, a tall, lean but muscular, dark-tanned young man with dark eyes and American Indian features, listened but said nothing.

As Zeke slowly scanned a wide swath of the desert landscape, he complained again, "If I see another coyote…"

"Whatcha gonna do, shoot 'em?!" Luís chuckled at his own comment.

Gonzales was assigned to the Ajo Station, Tucson Sector of U.S. Customs and Border Patrol in Why, Arizona. His present duty was the liaison officer for U.S. Drug Enforcement Administration Special Agent Zeke Sikes. Sikes had recently been given orders to report to the Ajo Station for a temporary duty assignment of undetermined nature and length. Presently he was surveilling from a low hilltop position about 100 feet above the Sonoran Desert floor, which provided him a good view of the U.S.-Mexico border fence and beyond.

"Funny man," Zeke replied without taking his eye off the scope. "It's not bad enough that I'm stuck here, slowly broiling in this desert heat while you're stretched out in the shade with your cap pulled over your face, having a nice afternoon siesta. Do you have to be a smart ass, too?"

"I can't help it, Doc. It's in my DNA. My family is full of smart asses."

"Why am I not surprised?"

In the distance a cactus wren sang its raw, scratchy song. High overhead, a red-tailed hawk made lazy circles in the still afternoon sky, crying hauntingly as it searched the desert floor for a tasty kangaroo rat, or perhaps a lizard for its evening meal.

Luís stood up and stretched, then rubbed his hand over his close-cropped, dark hair and dusted off his uniform with his green Border Patrol ball cap. "I'd like to point out, sir, that you are also in the shade of this beautiful mesquite tree."

"We may be in the shade, but I'm still hot," Zeke replied flatly, still peering through the spotter scope.

Then he leaned back, sneezed and looked up into the mesquite tree, "I must be allergic to these flowers."

Suddenly a flash of yellow caught their attention and the men watched as a bright yellow cloudless giant sulfur butterfly fluttered by.

"Desert plants are aggressive and produce a lot of pollen," Luís said, and then put on his sunglasses. "Well Doc, I say it's time to knock off. I hear a cold beer calling my name. Maybe two. Besides, your ass is numb."

"I can't argue with that," Zeke said as he got to his feet, dusted off his tan jumpsuit and rubbed his behind.

Zeke was slightly shorter than his companion and, at the age of 32, five years older. He had a medium build, a light complexion with typical Midwestern features, sandy brown hair cut military-style, and flashing green eyes.

Reaching into the pocket on his left sleeve, Zeke retrieved his aviator sun glasses and put them on. Then he looked out across the area that he had been methodically searching through his scope for the past six hours. "Scratch one more wasted day." He sighed. "I request an assignment to Central America and I end up here."

"Don't take it so personal, Doc. We're actually getting paid to do this."

Zeke retrieved his hat; a black ball cap emblazoned with the letters "DEA," hanging from a mesquite limb, then put it on and looked at Luís in amazement. "And you would do this for free?!"

It was the spring bloom, and the Sonoran Desert was painted

with yellow flowers blooming on almost every plant. Luís looked out across the distance, surveying the severely-clear late-afternoon sky, the forest of saguaro, cholla, staghorn and ocotillo cactus scattered among the yellow-tinted green paloverde and mesquite trees, and the endless sea of waist-high, dark green creosote bushes, commonly called greasewood, covering the "Green Desert" in all directions as far as the eye could see.

"Man, look at that sky! It seems like you can see forever."

He breathed in deeply and continued, "Doc, have you ever smelled greasewood on the breeze from a summer thunderstorm? Or watched a herd of pronghorn antelope running across the desert? Or listened to a male Gambles quail calling from the tip of an ocotillo cactus?

"I gotta make a living, just like everybody else, but I love the desert. I'd rather be out here than anywhere else in the world. To me, this is home."

Zeke smiled and slapped Luís on the shoulder, "You're a lucky man, Amigo; I envy you."

Zeke paused for a moment, and then asked, "How about you and I remove ourselves from this place? I'll get the tripod and the ice chest if you'll get the other stuff."

"Deal," Luís replied, then removed the spotter scope from the tripod, stowed it in the equipment case and grabbed Zeke's bandana. "Hey, Doc, you're right, it's dry!"

"What did you expect?" Zeke replied as he picked up the tripod and walked away, "It's been in the kiln…"

As they made their way down the hill toward the white and green Border Patrol truck, Luís, following Zeke a short distance behind, posed a question; "Doc, you do realize this is only mid-April, right?"

"I noticed that this morning when I checked my email." Zeke replied dryly.

"Man, you don't miss a thing; but then you are a trained observer."

"Yes, I am; professionally trained at the DEA Academy on Quantico."

"Did that training include desert survival?"

"No, it did not. But I asked about that when I received my orders."

Both men paused and watched as a startled pair of doves noisily flew up and dashed away.

Then Zeke continued, "I was told that desert survival training was only authorized for foreign assignments."

"Well that sounds like a government operation—is the DEA aware that the Southwest U.S. has deserts?"

Zeke ignored the sarcasm, and Luís continued, "I just wanted to warn you that it's not hot yet. Hell, it's not even warm yet. Next month will be a bit warm. And June will be damned hot."

"Lovely," Zeke replied sarcastically. "My orders state that I will be provided desert familiarization by Border Patrol personnel. Since you're my liaison, I'm assuming you're the Border Patrol personnel to whom they refer."

"That's the first I've heard of it," Luís said, sounding both surprised and disappointed. "Nothing like lots of warning—this is definitely a government operation."

"Amigo, exactly what did you mean by 'damned hot'?"

"115 Fahrenheit and higher. Usually in June and July—that's the hottest months. Typical daytime temps May through September will be 95 to 110. And we've seen summers with close to a 100 continuous days of over 100 degrees."

Zeke sighed in exasperation and moaned, "I have been assigned to Hell... I need desert survival training dammit!"

"Well, we're on the Organ Pipe Cactus National Monument right now. Have you been to the museum?"

"I haven't had time to do anything but spot coyotes, road runners, quail, and cotton tail rabbits."

Luís chuckled. "Well, if you ever decide to go hunting, you'll know where the game is. But seriously, the museum has a really informative display of the desert's flora and fauna, including cactus, rattlesnakes and a lots of other stuff. It won't teach you much about how to survive out here, but it's very educational nevertheless. I'll be happy to show you around. How 'bout we go this weekend?"

"Sounds like a good place to start," Zeke replied, then added sarcastically, "And I'll enter it into my training file as ad hock desert survival training."

Luís laughed out loud. "Doc, I love your sense of humor."

As the two men made their way toward the truck, parked about a quarter of a mile away, Luís paused to take a picture of a patch of desert wildflowers. Zeke continued on, making his way down into a narrow arroyo.

Realizing Zeke was out of sight, Luís called out to him, "Hey, Doc! You lost?"

"I'm over here, down in this gulch."

Luís hurried toward the direction of Zeke's voice. When he caught up to him, Zeke was just retrieving another bottle of water from his ice chest.

"Thirsty?"

"Yes, thanks." Zeke tossed him the bottle and reached for another one.

"I decided to walk through here," Zeke explained. "The ground is sandy. I'm tired of walking on rocks and stones."

They were standing in a narrow arroyo lined on either side by mesquite, salt cedar and paloverde trees. From the signs of erosion, it was obvious that rushing water had flowed often and abundantly where they now stood on the dry, white sand.

"There appears to be a lot of dry creeks in the Sonoran Desert," Zeke observed between gulps from his water bottle.

"Yep, you're right, Doc, except this isn't a creek. Around here it's commonly referred to as a wash, but more properly called an arroyo, especially by older Hispanic people. During the Monsoon season flashfloods are common after thunderstorms. Rain runoff will roar through here carrying trees, mud and anything else in its way, even vehicles."

"When is the Monsoon season?"

"It usually starts around the first of July and typically ends in late September. And, Doc, if you want to avoid being considered a pendejo, don't let anyone in the Arizona desert ever hear you call an arroyo a gulch or a creek."

"Pendejo—why would someone consider me a pubic hair?"

"Doc, you translate Spanish literally, don't you? A pendejo is a clueless dumbass."

"Oh. I'll definitely remember that. Since I now know what an arroyo is and the dangers of being in one during the Monsoon season, can we consider this my first lesson in desert survival?"

Luís chuckled. "And local language and customs as well."

"I should've taken a course in colloquial Spanish in addition to the formal Spanish classes," Zeke lamented.

Luís then pointed in the general direction of the truck. "Let's climb out of the arroyo here. We should be pretty close to the truck."

Zeke used his folded tripod as a walking stick and made his way up the low bank of the arroyo. Luís picked up the ice chest, along with the equipment case that he had been carrying, and followed. Upon reaching level ground, Zeke spotted the truck in the distance, partially hidden by creosote bushes and cholla cactus, and began walking in that direction.

Just as Luís climbed out of the arroyo, Zeke looked back toward him and said, "I see the truck, it's this way."

Then he turned back toward the truck and walked directly into a large cholla cactus.

"Ow! Son of a…!" Zeke yelled, "What in the Hell?!"

"Don't move!" Luís yelled back, "The spines will just go deeper."

Dropping the tripod, Zeke pulled his hands away from the cactus and several seed pods, looking like yellow sea urchins, came with him, now firmly attached to his skin by countless, needle-sharp spines. "This damn thing is attacking me!"

"That's why they're called jumping cactus. Stand absolutely still," Luís warned as he retrieved a pair of needle-nosed pliers from one of the small pockets of his dark green uniform pants.

"Damn this hurts!"

"I know. And pulling them out will hurt even more. Those needle-sharp spines are like fish hooks and not easy to remove. Just grit your teeth and brace yourself…"

One by one, Luís removed the seed pods and patiently pulled each spine out of Zeke's hands, arms, legs and torso, while Zeke provided very colorful and descriptive language concerning both the pain and what he thought of cholla cactus, the Sonoran Desert and the DEA.

When all of the cholla spines had been removed, Luís put his pliers away and said, "I think we can consider this your second lesson in desert survival."

As Zeke inspected one of his aching fingers, he replied, "And I'm certain I will never forget it!"

Luís smiled mischievously and said, "I'm guessing you're not going to enter this in your training file?"

Zeke just glared at him.

"I have a first aid kit in the truck if you need it. Unfortunately, there's not much you can do beyond pulling out the spines. Soaking in a warm Epsom Salt bath might help, but I'm guessing that your motel room only has a shower."

Zeke uttered a dismal sigh. Then, cautiously avoiding further contact with the cholla cactus, he carefully picked up his tripod and stood there for a moment looking at the offending cactus in disgust, then began walking toward the truck.

As Luís watched Zeke walking away he called after him; "Oh, by the way, Doc, welcome to the Sonoran Desert."

Zeke didn't bother to comment or look back; he just trudged on toward the truck, grumbling under his breath as he went.

After stowing the equipment in the truck, they drove a short distance south along a narrow, one-lane dirt trail that connected to the Border Patrol Drag Road, a wide, smoothly-maintained dirt ribbon paralleling the border fence, designed to show footprints of illegals crossing into the US.

Then Luís turned west on the Drag Road and followed it for several miles, which brought them to the Port of Entry at Lukeville. There, Luís turned north on Arizona Highway 85 and quickly headed toward Ajo Station in Why.

The trip of only 28 miles from Lukeville to Why (locally referred to as "The Y") seemed like an eternity for Zeke. As he slowly climbed out of the truck, he said in a mournful voice, "I need alcohol."

"Internal or external?"

"Internal."

"Now you're talkin'!

"Would you mind if I ride with you?" Zeke asked sheepishly. "My hands hurt too much to drive."

"No problem."

Fifteen minutes later they were in Luís' custom Silverado four by four headed for Ajo.

After a few minutes of silence, Luís spoke. "Doc, when we get to Ajo, I'll stop by the pharmacy. I'm sure they can recommend some kind of ointment that might help."

"Thanks Amigo, I appreciate that."

Luís parked in front of the pharmacy and said, "Hang on, I'll be right back."

Shortly Luís emerged with a small bag and handed it to Zeke. "The pharmacist said to apply this ointment to the wounds. It'll ease the pain and help prevent soreness. Also, if any redness or swelling doesn't go away in a few days, stop by and talk to her."

Zeke looked into the bag and said, "Thanks Amigo. What do I owe you?"

"Don't worry about it Doc. I think you've already paid enough."

Zeke looked at his hands and replied, "Hard to argue with that…"

As Luís backed out and drove away, he turned to Zeke, "You hungry?"

"I could eat."

"I'm starved. You like Mexican?"

"Sure."

"Great! I know just the place."

A few minutes later Luís parked in front of Marcella's Café and Bakery. "This place is great. It's like eating at my mom's. And the beer's cold."

As the two men walked in, every eye was on them. One of the staff said, "Hi, Luís."

He returned the greeting and asked, "Could we have two Coronas please?"

Presently the beers were brought to their table, along with menus, salsa and tortilla chips.

Zeke took a long drink of his beer, "Mmmm, that is cold." And then began perusing the menu.

Shortly, Zeke became aware that everyone in the restaurant was still looking at him. He lowered his menu slightly, leaned forward and quietly whispered, "What is everyone staring at?"

Luís, busily munching away at the chips and salsa, replied nonchalantly without even looking up from the menu, "You."

"Me?"

Then he lowered his menu and looked at Zeke. "Most folks around here are not accustomed to seeing a DEA Special Agent in the flesh."

Zeke paused for a moment, contemplating the answer, then glanced upwards at his hat, slowly removed it and placed it on his lap.

"Have some chips and salsa…" Luís suggested.

Zeke selected a chip, scooped up a generous portion of salsa, popped it in his mouth and began chewing.

"Mmm, this is very flavorful." Then he swallowed, and added, "And spicy!" as he reached for his beer.

8

Luís smiled, "You are definitely a gringo."

Zeke emptied his beer and replied, "Gringo. That basically means 'white boy', correct?"

"Right. But it's not derogatory, just a Spanish slang term for a fine, Irish-American like yourself."

"Actually, my ancestry is German, but that's beside the point. I'm obviously not Hispanic."

"So, you think this salsa is spicy?"

Zeke dipped another chip into the salsa and replied, "Yes. It's good, but spicy."

"Then my mom's salsa would send you to the emergency room."

"This salsa is seriously not that spicy?"

"It's about as warm as most people are comfortable with. The rest of us just have to deal with it. Besides, the delicious flavor makes up the difference."

"I like my dad's horseradish sauce. He makes it using fresh horseradish that he grows in his garden. At times it's so strong it will curl the hair in your nose."

"I've never eaten fresh horseradish sauce," Luís admitted.

"It has to be experienced. It seems to explode in your sinuses, and makes your eyes water. The effect is similar to Chinese hot mustard. Either one could be used to torture captured enemy prisoners."

"Yeah, I've had the Chinese mustard rush," Luís replied, "That can painful."

They both ordered more beer, then ordered food and ate. By the end of their dinner, Zeke had finished off six Coronas and was working on a seventh.

"Thanks for introducing me to this place, the food is delicious."

"Like I said, it's just like eating at my mom's."

"Your mom must be one helluva cook."

"She is indeed. You'll have to come with me the next time I go to my folks place. Mom and Dad live in Payson."

"My folks live in Michigan. My mom is a good cook, too. Mostly German dishes and Midwestern food."

Zeke then finished his seventh Corona and commented, "You know, I'm not feeling like a pincushion any longer."

"Well, if I had just finished off seven Coronas in just over an hour I probably wouldn't be feeling much either."

"How about another one?" Zeke offered.

"No thanks, two is my limit when I'm driving. And I think you've probably had enough as well. Why don't I drop you off at your motel?"

"Capitol idea, Amigo," Zeke replied as he grabbed his cap and picked up the check. "I've got this… remember I'm on per diem."

As Luís dropped Zeke off, he said, "I'll see you first thing in the morning for breakfast."

Zeke focused on the door and just waved as he walked.

Luís waited until Zeke actually made it into his room.

Chapter Two
A Trip Home

Above the predawn darkness of the Pozo Redondo Mountain Range east of Ajo the starry horizon was painted with the translucent purplish-blue glow of twilight. Luís sat on the tailgate of his truck, sipping coffee, enjoying the peaceful early-morning stillness of the desert and watching the birth of a new day. Nearby a solitary great horned owl quietly hooted.

Momentarily, Zeke emerged from his hotel room.

"Good morning, Doc!" Luís greeted Zeke enthusiastically.

"Good morning, Amigo," Zeke replied sleepily. "What time is it anyway?"

"It's 5:15; you have a clock radio and a smartphone, and you ask me what time it is?"

"I set both alarms for 4 a.m. a week ago." Zeke leaned against the tailgate and continued, "Since they alarmed, I assumed it was 4 a.m. I actually woke up during my shower when I accidentally misadjusted the water to cold. I think the only way that I could have slept comfortably was if I were weightless, perhaps sleeping in the International Space Station."

Zeke rubbed one of the cactus spine wounds on his left hand, "I've been having nightmares of an encounter that I had with a sea urchin while scuba diving in the Caribbean when I was 16. If not for the ointment that you gave me, I don't think I would have slept at all. My hands are so sore that I could barely shave, brush my teeth or wipe my butt! And my other wounds are only slightly less sore."

Luís sympathized, but remained silent. Then he hopped down from the tailgate, closed it, and said, "Climb in, Doc, let's go watch the show."

As Luís drove away from the hotel, Zeke asked, "What show?

"You'll see."

He drove a short distance east, where he found a suitable spot away from structures and lights, then he made a U-turn and parked the truck facing west. He grabbed his thermos and an extra cup out of the center console and said, "Come on, let's have some coffee."

His curiosity piqued, Zeke followed Luís to the back of the truck. Luís lowered the tailgate, sat down and poured Zeke a cup of coffee.

"I hope you like cream and sugar."

"Normally I just take milk, but cream and sugar is okay," Zeke replied. Then he stared into the cup and added, "I'm running about half throttle this morning; maybe the sugar will give me some energy."

Luís patted the tailgate and said, "Have a seat."

Zeke sat down and sipped his coffee, then looked out across the dark landscape and asked, "So, what are we looking at?"

"Beautiful sky, huh?"

Zeke paused to take in the scene, and then replied, "Yes, it is."

"Just keep watching."

Suddenly a tiny red spot peaked over the horizon. Second by second the spot grew, changing from red to gold and then bathing the landscape in the warm orange patina of early dawn. The movement of the sun could clearly be seen behind the dark silhouette of the mountains, creating the illusion that the sun was a radiant living being racing upwards into the morning sky.

Quickly the gold faded as the brightening sun bathed the desert scene, first in yellow, and then finally, white.

"Another beautiful Sonoran Desert sunrise," Luís observed, then slapped his knee and said, "Welcome to another day! How about you and I have a good, hot breakfast, whaddya say?"

"I could eat." Zeke replied unenthusiastically, then added, "By the way, that sunrise was amazing."

As Luís climbed into the truck he said, "Arizona sunrises and sunsets are two of my favorite shows in the West, so I try to catch 'em when I can."

After breakfast at Marcella's, as they passed by the New Cornelia Mine on the outskirts of Ajo heading south toward Ajo Station, Luís asked, "How're you feeling now, Doc?"

"Better, thanks. And I'm beginning to appreciate Mexican food. That was a fantastic breakfast. And you grew up eating food like that every day?"

"Yep, like I said at dinner; it's just like eating at my mom's house. And I have four brothers and two sisters, so my mom cooked every day, and in large quantities. My folks made sure we always had plenty to eat. My dad used to say, 'if you leave my table hungry, it's your own fault'."

They rode in silence for a few minutes while Zeke checked the email on his smartphone.

Then Luís broke the silence. "So, what's on the agenda for to-day, Doc?"

"I was just reminded that I need to send in a report. I'll do that first thing. Then we'll have to wait and see. I'll receive orders after my boss has read my report." Then he removed his cap and threw it against the windshield. "This is bullshit! I fail to see the necessity to micro-manage my assignment."

"I understand your frustration. Illegal drugs are pouring over the border. It's like you're a grizzly, standing by a river filled with fat salmon swimming upstream; there are so many fish swimming by, all you have to do is wade out and grab one, but you're not allowed to get in the water."

"Well, if this keeps up, I may turn into an angry grizzly…" Zeke said as he gazed out the passenger-side window.

"You already seem pretty grumpy to me."

At Ajo Station, Zeke went straight to his small office, opened his laptop and began working on the requested report. Luís fetched the keys to his assigned truck and began preparing it for another day in the desert, but not really knowing what to expect.

A short time later, having finished with his vehicle preparation, Luís got himself a cup of coffee and one for Zeke, walked into the office and sat Zeke's cup beside him on his desk. Without look-ing up from the computer screen, Zeke said, "Thanks." And then grumbled something directed at the computer, which sounded very uncomplimentary.

Luís picked up a multi-page document that was lying on the desk, sat down in the only available chair, propped his feet on the desk and began reading as he sipped his coffee.

Zeke finally leaned back in his chair, and speaking to the com-puter screen said, "Okay, sir; report delivered." Then he reached for his coffee and took a sip.

"What now, Doc? We wait?" Luís asked without looking up from his reading.

Zeke sighed, "We wait." And drummed his fingers on the desk.

Just then, Ron Addison, Assistant Patrol Agent in Charge, Ajo

Station, walked up and leaned on the door jamb. "Good morning, Special Agent Sikes, Agent Gonzales. How's the A-team this morning?"

Addison was middle-aged, of average height and build, thin-faced with a crew cut and a beer gut.

"Morning, Sir." Luís replied.

Zeke, unamused by Addison's 'A-team' comment, replied with a monotone, "Good morning."

"Sorry to bother you," Addison continued, looking at Zeke, "but Agent Breen needs to see you."

"Very well." Zeke picked up his coffee cup and headed out the door.

Luís leaned to look down the hall and called after him. "Have fun, Doc."

"Agent Gonzales, I've heard you call him 'Doc' on several occasions. Why is that?"

Luís looked up from his reading and replied, "Because he's a PhD."

"In what, proctology?" Addison asked, chuckling at his own sarcasm.

"Not MD, PhD," Luís repeated. "He has a Master's Degree in American Studies from Hillsdale College, a Doctorate of Philosophy in Politics from the Van Andel Graduate School of Statesmanship, and an Associate Degree in Criminal Justice from Lake Superior State University School of Criminal Justice."

"Well, ain't he the scholar. Why didn't he just go into politics?"

"Probably because he chose to become a special agent with the DEA instead."

"Humph!" Addison uttered, then and left.

Zeke walked up to the open door labeled Patrol Agent in Charge, but chose to knock before entering.

"Come in! Come in, Special Agent Sikes!" Ben Breen, Acting Patrol Agent in Charge, Ajo Station, called from within. "No need to knock. Come on in and pull up a chair."

As Zeke walked in, Breen stood up and offered his hand. Breen was a career Border Patrol Agent, tall and lanky, balding with a ruddy complexion. Known as a true professional, he was very serious about his job.

Zeke shook his hand, winced at the pain as Breen squeezed his hand, and said, "Good morning, Sir."

"It's good to see you. Please, have a seat. How is your assignment going? Is Agent Gonzales providing you with adequate support?"

"Oh, yes, Luís is invaluable. I couldn't accomplish my assignment—whatever that might be—without him."

"Excellent. I'm glad to hear that. He's a good man," Breen replied, then asked, "I assume you have yet to be given the specifics of your assignment?"

"Actually, I'm waiting for that as we speak. I'm just being a bit impatient this morning."

"I see. Well, Special Agent Sikes, we're down a man because of your mission. I'm willing to offer whatever help we can provide, I just want to make certain that Agent Gonzales is a necessary to meet your goals. I'd like to be read in to your orders."

"I would like to be read in as well, Sir."

"You mean to tell me that you were sent down here with no specific instructions?"

"I'm receiving daily assignments from my supervisor."

"Hmm…" Breen thought for a moment. "And you haven't yet received your assignment for today?"

"That's correct."

"Well, I suppose that you and I are in the same boat. But, I would appreciate it if you could keep me updated on a daily basis."

"I certainly will if I can, Sir."

"I appreciate that." Breen paused, then said, "Well, I'll let you get back to it. Just keep me in the loop."

"Yes, Sir," Zeke replied and headed back to his office.

In the hallway, Zeke met Agent Addison going in the opposite direction. Zeke nodded a silent greeting.

As Addison passed, he remarked, "Well, well, the doctor is in…"

Zeke paused, then continued without looking back.

As Zeke walked into his office, he looked at Luís and said, "I'm getting the distinct vibe of interagency rivalry and mistrust today."

Luís glanced up from his reading but didn't comment.

Then Zeke sat his coffee cup down, plopped in his chair and glanced at his computer screen.

"There haven't been any noises suggesting that email has arrived," Luís said.

"Crap!" Zeke slammed the lid of his laptop closed.

"Doc, I've been reading this addendum to your orders that's supposed to describe the conditions of your assignment. Yesterday, when I asked you if the DEA knew that the Southwest has deserts, I was joking. But apparently, they really don't know that the Southwest has deserts!

"The Sonoran Desert isn't mentioned even once. The US-Mexico border is discussed, and the term, 'vast stretches of uninhabited wilderness,' but that could describe Kansas. There's no mention of the summer temps or the arid conditions, or what is necessary to survive out there in the 'vast, uninhabited stretches of wilderness.'

"I also found the statement, 'familiarization to be provided by Border Patrol personnel.' Aside from that, this document is useless," Luís remarked and tossed it on the desk.

"That apparently describes my supervisor as well," Zeke commented dryly.

Zeke stood up and grabbed his cup. "Let's get some coffee."

Just then the computer dinged, indicating new email had arrived.

"Tell you what," Luís offered, "I'll get the coffee. You read your email."

"Hang on, this should be short and sweet."

Zeke lifted the lid on his computer, entered his password and opened the message.

Continue to monitor the border and report.

"Short and sweet, alright," Zeke commented in disgust, then spun the computer around so that Luís could read the message.

"This guy sure doesn't waste words."

Zeke turned the computer back, forwarded the message to Agent Breen and then shut it down.

"It's Friday," Zeke observed. "Let's go to the desert museum. I need some desert survival training. We'll 'monitor the border' after lunch."

After spending several interesting and educational hours at the Organ Pipe Cactus National Monument's Kris Eggle Visitor Center, Zeke and Luís had a long lunch in Ajo, then headed for the border.

As they approached Lukeville, Zeke suggested, "How about let's survey the border fence."

"Doc, I get the impression we're not planning to visit any hilltops this afternoon."

"Nope, I've seen enough desert wildlife for a while."

"Okay, where'd you like to go? Your wish is my command."

"Let's head west on the Drag Road."

"Aye, captain."

Luís drove to the port of entry, gained access to the Drag Road and headed west.

"According to my maps," Zeke said, "the Organ Pipe Cactus National Monument boundary parallels the border through here."

"That's right. The Organ Pipe boundary runs west from Lukeville for about 17 miles. Then it turns north. The Cabeza Prieta National Wildlife Refuge begins there and continues along the border for about 56 miles. The refuge is managed by US Fish and Wildlife."

"Does the Drag Road continue that far?"

"No, the terrain gets pretty rough on the western side of the refuge, especially through Christmas Pass."

"I remember seeing that on my map."

"The only road along the border through the refuge is the Camino del Diablo, or Devil's Highway," Luís continued. "That road has a lot of history; it was the original wagon trail from Tucson to Yuma."

They continued driving slowly along the Drag Road for a while, then Zeke commented, "I know that you love the desert, but you have to admit, this terrain gets a bit boring after a while."

"True, but no matter where you are in the world, I'd imagine the scenery becomes a bit repetitive after a while and tends to blend into the background."

"I guess you're right. Say, what kind of sensors and detection systems do you have out here?"

"Mostly these," Luís replied, pointing at his eyes with two fingers.

"So, how many Border Patrol Agents watch these open spaces along this section of the border?"

"Sadly, not many. We're spread pretty thin."

"I see… Now I understand why Agent Breen made it a point to tell me he was down one man. I think he would prefer that I do my mission alone."

"We're under a lot of pressure. Illegals and drugs are pouring over the border and Congress doesn't seem to care. American sovereignty matters. And that's our job, but we're not getting it done. We need four times our present manpower; and even with that, it would still be a challenge. We need a bigger budget, and we really need that wall built."

"I wouldn't hold my breath."

Luís sighed. "I know."

Presently they passed by the corner of the boundary between the Organ Pipe and the Cabeza Prieta.

"So, now we're at the southeastern boundary of the wildlife refuge?" Zeke asked.

"Right. And the refuge is pretty big; as I said earlier, it runs for 56 miles along the border from here to the southwest boundary, and its 860,000 acres if I remember correctly."

Zeke looked out across the vast mountainous expanse and commented, "That looks like rough terrain. My map doesn't show many north-south roads across the refuge. Illegals and drug mules actually cross into the U.S. through here?"

"Yes. Almost daily except in the summertime. Look out there…" Luís pointed across the border. Not far away traffic could be seen traveling along a paved highway.

"That's Mexico Highway 2 running for 125 miles along the border between Sonoyta and San Luis Rio Colorado. Drug smugglers, sometimes in caravans, will cut through the fence and drive north toward Interstate 8. Human traffickers also bring their cargo through here, or the people are just dropped off and cross on foot. And it's about 65 miles north to Dateland."

"That is a long walk."

"And a treacherous one."

"So, who patrols the refuge?"

"Just Border Patrol pretty much. Some of the older agents have told me that there used to be a couple of US Fish and Wildlife Law Enforcement Officers that patrolled the refuge constantly. They worked closely with Border Patrol, caught a lot of illegals and turned them over to us. They busted a lot of drug runners, too. But when those two officers retired that pretty much ended. Apparently, the new guys think that catching illegals and drug runners isn't their job."

"Why? Illegals and drug runners are breaking US law. Fish and Wildlife is a federal agency. It's every federal law officer's job to arrest anyone who violates federal law."

"Of course you're right, but I think the new guys just don't want to get shot at. And the shooting of the U.S. Park Service Officer on the Organ Pipe a while back didn't help matters much either."

"I remember reading about that. Are illegals often armed?"

"Not usually, but drug smugglers and drug mules are, and they won't hesitate to kill you. The smugglers have every type of weapon you can imagine, including rocks, which are damned deadly themselves. We have this;" Luís patted his Beretta 96D Brigadier service pistol in the holster on his belt.

"You mean that's the only weapon you're issued?"

"Yep, 'fraid so," Luís replied, then added sarcastically, "We're armed to the teeth."

"Well, just so you know, I'm carrying a Smith and Wesson 40, and I have a LAR-15 carbine and 200 rounds of ammo in my equipment case."

"Thanks, that's good to know." Then, Luís thought for a moment, "So that's why your case is so damned heavy!"

Zeke looked at him and smiled sheepishly. Then said, "So, I gather Border Patrol had to take up the slack."

"You got it, but after all, that is our job. And it's a big one; over half the illegal aliens entering the U.S. do so through Arizona. Unfortunately, it's not all we have to deal with. There's also a huge sex slave trade crawling across the border with the low-life animals that do it."

"I've heard that it's a lot worse than commonly known," Zeke said.

"One of my buddies is a Customs Agent at the port of entry in Nogales. Just recently they busted a sex slaver bringing in four young girls from the Ukraine. Those tall, beautiful blonde Slavic girls bring big bucks as sex slaves."

"Sex slavery is the most despicable crime that I know of."

"Well, it gets worse; last year they busted two women bringing in seven little girls. They claimed to be a Girl Scout troop, but something didn't look right, so he and a female agent brought the little girls into an interview room and asked them some questions. When one of the girls, who were all eight and nine years old, admitted that they were going to be sold as sex slaves, he just threw up right there on the spot.

"Another female agent was holding the two women in an adjacent room and saw him throw up. She asked his partner what was up. When she was told, before anyone could stop her, she attacked the two women and beat the living hell out of both of 'em before anyone could stop her. Put 'em in the hospital. She was suspended for a few days, but then allowed to return to duty. Turns out she had a nine-year-old daughter."

"It's hard to believe that humans could sink so low," Zeke said, "Every one of those animals should be executed. Slowly."

"I'm not sure about that," Luís replied. "After someone dies, people claim their troubles and pain are over. I think they should be imprisoned for life at hard labor, turning big rocks into small rocks for the rest of their miserable lives."

"You know, Amigo, that's not a bad idea."

Then, Luís swung the truck into a U-turn. "We'd better turn around here and head back."

On the way back, as they approached Organ Pipe, they met another Border Patrol vehicle driven by a female agent. As Luís met her truck, he leaned his upper body out of the window and yelled, "Jackie! What's up?!"

She stopped, smiled and replied, "Hello you lunatic, what are you up to?"

"Oh, just giving our guest the nickel tour." Then he leaned back to allow Zeke a better view and said, "Doc, this is Agent Jackie Williamson, the baddest agent at Ajo Station. Jackie, meet our temporary guest, DEA Special Agent Zeke Sikes."

"Pleased to meet you Special Agent Zeke Sikes. So, you're what all the buzz is about."

"Pleased to meet you, too. But I doubt I'm the source, there's not much going on with me to buzz about."

"Oh, I don't know about that…" Jacked smiled as she stretched to get a better view, then she said, "Hey, Wildman, let's get together for a beer or two. And bring Special Agent Sikes along."

"Just might take you up on that, Ma'm. See ya' later." Then, just as Luís pulled away he yelled, "Be safe out there!"

Jackie flashed a peace sign and yelled, "Will do!"

They drove along for a few minutes without talking, then Zeke commented, "Interesting agent."

"I think she found you interesting, too." Luís observed. "I can't remember the last time she invited me to have a beer."

"She just did invite you to have a beer."

"She only invited me so that I would bring you."

"She's single?"

"Yep, and I know she's interested in you because she knows that I'm taken."

"Oh?" Zeke replied, expecting more information.

"Bekah. She's a junior in Applied Criminology at NAU. She plans to get her masters."

"That's a good school. See her very often?"

"We meet as much as we can at my folks' place in Payson. Flagstaff isn't that far of a drive for her, so we have most of a weekend to be together."

"What about you, Doc? You have a young lady back in Virginia?"

"I did once. We were engaged. Cynthia was an intern with the State Department. She had been on an assignment to the US embassy in Bogota and was headed home when a bomb destroyed her commuter plane at 22,000 feet over the jungles of Columbia. They never found a trace of her or any of the other passengers. We were planning to be married after she returned. She was twenty two."

"Damn, Doc, I'm so sorry."

"Thanks. It's been ten years but I still miss her every single day. She was so beautiful…"

"I can't imagine. I don't know what I would do if I lost Bekah."

"You survive. Breathe in and out. Hold on to the good memories, forget the bad and do your damnedest to get out of bed every morning. Some days are really difficult, but you find a way. Eventually, you move on with your life - at least, that's what you tell yourself, anyway."

"Did they ever find out who did it?"

"No. The Columbian authorities suspected one of the cartels, but that's as far as it went."

"Is that why you became a DEA Special Agent?"

"That was my intention in the beginning, when I was in college. But over the years my desire for revenge lessened. In fact, they hit that subject pretty hard during my psyche evals. Tried their best to make me admit that I just wanted to use the DEA to find the murders that killed my Cynthia. But I convinced them otherwise."

"Do you think that's the reason they denied your request to be assigned to Central America?"

"I've wondered about that. Maybe. But it's been so long. There wasn't much evidence in the first place. Only a few pieces of the plane were ever found. Where would I start? What's left to investigate? No, there has to be another reason for sending me here. I just can't figure what it is…"

Day after day Zeke and Luís went through the same routine. The daily orders to monitor the border never changed. Finally, one Thursday morning Zeke had had enough…

Zeke walked into his office and sat down at his desk. Luís was already there, sipping coffee and reading the Ajo Copper News.

"Morning, Doc," Luís said without looking up from his paper.

"Amigo, I think it's time to go home."

Luís looked up, "Come again? Am I in trouble?!"

Zeke chuckled. "No, my mom's birthday is next week. I think I'll take a couple of weeks and visit my folks."

"Oh. It's kinda short notice, ain't it? If it were me, I wouldn't even bother; I have to put in for annual leave at least six months in advance. And they prefer a year. Four days? I'd be laughed out of the bosses' office!"

Zeke picked up his smartphone and put in the call.

"Hello Sir. How are things back at the ranch?—Yes, everything is going fine down here. Sir, I was wondering, my mom's birthday is coming up next week and I'd like to take ten days of annual to visit my folks.—Yes, Sir, starting this Monday.—Thank you, Sir. I'll be at my parent's home in Cambridge."

Zeke ended the call and put the phone on his desk.

"Damn! I want your boss."

Zeke looked at Luís and winked.

Then Luís asked, "Cambridge?"

"My dad is a professor of chemistry at MIT."

"MIT… cool! Massachusetts. Long trip."

"Right." Zeke replied, then began typing on his keyboard, studied the screen for a moment and looked at Luís. "Can you drop me off at Sky Harbor on Saturday morning?"

"Sure."

"Thanks. I'll let you know if I need you to pick me up when I return."

***

On a Saturday afternoon in late April, Zeke's flight touched down at Boston Logan Airport. A short time later he stepped out of his rental car in front of his parent's home in Cambridge, Massachusetts.

The house was a stately, New England-style two-story on a quiet street in an old neighborhood with large shade trees, finely-trimmed lawns, and hedges. Flowers were blooming everywhere. He walked up the steps and rang the doorbell. Behind the door, Zeke could hear Biscuit, the large, jolly, Golden Lab barking his alarm. Moments later his mother answered the door.

Anna Sikes' face lit up as she grabbed Zeke in a bear hug and squealed, "Ezekiel! You're home!" then she kissed his forehead and dragged him inside.

Biscuit bounced around Zeke, wagging his tail with a happy greeting.

"Hi, mom. It's good to see you," Zeke said and squatted down to pet Biscuit.

"Let me look at you." Anna grabbed his hands, stood him up and held him at arm's length to look him over. "How are you?"

"I'm—"

"You're a bit thin, but you're tanned and look very healthy." She kissed him on the forehead again and said, "Arizona must be good for you," then turned and yelled, "Bill! Look who just showed up on our doorstep."

"Well, who could it be?" Bill Sikes asked as he came down the hall.

He smiled when he saw Zeke and said, "Well, look at you!" then he hugged Zeke and said, "Good to see you, Son!"

"Hi, Dad. Good to see you. You're both looking great."

"What a scamp you are to just show up unannounced," his mother said as she wagged her finger at him, "but what surprise! How long can you stay?"

"Two weeks leave, starts Monday."

"Wonderful! Well then, put your things in your old room, freshen up from your flight and then we can sit and talk."

Zeke spent the entire week eating his favorite home-cooked dishes, visiting with his parents and paternal grandparents, who lived nearby. Their conversations were mostly about Arizona and catching up on family news. Since his dad was busy with classes at MIT during the day, they visited during the evenings and on the weekend.

On the following Sunday evening during dinner, Zeke announced, "I have to fly down to Virginia tomorrow morning."

"Oh?" His dad replied. "Any problems?"

"No Sir, I just need to get some things from my locker and take care of paperwork with the travel office. I'll be back tomorrow afternoon."

After breakfast, Zeke departed on a flight from Boston Logan to Reagan National, Washington, DC. Later that morning, he entered DEA headquarters, went straight to Senior DEA Special Agent Ray Alexander's office and walked into the reception area.

Ray Alexander's Administrative Assistant, Kathleen O'Connor, a tall and attractive redhead, greeted him with a warm smile. "Good morning, Special Agent Sikes. May I help you?"

"Good morning, Kathy, I'd like to see him if he's in."

She stopped smiling and asked, "Aren't you supposed to be on leave in Cambridge?" then added, "He's not expecting you."

"No, he isn't."

"I see. Just one moment."

She touched the screen on her computer display and said, "Special Agent Sikes is here to see you, Sir."

There was a momentary pause, then she smiled again and said, "You may go in."

Zeke walked in to the spacious office and closed the door behind him.

Senior DEA Special Agent Ray Alexander, Zeke's supervisor, a tall, athletically built, balding black man with glasses and a friendly demeanor, stood up from his large desk and said, "Special Agent Sikes! I didn't expect to see you here. Aren't you supposed to be on leave up in Cambridge? Please, make yourself comfortable."

Alexander touched his computer screen and said, "Thank you, Kathy. No calls please."

Zeke sat on a large, plush leather sofa facing the desk. "I'm still on leave, sir, I just flew in for the day to take care of a few things."

"Well, how is your family?" Agent Alexander asked as he studied Zeke's face.

"They're all very well, sir, thank you."

At that point the conversation dwindled and Agent Alexander went right to the point. "Something is on your mind, Zeke. Let's have it."

"Well, Sir—"

"We can be informal here, call me Ray."

"Well, Ray, frankly I don't understand what I'm doing at Ajo Station. And why the day to day assignments? Always the same; monitor the border, monitor the border. What am I looking for? Customs and Border Patrol are in a better position to apprehend illegals and drug smugglers. I realize this is my first solo field assignment. Am I being tested or something?"

Ray glanced down at his desk for a moment, picked up a pen and started writing, then began speaking, "I understand your confusion and frustration. This hardly compares to your previous support roles, but I assure you that you are fulfilling an important mission objective…"

As Ray spoke, he scribbled something on a note pad. As he continued to speak, he carefully removed the note from the pad, walked over and handed it to Zeke, then finished by saying. "Do you have any questions?"

On the note, he had written, say, 'I think I understand, but right now I'd like to get a cup of coffee.'

Zeke studied the note briefly, then repeated the words verbatim.

"Great idea! Me, too. Let's take a break and go to the coffee shop."

As Zeke stood up, Ray took the note from his hand, folded it and put it into Zeke's coat pocket.

After they got their coffee, Ray said, "Let's go out on the quad."

Zeke walked along with Ray to a remote park bench beneath a large shade tree.

Ray sat down and said, "Have a seat, now we can talk."

"What's the deal, Ray? Is your office bugged?"

"Maybe. I can't take the chance that it's not. Zeke, I've been following you closely. I picked you for this assignment because I know I can trust you."

Zeke exhaled through his pursed lips. "Thank you. I was beginning to think that I had been shuffled off to a backwater assignment to keep me out of Central America."

"No. Absolutely not. Your integrity is impeccable. Something big is on the horizon, and it's centered in Northern Mexico. I'm certain that it involves the warring cartels there. But the Mexican government is also involved. And I believe there's another foreign government involved, as well; maybe the Russians, or even the Chinese. I'm just not certain because right now all I'm getting is disjointed intel chatter."

"With all due respect, Ray, this sounds like something for the FBI or CIA, maybe DIA. Why are we getting into this?"

"The DEA isn't getting into this, Zeke, we are, you and I."

"Come again?"

"The CIA has been compromised. One of their special agents was just caught selling secrets to several Asian governments. No one knows how deep that will go until a thorough damage assessment has been done. And you know what's been going on with the FBI; they can't be trusted to empty a piss pot.

"Unfortunately, I don't have any reliable contacts with DIA. I need you to be my eyes and ears in Arizona. I know it's an unlikely place, but something is developing along the border. There's a Russian listening post in Bogota, focused on the US embassy. And there are reports that the Russians are selling the intelligence they gather to Red China. The thing is, the Chinese are moving companies into Mexico. They're spending big bucks down there, but satellite data only shows typical office building and factory construction and the like. Nothing suspicious."

"I'm just not sure what I can do, Ray…"

"I know I must sound like I've gone off the rails; when you throw all of this out there, none of the pieces fit. But I've had my ear to the ground on this for a while. The pieces are slowly coming together; it's just that the intel is only trickling in. It's very frustrating. However, if something is being lined up to make a run at the U.S., they have to show up at the border at some point. You don't just plow into a situation blind, you do recon… take surveys… reconnoiter. Satellite images and drone video can't provide everything. Some things have to be seen through human eyes, with boots on the ground. And you must have infrastructure. That sort of thing can't be easily hidden."

"Are we talking infiltration by the cartels to bring in more illegal drugs?"

"I don't think illegal drugs are even involved. It's something else. Something bigger. Call it intuition, or paranoia… hell, I don't know. I just need your eyes and ears down there. I know you're just one man, and you're just getting your feet wet in field operations. And you can't be there 24/7, but I don't expect that. The thing is, I can't assign more agents. Normal DEA channels have suddenly gotten cloudy. They may be compromised. So I can't make noise about this because I don't know who I can trust. Except you."

"I appreciate your confidence in me, Sir."

"Maybe it won't amount to anything and you'll have just wasted your time down there. But just watch for something, anything, out of the ordinary. And report directly to me, using our coded method only. Trust no one else."

"Well, I do have a liaison."

"Good man?"

"I think so."

"Then I'll trust your judgment."

"Yes, Sir."

Then Ray stood up. "Enjoy the rest of your leave. You'll hear from me when you get back to the border."

Just as he started to walk away, he added, "Oh, and when you get back to the airport, flush that note."

***

Late that afternoon, in the back yard of his parent's house, as birds flitted about in the budding trees, shrubs and flowers of the lush landscape, Zeke sat at the patio table, idly fidgeting with his glass of wine, oblivious to his surroundings. At his feet, Biscuit lay curled, sleeping.

Presently, Bill sat down across from him with a glass of wine, took a sip, and then studied his son for a moment.

"What's on your mind, son?" He asked.

Zeke stirred from his contemplation, looked at his dad and smiled, "Oh, nothing really. Just thinking."

"I don't mean to pry son, but something is bothering you. You've barely spoken since you returned from Virginia. It's obvious that it's not nothing. So, what's on your mind?"

Zeke paused for a moment, then spoke, "I met with my boss today. I needed to know the real reason for my assignment on the border. His answer was not what I expected."

"Good, or bad?"

"The jury is still out on that." Then he grew serious, looked at his dad and said, "Things could get a bit dicey in the coming months, Pop. But don't worry, I'll keep you in the loop."

"That's good enough for me."

Zeke was scheduled to fly back to Arizona on Sunday. So, on Friday, the family gathered for a backyard, farewell dinner, with grilled steak and all of the trimmings. Everyone was there, except Zeke's grandfather, Ezekiel, 'Ezzy' Sikes. Ezzy was a Vietnam War vet and a wily, sharp-minded, retired Bird Colonel, formerly with US Army intelligence.

"Ezekiel?" Anna called.

"Yes, Mom?"

"Would you please go out front and greet your grandfather? He just called and said he would be here momentarily."

Zeke walked out of the front door just as a Ford F-150 Raptor 4-door pickup, silver with black trim, rumbled up the driveway and parked. Dark-tinted windows obscured the driver. Just then the driver's door opened and out stepped Ezzy.

"Grandpa?!"

"Hey, Zee! How fortuitous that you're here now. What do you think of my new toy?"

(Ezzy had called his grandson "Zee' since Zeke was in elementary school)

"I… um… wow!"

"Speechless, eh? Ain't she fine?"

"Yes, Sir… and… then some. But how? … Why? …"

"Still speechless. Well, while you try to get your brain in gear, let me tell you about this baby's gear; it's a 2017 Super Crew, with a blueprinted and balanced, fuel-injected, supercharged, 588 cubic inch big block, pumping out around 900 horses, and 950 foot-pounds of torque. That monster motor is tied to a hardened 10-speed automatic tranny, with all-wheel drive, race-proven differentials, race-series brakes, and Z-rated off-road tires."

"Wow…" Zeke exclaimed in an astonished whisper. "This is… amazing! But, I thought the new Raptors had that high-output V-6 motor."

"This one started out so equipped. Some spoiled kid blew it up, along with the transmission. I got it for a song and called an old friend of mine that has an auto shop over in Medford. He builds off-road racing trucks as a hobby, so I asked him if he could do something with the Raptor. I told him that I didn't care what it cost. He's had it for a couple of months, and just finished with it last week. When he brought it to the house and I asked what I owed him, he just handed me the keys and said, 'no charge, it's my pleasure'.

"Really," Zeke replied in a sobering tone, "He must be some friend."

"I saved his life, along with a few others, in Vietnam. That's why I was awarded the Medal of Honor. We became friends after that. John is a good man and a good friend."

"I'll say!"

28

Then Ezzy tossed Zeke the keys.

"Grandpa, can I take it for a spin around the block?"

"You can take her for a spin whenever and wherever you want… she's yours."

"Beg your pardon?"

Ezzy walked over to the truck, opened the driver's door and retrieved a large envelope, then he handed it to Zeke. He opened it and pulled out a personalized license plate that matched the colors of the truck and read, Zeez, along with the vehicle's title, in Zeke's name, and a custom-made booklet with a picture of the Raptor on the cover, and inside, all of the technical data on the truck, including build-sheets on the motor, transmission and drive train.

Zeke whispered, "Oh, wow…"

Then Ezzy put his hand on Zeke's shoulder and said, "Zee, you've been too serious for far too long. You lost that wonderful girl you were planning to marry. Then buried you head in the books for all those years. But you've been alone too long. Make no mistake. I'm proud of you, proud of your scholastic achievements, proud of where you are and what you've accomplished. But now it's time for you to live a little. Kick up some dust. Stretch your legs. Get out there and have some fun! Then find yourself a nice girl, get married and start making babies… I want more great grandkids!"

"Zeke looked at the keys and the tag and said, "Grandad, I don't know what to say… thank you so much! But this must have cost..."

"Aw, hell! I don't care about the money. I've had funds rat-holed since before I retired from the Army. And for what? Your grandmother is well provided for. I'm eighty two years old. What, pray tell, do I need all of that money for?"

Zeke hugged Ezzy and said, "Thank you so much, Grandpa."

Ezzy chuckled and replied, "You're welcome, Zee. Actually, I'm glad that you're here to take possession. I really didn't want to drive it all the way to Arizona.

"And, by the way, if anything goes wrong with the engine or drivetrain, there's a number in that book. Just call John and he'll recommend a shop. And if you can't get satisfaction, he'll send a mechanic out to diagnose the problem and supervise the repairs."

"Amazing," Zeke commented.

As they both stood, admiring the truck, Ezzy said, "Oh! Before I forget…" Ezzy pointed at the driver's side of the truck. "You see the fuel filler there. The factory tank holds about twenty seven

29

gallons, give or take. Well, when you lift the tonneau cover, just inside the bed, adjacent to the fuel filler, there's another fuel filler attached to a 50 gallon tank inside the bed. The fuel management system starts out pulling from the big tank. When it's down to five gallons remaining, it switches to the main tank. Both tanks use the same fuel gauge. There's an indicator on the instrument panel that tells you which tank you're using. Cool huh?"

"I'll say."

Then Ezzy slapped Zeke on the back and said, "Come on, Zee, let's take this monster for a spin!"

Just before they drove away, Ezzy said, "Now, take it easy until you get a feel for this power; otherwise, before you can snap your fingers, she'll be jerked a link out of your chain!"

Sometime later they returned. Zeke stepped out of the truck and yelled, "Whooo! What a rush! This truck is awesome!"

As Ezzy and Zeke walked away from the truck, Ezzy patted the truck on the hood and said, "A buck fifty on I-93—sweet!"

Zeke stopped in his tracks. "Wait! What?! You drove this Raptor doing 150 miles an hour on I-93?!"

"Well, the speedometer only goes to 120," Ezzy admitted. "But the needle went past that and was pointing straight down, so…" Ezzy shrugged his shoulders and turned to go inside.

"Unbelievable…" Zeke whispered in amazement as he watched his grandad walk toward the front door.

Suddenly Ezzy turned back and whispered, "Do not tell your grandmother! As far as she knows I haven't driven it over sixty."

Early the following morning, Zeke sent a quick text to Luís letting him know that he wouldn't need to be picked up at Sky Harbor on Sunday. Then he cranked up the music, pulled out on Interstate 90, set the Raptor's cruise control on 80 MPH and let her run.

Chapter Three
Abril

Just before 4 a.m. Monday in early May, Zeke parked his Raptor in front of his hotel room in Ajo, completing the 2,790 mile drive from his parents' home in Cambridge in 35 hours. He went directly inside and crashed. Three hours later his smartphone alarm sounded. He quickly showered and shaved, then texted Luís, "on my way." At 8 a.m. Zeke walked into his office.

"Morning, Doc!" Luís said as he sat having coffee and reading a report. "Welcome back. When did you get in?"

"About four this morning."

"Man, your ass must be draggin' big time."

Zeke looked at Luís through bloodshot eyes and said, "I need a caffeine I-vee drip."

"Well, my coffee needs a warm up. I'll get you a cup… with a shot of caffeine."

Then he tossed the report that he had been reading to Zeke and said, "You might find that interesting."

Zeke began reading the report, but only made it through a few pages before Luís returned with the coffee.

"Here you go, Doc."

Zeke took a sip, then looked at the report and said, "I can't concentrate enough to make any sense out of this. How about giving me the condensed version."

"Well," Luís took a sip of coffee and began. "While you've been gone, an all-out territorial war between the drug cartels has erupted in Northern Mexico. Open gun battles with heavy machine guns, rocket launchers, helicopters, you name it, have been reported in cities and towns across the states of Sonora, Chihuahua and Baja California. In some cases the Mexican Army is in the fray, but no one is certain whose side they're on.

"The state department has banned travel in Northern Mexico, so there's no traffic going south, but the border is being flooded by people heading north seeking refuge. Customs is screaming for help because every port of entry from San Diego to Brownsville has been slammed with refugees requesting sanctuary, and evacuees requesting visas.

"Illegals are flooding over the border. But due to the escalating hostilities, the detainees are being held in the U.S. instead of being bussed back to Mexico, which is causing complaints across the political spectrum.

"The thing is, the visa applicants, refugees, and illegals are not just citizens of Mexico; they're also from South America, Afghanistan, Iran, Iraq, Syria, Yemen, Asia, and East Asia. That's nothing new, but the up tic includes all of those countries, and that doesn't make any sense.

"The prevailing theory is that the bedlam and confusion created by the surge of refugees from Mexico is being used as an opportunity for undesirables to slip undetected through the system due to the rush to process visa applications.

"Also, recent reports from the Minutemen Project indicate an increasing number of people, appearing to be Chinese nationals, have been spotted in remote areas along the border. Around here they're making jokes about it, calling them 'salt-backs' because they have to swim the Pacific Ocean all the way from China."

When Luís finished, Zeke was just staring at his desk. Luís waited a moment, then asked, "So, what do you think, Doc?"

Zeke continued staring.

"Doc? Are you with me?"

Zeke suddenly grabbed his smartphone and said, "It's begun."

"What has begun? Doc, I don't follow you."

Then Zeke hesitated, put his phone back down and mumbled, "No, I can't do that yet."

"Can't do what yet?" Luís asked, thoroughly confused.

"Eyes and ears on the ground…" Zeke mumbled to himself, then looked at Luís and asked, "Can you get in touch with the Minutemen Project?"

"Sure. There's a post in Bisbee. Lots of border problems down there. You want to call, or meet them in person?"

"Neither one."

"Come again?"

"I can't be involved."

"Doc, what's going on? You just said, 'It's begun.' What has begun?"

Zeke glanced at Luís again, and then looked away, as if staring into space.

"Doc, you sure you don't need to get some sleep? When did you say you got in this morning?"

"Around four," Zeke answered as if in a trance.

"Wait a minute—didn't you text me just before you left Cambridge? That was Saturday morning…"

Luís looked at his phone and pulled up the message. "Yeah, 5 a.m. on Saturday morning. And you got in this morning at four. That's… 35 hours. Seems like that drive should take longer than 35 hours."

He then pulled up a maps program on his phone. "The distance from Cambridge to Ajo is… 2790 miles."

Then he brought up the calculator. "2790 miles… in thirty five hours… holey socks, Doc! You averaged 80 miles an hour for almost 2800 miles! What are you drivin', a Ferrari?!"

"A Raptor."

"Come again? Did you say a Raptor? As in Ford F-150 Raptor Pickup?"

"Yes."

"Doc, are you sure you don't need more sleep?"

Zeke suddenly came out of his contemplative daze and said, "It's time to read you in."

"Read me in to what?"

Zeke then told Luís the whole story of his trip, in detail. When he finished, Luís leaned back in his chair and exclaimed, "Wow! Doc that was one helluva trip! Can we go check out your Raptor now?"

"Sure," Zeke replied, then got up immediately and headed out of the door.

As Luís walked around the Raptor, he was awestruck. "Unbelievable," he muttered, "your grandad is awesome."

"Grandad Ezzy is one of a kind."

"And apparently he's really fond of you."

"We've always had a special bond. It's hard to explain. He gave me the nickname, Zee. And he's the only one who has ever called me that. I think he confides personal aspects of his life to me and no one else. That makes me feel pretty darn special. I have a deep and abiding respect for him that I've never felt toward anyone, even my dad."

"Hold on to that relationship for as long as you can, Doc. Something like that comes only once in a lifetime. For some, it never comes at all."

Zeke looked at Luís and said, "Climb in, I'm hungry."

Zeke covered the ten miles from Ajo Station to Marcella's Café in Ajo in about five minutes.

As the two men were looking over the breakfast menus, Luís said, "That is the quickest I have ever made the trip from the Y to Ajo. You do realize that we became airborne every time we went through a wash? Your Raptor is a rocket. Now I see how you made it from Cambridge to here in 35 hours."

"I really love that truck," Zeke confessed. "But I almost maxed out my credit card buying gas. That thing eats premium like you eat chips and salsa."

"You know, it might help if you drove a little closer to the posted speed limit."

"Yeah, but what's the fun in that?"

When they returned to Zeke's office after breakfast, Luís said, "So, you need me to coordinate with the Minutemen Project and get as much data on sightings of Chinese nationals in Mexico as they can provide?"

"Yes. Just tell them that you're collecting data for a census report or some such," Zeke suggested. "As soon as we get enough verifiable data, I'll compile it and send the report to Ray."

"Verifiable. How do we get verification of the sightings?"

"If two or three different reliable sources see the same thing then I'll be able to justify that as verifiable data. Who knows, maybe we'll get lucky and you and I will be one of those reliable sources…"

Four days went by and Zeke had not learned anything new. During their daily recons; whether it was hilltop surveillance or running the Drag Road, nothing out of the ordinary appeared. Luís hadn't received anything from the Minutemen Project either. Both men were disgusted and bored.

On Thursday afternoon, Luís suggested, "Why don't you come up to Payson this weekend with me to visit my parents and eat some of my mom's world-class cooking?"

"That's a tempting offer," Zeke replied.

"Why don't we make it a three-day weekend and head out tomorrow morning?" Luis suggested.

"Amigo, you just sold me on your idea. I'll shoot an email to Agent Breen that we have to go to Phoenix tomorrow to look at some surveillance equipment."

"Great! I'll call my mom and tell her we'll be there for breakfast."

Early Friday morning, long before sunrise, Zeke and Luís loaded their travel bags in the back of the Raptor and headed north on Highway 85, then turned east on Interstate Highway 8 at Gila Bend. Zeke ran the Raptor up to 90 mph and shortly they were turning north toward Maricopa. From there they continued on toward Phoenix and the Valley of the Sun.

In Phoenix, their journey turned west, traveling across the Phoenix Metro area to Highway 87, called the Beeline Highway, which is a four-lane, divided highway that winds through the mountains to Payson and beyond.

The Beeline climbs from an elevation of 1200 feet in the Valley of the Sun to 5000 feet in Payson. Along the way it winds through the picturesque Mazatzal Mountains. Along with the scenic view, the road provides an interesting drive for high-performance vehicles in the form of a number of sharp curves, commonly called switchbacks, climbing through the mountains.

Although Zeke had never driven the Beeline, Luís told him what to expect, so Zeke set the cruise control for 80 mph. The Raptor sailed passed vehicles traveling a more reasonable 70 mph (five mph above the posted speed limit).

Luís watched in fascination as some drivers unsuccessfully tried to keep up with the Raptor.

"Man, this truck is amazing! It doesn't feel like we're taking these curves this fast."

"The racing seats have something to do with that, but it's mostly the suspension and tires. I couldn't drive a normal vehicle like this if you held a gun to my head."

Then he added, "Speaking of that, would you like to drive?"

"Really?!" Luís replied with the excitement of a little boy.

"Most certainly."

Zeke stopped at the next pullout and Luís enthusiastically jumped into the driver's seat. As he pulled out onto the pavement, Luís burned rubber in first, second, and third gear using the paddle shifter.

He looked sheepishly at Zeke and said, "Sorry about that." Then he smiled and said, "I've never burned rubber with all four tires at once. That's pretty cool. This truck has some serious torque."

"You're doing really well. I'm not going to tell you how many times I lost control of this thing before I became accustomed to all of this power."

"Wow!" Luís exclaimed as he entered a sharp curve. "The way this truck handles is unreal!"

"It's the all-wheel drive; it pulls and pushes through a curve. You can run it up as much as you like, as long as the tires maintain traction. But it's not pretty when the tires break loose."

At that point, Luís eased up slightly on the throttle.

As they climbed Mount Ord, the last steep grade before reaching the town of Payson, Luís asked Zeke, "Have you noticed the thermometer? The outside temp has dropped a bit."

The digital display indicated 62 degrees F.

"Time to turn off the air conditioning and open the windows," Luís suggested.

Just as they lowered the windows, Payson came into view, with the grand backdrop of the Mogollon Rim gleaming in the light of the sunrise.

"Now this is more like it!" Zeke exclaimed as he breathed in the crisp, pine-scented mountain air.

"Luís, thanks for driving. I've really enjoyed the scenery."

"Don't mention it," Luís replied and smiled, certain that he received the best part of the deal.

As Luís turned into the driveway of his parents' house, he said, "Oh, by the way, I forgot to mention that my younger sister, Abby, and her son, Javi, are living with my folks right now. But she's a sweetheart and Javi is a great kid."

"I'm looking forward to meeting your family," Zeke replied.

The house was a large, six bedroom log cabin-style home, with dark brown stained logs and a green metal roof. It was sitting on the side of a low hill facing northeast, with a grand view of the Mogollon Rim. Two tall blue spruce trees stood on opposite sides of the stone-paved circle driveway leading to a three-car garage. Large oaks and maples shaded the property in selected locations and well-manicured flowering hedges lined the front of the house on either side of a wide front porch, featuring two large oak rockers and a large oak porch swing.

Luís walked in the front door and Zeke followed. The living

room was warm and spacious, featuring Southwestern style furnishings, paintings and family pictures lining two of the walls and continuing down the wide hallway. Sculptures and other artifacts were visible inside several lighted antique wood and glass display cases.

Two large oak rockers with overstuffed cushions faced a large fireplace with a hand-hewn log mantle. Leather furniture, with iron and flagstone coffee tables and end tables filled the center of the room, facing a large-screen TV in one corner. A grand view of the Mogollon Rim could be seen through two large picture windows in the front wall. Just above the wide, solid oak front door, two tall windows reached to the top of the vaulted ceiling, filling the room with light from the rising sun.

Luís yelled, "Mama, your favorite child is in the building!"

"I'm in here," she replied.

"Mijo!" Mama smiled and hugged him as he walked into the kitchen. "It is so good to see you! How are you?"

"Hungry!" Luís gave her a peck on the cheek, perused the stove to see what was cooking, grabbed a freshly-made tortilla from a pile on a platter beside the stove and then asked, "Where's Papa?"

"He's out in his shop as usual. I was about to call him to breakfast."

Just then, Zeke walked into the kitchen. It was a large, ranch-style kitchen with a flagstone floor, a center island with a sink, dishwasher and a marble countertop with a large, stone cutting board. Above the island, a large, stainless steel hood with a skylight hung from the ceiling, providing ample light and hooks containing an array of pots, pans and cooking utensils.

A rich variety of delicious aromas from coffee, tortillas, bacon and beans filled the air, joined by the spicy aroma of chorizo and eggs simmering on the stove. The stove was in the center of a long marble countertop, with cabinets and drawers underneath, that ran the length of the wall and continued along an adjacent wall where it ended at a doorway leading into a large pantry. Oak cabinets filled the space above the entire counter. On the opposite wall sat a long, rectangular oak dining table with twelve oak chairs. The table was covered with a tan table cloth trimmed with lace and decorated with Kokopellies around the edge.

The walls were decorated with paintings and pictures. Above the counter beside the stove a wooden plaque read; Mama's kitchen: wipe your feet, wash your hands and mind your manners!

Mama was a lovely American Indian lady of the Pascua Yaqui Tribe, with salt and pepper hair, light brown eyes and a well-rounded figure. She elbowed Luís in the ribs and said, "And who is this handsome young man?"

In between bites of tortilla, Luís managed to mumble introductions.

"Mama, this is my friend and associate, Zeke Sikes. Zeke, this is mi Madre, Adelita Gonzales."

Mama smiled and said, "I am very pleased to meet you." Then she offered her hand. "Please, call me Mama."

Zeke took her hand and replied, "The honor is mine, Mama."

"Oh, what nice manners! Mijo, I like this one." Then she put her arm around Zeke's waist, pulled him to the stove and said, "Have a tortilla," and handed him one.

Just then, Papa came into the kitchen through the back door.

"What's this?!" Papa bellowed, "While I'm slaving away in my shop, my sweetheart is fooling around with a young stud!" then he winked at Zeke, kissed his wife on the cheek and grabbed a tortilla.

Luís walked over and hugged his dad, "Great to see you, Papa. You're looking healthy."

"I'm well for an old fart! How are you doing, Mijo?"

"I'm great. And these tortillas are delicious, Ma!" He said as he reached for a second one.

"Papa, this is my friend and associate, Zeke Sikes. Zeke, this is mi Papa, Bernardo Gonzales."

"Please, call me Bernie," he said and shook Zeke's hand with a powerful grip. Then he said, "Have a seat. Make yourself at home."

Zeke chose a chair on the side of the table facing the stove and sat down.

Bernie, a broad shouldered, six-foot tall, American Indian gentleman of the Navajo Tribe, with dark eyes and a wicked sense of humor, sat down across the table, facing Zeke and said, "'Associate,' Luís said. So, you're also with Border Patrol?"

"I'm a federal law enforcement officer," Zeke replied non-specifically, "TDY to Ajo Station."

"Zeke's only here for a short time, Papa. He's working with me while he's here, or I should say I'm working with him."

"Where's home, Zeke?" Bernie inquired.

Then, Mama interrupted. "I'll bet your mother calls you Ezekiel, doesn't she?"

"Yes… Mam," Zeke replied, taken somewhat off guard.

"I thought so," She replied, quite pleased with herself.

Then he answered Bernie's question; "I was born and raised in Hillsdale, Michigan, Sir. Right now I'm living in Arlington, Virginia."

"You're a long way from home. Is this your first time visiting Arizona?"

"Yes, Sir."

"How do you like it so far?"

"I'm enjoying my visit." Zeke gave Luis a self-conscious look, but he just smiled and winked. Zeke quietly sighed knowing that his cactus encounter story would not be revealed.

"DC is a fair hop from here," Bernie commented.

"Yes, Sir, about 2000 miles from Payson."

"My husband used to fly airliners from Sky Harbor to DC and many other places," Mama informed Zeke, explaining the term "hop" that Bernie used.

"Are you retired?"

"After 35 years," Bernie replied proudly.

"You must have a lot of hours."

"32,000, give or take."

"That's a lot. I can't even imagine."

"You fly?"

"I'm not a pilot, if that's what you mean. I used to fly with my college roommate. He had a Cessna 172 and we flew it everywhere. He wanted to be an instructor, so he would always fly right seat. On a typical trip, I would plan the flight and fly the airplane from chocks to chocks. As soon as I got the aircraft leveled out and trimmed for cruise, he would get on the phone with his girlfriend."

"Well then, Ezekiel, you actually are a pilot," Bernie explained, "You're just not certified. You obviously like to fly. You should go ahead and take the next step. Go to ground school. Find an instructor and earn your wings."

At that moment, Luís' younger sister, Abby, walked into the kitchen. Zeke immediately stood up and watched intently as she walked over to her mother and gave her a kiss on the cheek.

"Good morning, Mijita!" Mama said, "How is my beautiful daughter this morning?"

"Good Morning, Mama. I'm okay. You look lovely today."

"Thank you, Mija, you're so sweet."

Then Abby walked over to the table, placed her hand on Bernie's shoulder, leaned over, gave him a peck on the cheek and said, "Good morning Papa."

"Good morning, Mija," Bernie replied, as he lifted her hand from his shoulder and kissed it.

Then she turned her attention to Luís, now sitting at the table beside his dad. She gave him a peck on the head, patted him on the cheek and said, "Hi, Big Brother."

Luís leaned back in his chair and looked straight up at Abby, "Hi, little sis."

Then, Abby and Luís both looked at Zeke, who was still standing and staring at Abby, completely dumbfounded.

"Abby, this is Zeke. Zeke, this is my little sister, Abby."

Zeke attempted to walk around the table in order to properly greet her, but almost fell over his chair. Abby quickly went around the table to him, smiled sweetly, offered her hand and said, "Welcome to our home, Zeke. It is a pleasure to meet you."

Zeke took her hand very gently and replied, "The pleasure is most assuredly mine, Abby."

Zeke's entire personality somehow softened as he gazed into Abby's big, beautiful, honey-brown eyes. She was 5 feet 4 inches tall, about 120 pounds, and dressed very casually, wearing an Arizona Sun Devils football jersey, old faded torn blue jeans and thick white socks. She was stunningly beautiful, with olive skin, and long, straight, chestnut-brown hair that fell over her shoulders and partway down her back. She radiated a down-to-earth, country-girl beauty and simple charm that was almost indescribable and yet, undeniable.

After his initial greeting, Zeke was rendered completely speechless and just continued staring at Abby's beautiful face, thinking she looked like an Indian princess.

Abby slowly retrieved her hand from his, and then said, "Please, sit down, Zeke. Make yourself at home."

Zeke immediately sat down. Then, standing on his left side, Abby rested her right hand on the back of his chair and placed her left hand on the table in front of him. She cocked her head sideways, causing her hair to shift and fall over her left shoulder, then sweetly asked, "Can I get you a cup of coffee?"

Gazing up at her face, no more than two feet from his, Zeke was still speechless.

Recognizing his sister's coy flirting that he had seen many times before, Luís said, "Doc, you still with us?"

Zeke looked at Luís and blushed, then looked back at Abby and replied, "Yes… Yes, Mam, I would love some coffee."

Everyone watched Abby as she flitted like a little bird across the kitchen toward the coffee pot. Mama and Bernie exchanged surprised, silent glances.

Abby turned and sweetly asked, "How do you like your coffee, Zeke?"

"Just a splash of milk, thank you."

Abby quickly brought his coffee and placed it in front of him, then rested her left hand on his left bicep. She touched his right shoulder with her right hand and then slid her hand up his neck until she touched his hair, leaned very close to his left ear and whispered in a soft, alluring voice, "Enjoy…"

Zeke blushed, looked up at her and replied, "Thank… thank you, Abby."

After witnessing that moment between Abby and Zeke, Mama's eyes gleamed as she smiled at Bernie. He returned her smile and winked.

Abby then went to the hallway entrance, stopped and called, "Javi, hurry up! It's almost time for school and you haven't eaten breakfast yet. What would you like?"

"Cereal, please," came his reply from down the hall.

Abby prepared a bowl of cereal and a glass of orange juice and placed it on the table just as Javi came in the kitchen. She pulled out a chair for Javi beside Zeke and said, "Zeke, I would like you to meet my son, Javier."

Zeke stood up and Abby continued her introduction, "Javi, this is Mister Zeke Sikes."

Zeke turned to Javi, reached out for a handshake and said, "Pleased to meet you, Javier."

"Hello." Javi said, and instead of returning Zeke's handshake, he put out his fist. Zeke responded immediately and bumped fists.

Javi looked up at him and said, "Cool!" and then sat down and started eating his cereal.

Then Bernie said to Javi, "Squirt, as soon as you're ready, I'll take you to school."

"Okay, Grandpa."

"Thanks, Papa," Abby said, smiling gratefully at her dad.

Bernie just smiled at her and winked.

After a very enjoyable breakfast, Abby offered to show Zeke around Payson. Luís volunteered to help Mama clean up the kitchen, which actually meant that he was going to continue eating.

Abby's comprehensive tour of Payson ended at Green Valley Park, where she and Zeke walked around the park and picturesque lake several times, then sat beside the lake on the well-manicured lawn and talked for a while. Then he drove her to Saw Mill Crossing for ice cream at Scoops.

As Abby nibbled at her ice cream cone, she asked, "Is Zeke your nickname?"

"Yes. My full name is Ezekiel Bartholomew. I'm not overly fond of it, but that's my heritage. My paternal grandfather is Ezekiel. Everyone calls him Ezzy. He calls me, Zee. I think my little sister called me Zeke because she couldn't pronounce Ezekiel, and it stuck. Thank goodness I wasn't nicknamed 'Bart'."

Abby giggled.

"My great-grandfather was Bartholomew. He was a medical doctor, born in Germany."

"Is Abby a nickname, too?" Zeke asked.

"Yes," Abby replied, "My full name is Abril Esmeralda."

"That's a pretty name."

"Thank you, you're sweet."

"No, really, your name is beautiful, Abril Esmeralda, just like you."

Abby blushed, glanced away and said, "It's been a long time since any guy told me that I was beautiful…" Then she smiled at him and said, "Thank you."

"Well then, there are a lot of really stupid guys in Arizona."

Abby laughed. "I can't argue with that!"

Then she changed the subject. "Tell me; at breakfast, why did Luís call you Doc?"

"He started that right after we met."

"But why, Doc?"

"I have a PhD."

"Oh!" Abby reacted with surprise. "I thought you were a Border Patrol Agent like Luís."

"I'm a federal law enforcement officer, but I also have a Doctorate of Philosophy in Politics."

"That sounds very important."

"Along with five bucks," He replied, "It will buy you a cup of coffee, most places."

Abby reached across the table, tenderly touched Zeke on the hand and said, "Oh, I'm sure it's more important than that."

"Only to certain people," He replied and shrugged.

Abby reached across the table with her other hand, gently touched his chin with her fingertips, looked into his eyes and said, "Well, I'm one of those people."

Zeke took her hand in his and simply smiled.

Then he looked at her introspectively, "You know, it's strange, but I feel like I've known you for a long time. And yet, we met for the first time, what... four hours ago?"

"I know." Abby agreed. "I feel the same way. And it is strange, but I like this kind of strange."

"Me, too." Zeke replied, and smiled. Then he suggested, "We probably should be getting back."

As he opened the door of his truck for her, he commented, "We've been gone so long they'll think I've kidnapped you."

Abby laughed, "They'd probably say, 'Hooray! Keep 'er!'"

Zeke walked around the truck, opened his door, and as he was climbing in said, "I'd be most happy to take them up on that offer."

As they drove away, Abby smiled and quietly studied him for a long moment.

Back at the house, Luís was already eating lunch when Zeke and Abby walked into the kitchen,

"I couldn't wait on you two." Luís said. "Mama made tacos. You'd better get some before I eat 'em all!"

"I see your appetite hasn't changed any," Abby commented to Luís as she handed Zeke a clean plate.

"What can I say, Sis, I'm a growing boy."

Abby looked at Luís with a raised eyebrow as Mama said, "Everything is on the counter, so help yourselves."

Zeke walked up to the counter with his plate. Abby followed and stopped beside him. She leaned on the counter, selected a taco with her left hand and took a bite, then reached up with her right hand and gently caressed Zeke's back and shoulders.

Mama immediately noticed, silently motioned to Luís and pointed at the couple. Luís turned to look, then glanced back at his mother with a surprised, but pleased expression. His mother smiled back and gave him a thumbs up sign.

There was also a bowl of corn chips on the counter, along with a bowl of Mama's homemade salsa.

Abby handed Zeke a chip and said, "Try Mama's salsa. It's delicious." Then scooped some salsa onto a chip for herself.

Zeke scooped up a generous portion onto the chip and popped it into his mouth. Seconds later his eyes grew a bit wider and he immediately looked at Luís.

Luís smiled and said, "I told you; Mama's salsa's a bit hot."

Zeke nodded, swallowed and cleared his throat.

Abby handed Zeke a glass of iced tea and said, "Here you go Sweetie."

Zeke gratefully accepted the glass, took a long drink and then hoarsely whispered, "Thank you."

"So, Ezekiel, what do you think of my salsa?" Mama asked.

Zeke looked pleadingly at Abby. She smiled and said, "He thinks it's delicious, Mama."

"Refill?" Abby asked, holding the tea pitcher as she contained her amusement.

"Yes. Please." Zeke whispered as she filled it, then he immediately took another drink and sighed.

Abby smiled, patted him on the cheek and said, "You'll get used to it."

Later in the afternoon, Abby said to Mama, "It's time to pick up Javi from school."

"Do you want Papa to go get him?"

"I'll take you." Zeke quickly offered.

"Great!" Abby replied and took his arm. "Javi is going to love your truck."

***

Zeke and Abby had just returned with Javi when an older, somewhat rundown Toyota pickup with two men inside pulled up behind the Raptor. A big guy with broad shoulders got out of the passenger side and yelled at Abby, "Who the hell is that asshole?"

Zeke looked at the guy and then at Abby. Abby grabbed Javi's hand, looked at Zeke apologetically and said, "I'm so sorry, Ezekiel, that's Jack, my ex-husband."

The big guy yelled again, "Did you hear me, bitch? I said, who is that asshole?"

"Jack, will you please stop cursing?" Abby pleaded.

He spat on the ground and replied, "Screw you."

At that point, everyone in the house came outside to see what was going on.

Zeke, now visibly annoyed, looked at Abby and whispered, "Jack needs to shut up."

Jack watched as Luís slowly walked over to the driver's side of the pickup and spoke to the driver, "Hello Frank."

"Yo, Bro, whaz up?" Frank replied.

Luís didn't reply, but just leaned against the truck.

Abby whispered pleadingly to Zeke. "Ezekiel, please, don't do anything. Jack is very violent. He's already been in jail a number of times for assault."

Zeke took Abby's hand and pulled her aside, intending to speak to her confidentially.

Jack yelled, "Get your paws off of my bitch, ass hole!"

Zeke looked at Jack, then looked back at Abby for a moment, then turned to Jack and said calmly, "I am speaking with Abril right now. I will deal with you in a moment."

Mama and Bernie looked at each other with surprise and simultaneously whispered, "Abril?"

Abby started to plead with Zeke again but he gently placed his fingers over her lips and said. "Abril, I'm a Special Agent with the DEA. I can handle this. Trust me. Okay?"

Abby raised her eyebrows in surprise and just nodded.

Zeke then started walking toward Jack and Jack met him halfway. As they came face to face, no more than three feet apart, it was apparent that Jack was at least twice Zeke's size.

In the truck, Frank looked up at Luís, "Whaz up with this dude? He nuts?"

"No, Frank, he's not nuts. He's a nice guy. And someone that you really don't want to screw with... ever."

Jack looked down at Zeke and asked, "What's your problem, asshole?"

"My name is Zeke." He replied sternly.

Jack didn't comment.

"So," Zeke continued. "What's your problem...Jack?"

"You, and that bitch over there."

Zeke gritted his teeth and growled, "Her name is Abril!"

"So f***ing what." Jack flippantly replied, then reached out toward Zeke with his right hand, intending to shove him backwards.

Zeke grabbed Jack's hand at the wrist with his right hand, gave it a small twist and then grabbed his elbow with his left hand. Jack's eyes grew bigger as pain ran up and down his arm from his shoulder to his wrist.

Quietly, Zeke spoke: "Okay, Jack, here's what's going to happen; either you're going to be on the ground crying like a little girl, or we're going to come to a meeting of the minds. Do you understand?"

Jack nodded.

"I'm guessing that you want to speak to your son?"

Jack nodded again.

"Do you realize that he has heard the filth spewing out of your mouth and the despicable names that you just called his mother?"

Jack nodded again as beads of sweat began to roll down his forehead.

"You and Abril are divorced, correct?"

Jack nodded again.

"Consequently, you have no right to tell her anything about what she does or doesn't do, correct?"

Jack hesitated, Zeke tightened his hold and Jack winced, then nodded again.

"Jack, if you don't want your son to see you on the ground begging me to release you, you're going to apologize for your inexcusable behavior. First to his mother, then to his grandparents, and finally, to him. Then, if Javier wants to speak to you, you'll be allowed a few supervised moments with your son. Are we on the same page now, Jack?"

Jack nodded slowly.

"Good. Now, I'm going to release you, but know this; if I ever hear that you have spoken to Abril in the manner in which you have today, I'll be coming to see you. And if you ever as much as lay one finger on her, you will wake up in the desert, staked over an ant hill, having the agonizingly painful opportunity to experience being eaten alive by hungry ants. Are we clear?"

Jack hesitated. Zeke tightened his hold considerably. Jack whimpered, and Zeke repeated his question, "Are we clear?"

Jack nodded and Zeke released him. Jacks right arm dropped, limp at his side. He stepped back a few paces and tried, unsuccessfully, to move his arm. Then, he stepped forward, looked at Abby and said, "I'm sorry for the way I've acted and the names that I called you."

Then Jack looked at Bernie and Mama, "Sir, Mam, I apologize for my behavior."

Then he slowly knelt down, looked at Javi and said, "I'm sorry son, the way I've been behaving is wrong. I shouldn't call your mom names. Can I see you for a little bit?"

Javi hesitated momentarily and looked at Abby. She smiled at him and said, "It's alright Mijito, talk to your dad a little bit if you want."

Abby watched Javi as he slowly went to Jack and hugged him. Then she turned to Zeke, placed her hands on his cheeks, kissed him tenderly on the lips and whispered, "Thank you."

Javi and Jack talked for about ten minutes. Finally Jack kissed Javi goodbye, thanked Abby, and gave Zeke a respectful nod as he left.

As Jack drove away, Luís walked up to Zeke.

"Thanks, Amigo," Zeke said, "I appreciate you covering the driver."

"No problem. I figured you had your hands full with the Jackass." Then Luís slapped him on the shoulder and said, "Nicely done, Doc. But, I don't know how you kept from killing the bastard."

"I considered it," Zeke replied as he stared in the direction that Jack had departed.

Abby, standing beside Zeke with her arm around his waist, looked up at him and wondered if he was kidding or not.

Back inside, Bernie shook Zeke's hand and said, "Thanks for handling that. Every time I tangle with Jack-ass we end up calling the police." Bernie turned to walk away, then turned back and asked, "By the way, how did you do that wrist and elbow thing?"

"It's just a matter of pain centers and pressure points. It's like hitting your funny bone really hard, only more painful. Although your elbow isn't really injured by a bumped funny bone, your arm feels weak and almost useless because of the pain. Add more pain and it gets serious. It can be an effective way to control some people. Jack puts on a big bad act, but he's really a coward. It doesn't take much pain to control him."

"What if that trick hadn't worked?" Bernie asked.

"Take it to the next level." Zeke replied.

Just then, Javi turned to Abby and asked, "Mom, why was Daddy and Mister Zeke holding hands?"

"Holding hands?" She asked, confused for an instant, then she gave Zeke a distressed glance, turned back to Javi and replied, "Well, Ezekiel was just helping your daddy adjust his attitude, Mijo."

Zeke was concerned by the look on Abby's face and came to where she and Javi were standing.

Javi looked up at Zeke and said, "Mister Zeke, I hope that you and my Daddy hold hands again so that you can adjust his attitude. He was much nicer after that."

Zeke knelt down, smiled and held out his fist for a fist bump. Javi obliged, then smiled back at Zeke and walked away. Zeke looked up at Abby just as tears began rolling down her cheeks. He quickly stood up and held her close, then he wiped away her tears and whispered, "Don't worry, Beautiful, everything will be okay."

Abby held him tighter and buried her face on his chest, then she broke down and wept. Zeke immediately scooped her up into his arms and headed down the hallway.

Luís saw what was happening and said, "Her room is the second door on the left."

Zeke closed the door and gently laid Abby on her bed. She immediately turned over and buried her face in her pillow, still crying. Zeke sat beside her on the bed and slowly massaged her back and shoulders long after she had stopped crying. It was the first time that he had touched a girl with such affection in ten years. Suddenly, he stopped, stood up and quickly left her room, closing the door behind him.

Several hours later it was late afternoon. Zeke was alone in the back yard, reclining on a chaise lounge, drinking a beer and watching humming birds darting about and feeding from several feeders hanging from tree limbs around the yard. The entire back yard was bathed in an orange glow from a beautiful, multi-colored, Arizona sunset.

Abby quietly walked up behind him, slid her arms over his shoulders, gently kissed his ear and whispered, "Beautiful sunset."

Zeke put down his beer, took her hand and pulled her on top of him. "Not as beautiful as you," He whispered, then wrapped his arms around her and kissed her long and deeply.

In the kitchen, Mama was preparing dinner. She happened to glance out one of the kitchen windows, saw them kissing and whispered, "Madre Mia! Papa! Papa!" She then ran into the hallway and called again in a loud whisper. "Papa! Come see! Andale! Come see!" and excitedly ran back to the kitchen window.

Then Bernie rushed into the kitchen asking, "What is all the fuss?!"

"Look! Look!" She pulled him to the window and pointed. Zeke and Abby were still kissing. And very passionately. Bernie and Mama looked at each other in amazement. Then they hugged each other and Bernie said, "Mama, our little girl has finally come out of her shell."

Zeke and Abby cuddled, neither one speaking.

Finally, she said, "Thank you for carrying me to my room."

"I couldn't bear to see you crying. I wanted to ease your pain, but I didn't know how. I felt so helpless."

"You comforted me more than you know. It's been so long since a man showed me tenderness and compassion. I fell asleep feeling your touch and dreamed that you were holding me. I can't remember when I've had a dream like that."

Then she whispered in his ear, "I think I was having an orgasm when I woke up."

After admitting that, she buried her face against his neck in embarrassment. Then she giggled, lifted herself up so that her face was about six inches from his, looked into his eyes and confessed, "I don't believe I just told you that!" and buried her face against his neck again.

Zeke ran his fingers through her long, silky hair, then pulled her to him and kissed her deeply once more.

A while later, still cuddled together on the chaise lounge, they were talking softly. Zeke was trying to come up with something funny to say because he loved to hear Abby laugh.

Suddenly he grew serious and said, "I'm sorry that I left your room so abruptly this afternoon. I wanted to stay and comfort you, but I just couldn't."

"By that time I think your wonderful massage had just about put me to sleep. I was only vaguely aware that you left. Then I fell fast asleep. Was something wrong?"

"Believe it or not, touching you like that... I became lost in you. But, it didn't seem right, it just doesn't seem all that long ago since—"

"Since you touched Cynthia that way?"

"Yes... But how...?"

"Luís," She confessed. "He came up while you were gone to

Massachusetts. We were talking about his job and then he began telling me about you. I became so fascinated that I kept prodding him until he told me everything. But don't blame him, I've always been able to get Luís to tell me anything."

Then Zeke began to explain. "Cynthia has been a part of me for such a long time. When I was touching you, I suddenly felt like I was being unfaithful. I just couldn't deal with it. So, I walked around a while, then came out here to think. Some of the words that my granddad said to me just before I left Cambridge kept echoing in my mind.

"Then suddenly, I got it. I realized that I've been holding on to her memory for the wrong reasons. I'm blessed to have loved her and to have been loved by her, but I've been living in the past, holding on to her memory as if that was enough to sustain me for the rest of my life. Cynthia wouldn't have wanted that. She loved life and would've wanted me to live it to the fullest.

"I suddenly realized that I don't have to let her go. She will always be a part of me, but that's okay. That's how it should be."

"Yes, I agree. So, what did your grandad say to you?"

"He said, 'you've been alone too long. Get out there and have some fun. Then find yourself a nice girl, get married and start making babies. I want more great grandkids!'"

Abby threw her head back and laughed out loud, then she said, "Your granddad sounds like a rascal. But he's also very wise. I, too, have been hiding from life and living in a shell. But now that I've met you, I don't want to hide any longer."

Then she leaned in and whispered in his ear. "And when you're ready to get married and start making babies, let me know." And then kissed him deeply.

They were just about to kiss again, when Mama called everyone to dinner.

And just then, Luís' girlfriend, Bekah, arrived from Flagstaff. Luís introduced her to Zeke and then everyone sat down to have dinner.

During dinner, Javi said, "Mister Zeke, I sure did like riding in your Raptor today. That thing is awesome!"

"Well, thank you, Javi," Zeke replied, "I'm glad you enjoyed it. I enjoy driving it, too."

"Can we go for another ride tomorrow?" Javi asked.

"I don't see why not… tell you what, since Bekah is here, and if it's okay with your mom, why don't you, your mom, Bekah, Luís and I take a ride up on the Rim tomorrow morning and do some off-roading?"

"Cool! That would be awesome!" The Javi looked at his mom pleadingly and asked, "Could we, Mom?"

Abby smiled and said "Sure."

"Hurray!" Javi shouted.

"Not so loud young man!" Abby scolded. "You're at the dinner table." Then she added, "You'll need to go to bed early tonight if you want to go four-wheeling tomorrow."

"Yes, Mam." He replied. "I'll go to bed now," and started to leave the table.

"No, wait. Finish eating. Then get ready for bed."

"Okay Mom."

After dinner, Abby and Zeke tucked Javi in for the night, and then the adults went out to the patio to have some wine and visit. After a while Bernie and Mama decided to turn in, but Abby, Zeke, Bekah and Luís remained on the patio, talking and drinking more wine.

It had been over two years since Abby had drank any alcohol. Before long she was silly drunk, and becoming very amorous. Finally, Zeke scooped her up in his arms and carried her to her room. She was very insistent that Zeke sleep with her, and it took him some doing to get her settled down. Then he quietly left her room, shut the door and went to his room.

Early the next morning, Zeke was having coffee in the kitchen with Mama when Bernie came in and sat across from Zeke. Bernie was sipping his coffee and not saying much, then finally he looked at Mama, then at Zeke and said, "I want to thank you for taking care of our daughter last night. We couldn't help but hear. She must have been a handful."

Zeke smiled, "Yes, Sir, she was. I gather she doesn't drink very often."

Then Mama joined the conversation. "Abril hasn't been doing anything but hiding away in her bedroom, living like a hermit. Jack was abusive. And if that wasn't bad enough, he invited a friend over for dinner one night. He and his friend got drunk, and then Jack— the pinche bastard, offered to share Abril with his friend. She just couldn't cope with it. She got the baby and came back home that night. She never went back. We got the rest of her things a few days later.

"Since the divorce she has had nothing to do with men, period. She goes nowhere except to take Javi to and from school, and she does nothing, except mope around here. It's been almost three years. We've all been very worried about her."

Then Bernie said, "Ezekiel, I want to thank you for bringing our daughter out of her shell. It is so wonderful to see her happy and smiling again. But I especially want to thank you for last night. It was very obvious what she wanted, even though it was the alcohol talking. You could easily have taken advantage of her. Now, don't get me wrong, that's none of my business; she's a grown woman and can make her own decisions. But last night, alcohol was making those decisions for her. And you were a perfect gentleman. So, thank you for respecting our daughter."

"It was my honor, Sir. I could never take advantage of Abril like that. I can't even stand to see her upset, it would kill me to know I had done something like that to her. Truthfully, she has brought me out of my shell, too. I guess you could say that we've saved each other. And, just so you both to know, I think I'm falling in love with her."

Bernie and Mama looked at each other knowingly, then Mama replied, "It's quite obvious young man. We see the way you look at her. And we also see the way she looks at you. I think she's falling in love with you as well.

Then Mama grew very serious. "This is all very sudden. Abril is very vulnerable right now. And, apparently, you are as well. Just go slowly. Take your time. Get to know one another. You're young, you have all the time in the world.

Then she narrowed her eyes, pointed her finger at Zeke and said, "So don't break my little girl's heart!"

"Oh no, Mam. You don't have to worry about that."

Just then, a very hung-over Abby, wearing her robe, looking disheveled and miserable, dragged herself into the kitchen, sat on Zeke's lap and laid her head on the table.

"Good morning, lover girl!" Bernie said.

"Uhnnnn." She groaned.

"My poor Baby Girl," Mama teased, "can't hold her wine."

"Uhnnnn."

Zeke leaned over, pulled her tangled hair aside, kissed her softly on her cheek and whispered, "Good morning Sunshine."

"Not that good," she moaned hoarsely.

Then Zeke slid his coffee cup in front of her. She raised up and looked at it, then made a nauseated noise, covered her mouth with her hand and ran toward the bathroom.

Zeke looked at Bernie and Mama, raised his eyebrows and sighed, then said, "I think she might need some help," and followed her.

The bathroom door was open. Zeke looked in to find Abby kneeling in front of the toilet, retching and trying to keep her hair out of the way. He quickly came to her aid, gathered up her hair and tucked it down the back of her robe. Then he reached into the linen closet, grabbed a washcloth, soaked it with cold water, folded it, and pressed it against her forehead.

Momentarily her retching stopped. She raised up, put her hand on Zeke's hand and hoarsely whispered, "Thank you."

Zeke helped her stand up, and then fetched a cup of water so she could rinse out her mouth.

Zeke carefully wiped her face with the wash cloth, then she leaned against him, laid her head on his shoulder and whispered pleadingly, "Please don't ever let me drink that much wine again."

Zeke scooped Abby up in his arms, took her to her bedroom and sat her down in front of her vanity.

She looked in the mirror, then covered her face with her hands and moaned, "Oh, God…"

Zeke took her hair brush from the vanity, then kneeled down, kissed her cheek and whispered, "You're beautiful." Then he began to gently untangle and brush her hair.

"Owww…" she moaned, "even my hair hurts!"

"I'll be easy." He softly reassured her.

As he gently brushed the full length of her hair, she closed her eyes and said, "That feels so good."

"You have such beautiful hair, it's so soft and silky." Then he placed his hands on her shoulders and tenderly kissed her on the back of her head.

She opened her eyes and met his in the mirror, they lingered for a long moment, just silently gazing at each other, and then she asked, "Why are you being so good to me?"

"Because I want to. And you need it. This is the way you should be treated. Always."

She smiled demurely, reached up and took his hands in hers,

then she closed her eyes and cuddled his right hand against her cheek.

He kissed her on top of her head once more and said, "Okay, let's see if I can get your hair organized just a bit—at least as well as my feeble skills will permit."

Then he picked up a hair tie from the vanity and tied her hair into a ponytail.

"There," he declared, "much better."

She looked at her reflection in the mirror and frowned. He bent down, kissed her gently on the lips, and repeated, "You're beautiful."

Then he scooped her into his arms again and headed out the door toward the kitchen.

She put her arms around his neck, kissed him on the cheek and said, "I could get used to this."

"So could I…" He replied and she kissed him again.

In the kitchen, Bernie, Luís and Javi were sitting at the dining table. Mama and Bekah were preparing breakfast.

Zeke gently lowered Abby into a chair at the table and took a seat beside her.

Luís said, "Well, good morning, your highness."

"Good morning again, lover girl," Bernie said, "You look much better now."

"Thanks to Ezekiel," She replied and squeezed his hand. "Now if I only felt better."

Bekah brought Abby a cup of black coffee, stroked her ponytail and then smiled and said, "Good morning, lover girl."

Abby looked up at her and said, "Thank you, sweetie."

Then she wrinkled her forehead and asked, "Why is everyone calling me 'lover girl'?"

"Well…" Zeke began and looked down at the table.

From the stove, Mama said, "Your highness was just a bit amorous when Ezekiel carried you to your boudoir last night."

"I was?" She replied and then looked at Zeke.

"Afraid so," Zeke replied sheepishly, then he added, "You were quite the little handful."

Embarrassed, Abby blushed, covered her face with her hands and admitted, "I don't remember anything except sitting on the patio drinking wine with everyone."

Then she peaked apprehensively through her fingers at Zeke.

He reached out and caressed her shoulders. "After I tucked you in, you went right to sleep. Well, passed out might be a more accurate term. As I closed your door, you were snoring."

Abby smiled and caressed his cheek, then her expression suddenly changed to shock as she exclaimed, "Snoring?!"

"Just a little bit. Actually, it sounded more like you were purring."

"Oh," She said, sounding somewhat surprised, then she took a sip of coffee and made a yucky face,

"This tastes awful!"

"It's black," Bekah informed her. "I thought something sugary might not go down so well."

Abby got out of her chair with her cup, then picked up Zeke's cup and went over to the coffee pot where she added several teaspoons of sugar to her cup, and then poured in French vanilla creamer as well.

As she filled Zeke's cup, she asked, "You just take milk, right, Honey?"

Bekah looked at Mama with a surprised, inquisitive expression and silently mouthed, "Honey?"

Mama just smiled and nodded.

"Yes, Sweetheart, that's right, just milk," Zeke replied.

Bekah looked even more surprised and Mama gave her a thumbs up sign.

Abby returned to the table, gave Zeke a peck on the cheek and put his coffee in front of him. Then Javi asked for cereal, so she served him a bowl.

As he ate, without looking up, he asked, "Mom, what does 'amorous' mean"?

Abby got a terrified look on her face and replied, "Just never you mind!"

"He doesn't miss a thing, does he?" Zeke commented.

"Apparently not," Luís replied and bit his lips to hide his amusement.

Abby gave Luís a threating look, grabbed a folded dish towel and smacked him the top of his head with it.

After breakfast, Abby, Zeke, Javi, Luís & Bekah went four-wheeling on the Raptor. Everyone got to drive it, even Javi drove while sitting on Zeke's lap. Later on that evening, everyone was watching a movie in the living room. Javi sat between Abby and

Zeke. Then he snuggled up against Zeke and fell asleep.

Mama looked at Javi and said, "Ezekiel, I think you've made a friend."

Abby looked at Javi and said, "Awww, how sweet. I think we'd better put him to bed."

Zeke gently lifted Javi in his arms and followed Abby to his bedroom.

After Javi had been tucked in, they stood holding each other, watching him sleep.

"He had so much fun today," Abby said. "Thank you for being so good to him."

"He's easy to be good to, just like you. He's a great kid. And you're a good mother. I don't understand why Jack doesn't try to be a better father. I'd be proud to be Javi's dad."

Abby looked up at Zeke and whispered, "Really?"

Zeke looked at her, gently caressed her cheek and said simply, "He's your son."

Then Abby kissed him.

Javi stirred and, without even looking, said, "No kissing in my room!" then rolled over and snuggled into his pillow.

They both looked at Javi, and then at each other.

"I think we've just been scolded," Zeke whispered.

Abby took Zeke's hand, and as she led him out of Javi's room, whispered, "I know we have!"

Sunday afternoon came and it was time to go. The sun had just disappeared behind the mountains, bathing the scene in the golden half-light of the fading day.

Zeke thanked Bernie and Mama for their wonderful hospitality and said his goodbyes. Luís walked Bekah out to her car, and as they were saying their goodbyes, Zeke and Abby stood by the Raptor, silently looking into each other's eyes, both reluctant to part and searching for something else to say besides goodbye.

Finally, Abby slid her arms around Zeke's waist, laid her head on his chest and said, "This whole weekend seems like a fairytale dream. It's hard to believe that so much could happen in just three days. My whole life has changed. But I'm just so afraid that after you go, I'll find that it's all been a mistake and we'll never see each other again."

Zeke gently turned her face up to his. Then he kissed her ever so tenderly and said, "Beautiful, the only way you'll get rid of me is if you chase me away with a big stick!"

Abby giggled and Zeke said, "I love your laugh." He kissed her on the tip of her nose.

Then he said, "Do you remember when we were having ice cream, and I told you that I felt like I've known you for a long time?" Abby nodded and he continued, "And you said that you felt the same way about me."

"Yes. And I do feel that way."

"Well, it's actually more than that. It seems as though I've known you my whole life. Being with you feels so natural, just like right now; your body pressing against mine, your touch, your smell, hearing your voice. I feel like we've always been this way, and this is where I'm supposed to be, with you, together always. What I'm trying to say, Abril Gonzales, I have fallen head over heels in love with you."

A big smile brightened her face and she replied, "And I have fallen in love with you, Ezekiel Sikes."

They kissed long and passionately. And were still kissing when Bekah drove away and Luís walked over to the Raptor. He stood there, trying to be discreet and allow them privacy, but then finally cleared his throat a couple of times and said, "We are planning to get back to Ajo tonight, right?

Zeke and Abby stopped kissing and looked at the ground, touching their foreheads together.

Then Zeke looked over at Luís, "Time to go, huh?"

"Sorry, Doc, but yeah." Then he climbed into the Raptor.

Zeke also got in, cranked the engine and the Raptor rumbled to life.

"I'll see you just as soon as I can, Beautiful."

Abby stood on the running board, leaned through the open window, kissed him again and whispered, "I love you. Be safe and come back to me." Then she pointed at Luís and said, "You take care of my Ezekiel!"

Abby stood on the driveway, waving goodbye and watching as the Raptor disappeared from sight, then she turned and ran partway up the driveway, jumped high in the air with her arms raised and yelled, "Yeeeeesss!!"

"Want coffee?" Zeke asked as he pulled in to a convenience store to fuel up on the way out of Payson.

"Sure. My treat," Luís replied and went in to get the coffees.

Zeke had just finished fueling when Luís returned and got in. Then Zeke got in and was about to start the Raptor when he heard a loud voice coming from behind the gas pump. Suddenly someone approached the driver's side window.

"Heads up, nine o'clock!" Luís warned.

Zeke looked left just as Jack stopped beside the Raptor. He was barefoot, wearing jeans and no shirt. He took a defiant stance, with his legs apart, looking down a Zeke. Then he remarked, "Well, well. If it isn't the new boyfriend drivin' his cute little toy truck."

As Zeke lowered his window he pulled his handgun from the holster along the side of his seat, put it between his legs, and then said, "Hello, Jack. What can I do for you?"

Jack was attracting the attention of the other customers as he said, quite loudly, "How 'bout eat shit and die!" and then laughed.

"Jack…" Zeke motioned with his finger for him to come closer. Jack leaned over, with his face at the top of the window, one hand on the windshield post, the other on the top of the cab and asked, "What the hell do you want?"

"He's drunk," Luís commented as he smelled the liquor on Jack's breath.

"I ain't drunk! I just had a few shots."

"More like a few dozen," Luís mumbled under his breath.

"Jack, do you remember the discussion that you and I had on Friday?" Zeke asked.

"What of it?"

Zeke slipped his DEA Special Agent badge off of his belt and held it up for Jack to see. At the same time, he brought his handgun into view. "I am very serious about Abril's wellbeing. I am also very serious about that ant hill. Don't make me have to show you just how serious I am…"

"Shit!" Jack said as he shoved himself away from the truck, then yelled, "You're a damn fed!"

Then he held his hands above his head. "Peace brother. No harm, no foul. I'm just screwin' with ya', man, don't mean no harm. Don't mean no harm."

Zeke started the Raptor, revved it up a couple of times, and then said, "Remember what I said, Jack," and drove away.

As Zeke pulled out onto Highway 87 heading south, he said, "Something's not right with that boy."

"Jack was a star quarterback in high school," Luís said, "and a fairly decent guy for an arrogant, entitled, self-important jock. But something happened just after he and Abby were married. He suddenly turned mean. And he's really mean when he's drunk. A total loose cannon."

"There's something about his eyes," Zeke observed. "When he looks at you, he has a thousand-yard stare. It's like there's someone else in there with him, looking back at you. He is one scary dude. And Abril has to deal with him wanting to see his son. He's going to be trouble…"

"By the way," Zeke continued, "Yesterday, Mama called Jack a 'pinche bastard'. I didn't want to ask what that meant. She obviously said it in a derogatory way, but I interpret 'pinche' as 'kitchen boy'. Kitchen boy bastard doesn't make much sense."

Luís laughed. "I see your confusion. Pinche is slang for worthless or insignificant. But when Mama refers to Jack like that, she's calling him mean and worthless."

Zeke nodded in agreement. "I think she has him nailed perfectly."

Luís continued. "When Mama says, 'that damn pinche gringo', everyone knows who she's talking about. She probably didn't say 'gringo' yesterday because she didn't want to offend you. Mama has a great deal of respect for you."

Zeke smiled and said, "Hmm…"

During the ride down the mountains, Zeke was quiet, just listening to music.

Luís had been studying him for a while and finally said, "I think it safe to say that you and my sister are an item."

"Amigo, your sister is…" Zeke searched for the right adjective.

Luís offered, "Amazing?"

"Yes! Yes, she is! I've never…" again he searched for the right words.

Luís added, "In your life ever met anyone like her?"

"Yes! That's it exactly! Abril is simply perfect in every way." Then Zeke smiled at him and said, "Amigo, I'm in love!"

"I'm pretty sure I noticed that."

Then Zeke's expression changed to apprehensive and he asked, "How do you feel about that, Luís?

I mean, you've known me longer than Abril has and that isn't very long at all. I know how protective brothers are over their sisters—I've intimidated several guys for wanting to date my sister, Allie. And Abril and I just met on Friday; that was just two and a half days ago!"

"Doc, I've known you long enough to know that you're a good guy. And you have integrity. That's a rare commodity these days. And you've made Abby happy again. It's been tearing my heart out to see how depressed she's been in the six years since her divorce.

"When we were growing up, she was bright, energetic and as happy as a little bird. She was our own little ray of sunshine. Then Jack got abusive and she just went dark. Now, our little ray of sunshine is back and I couldn't be happier."

"Well, how would you feel about me being your brother-in-law?"

"Caramba! I didn't realize you were that serious… well… I could do worse. Hell, what am I saying? We had Jack!"

Zeke looked at Luís and punched him on the arm.

Chapter Four
A Wedding and a Funeral

Zeke and Luís returned to work and back to the same day to day routine. The daily directive email message from Zeke's supervisor never varied. The cartel turf war for Northern Mexico raged on, with increasing carnage and casualty figures. Evacuees claiming refugee status continued to flood U.S. ports of entry, but Customs reported nothing out of the ordinary except the increased volume of applicants, and even those numbers were beginning to decrease.

The Minutemen Project provided the additional eyes and ears that Zeke had hoped for, far exceeding his expectations for meeting his mission objective, yet their daily reports to Luís never mentioned sightings of Chinese Nationals or anything else out of the ordinary.

Zeke and Luís established a schedule alternating between cruising the Drag Road one day and utilizing various stationary surveillance positions along the border the next. The strategy wasn't intended to increase mission effectiveness but to stave off boredom as much as possible. However, the strategy was only marginally effective, with the possible exception that Zeke was becoming extremely familiar with bird and animal behavior in the Sonoran Desert. Due to the increasing day-time temperatures of early June, they began their workday before dawn and were back in the comfort of the air conditioned office at Ajo Station during the heat of the afternoon.

Zeke thought of Abby constantly. His affection for her grew with each passing day. Early morning text messages and late-night phone chats with Abby kept him sane, centered, and hopeful. Every weekend he and Luís were in Payson and every minute that he spent with Abby was more precious to him than mere words could possibly convey. More and more he realized that living without her was becoming entirely unbearable. Yet, he also realized that he and Abby had known each other for just over one month. The thought of asking her to marry him at this early stage in their relationship was absurd in the extreme, yet the more he thought about it, the more he liked the idea.

One rare midweek day away from work in late June, Zeke, Abby, Javi, Luís and Bekah went tubing on the Lower Salt River, which originates at Roosevelt Lake in Central Arizona northeast of Phoenix.

The river flows west from the Theodore Roosevelt Dam, feeding three lakes downstream; Apache Lake, Canyon Lake and Saguaro Lake. Flowing from Stewart Mountain Dam, which creates Saguaro Lake, the Lower Salt River continues carving a winding, scenic westerly path through the Sonoran Desert landscape of soaring rocks, beautiful mountain vistas and a forest of saguaro cactus, mesquite and other desert flora.

Zeke, Abby and the others were all floating along together on the tranquil river, enjoying the cool, clear-flowing water. The guys were dressed in long, baggy swimming trunks and ball caps. Bekah wore a yellow bikini and a matching sun hat. Abby wore a white, one-piece swim suit with a large, floppy-brimmed white hat.

Suddenly Abby spotted a unique rock on the river bottom. She and Zeke stopped and he retrieved it for her. Seeing that they had fallen slightly behind, Abby waved to the others and yelled, "We're coming! We'll catch up to you for lunch."

As they floated along, admiring the picturesque scenery and casually talking, Abby stretched her legs across Zeke's tube, placing her feet in his lap, which put her in a position so that they could make eye contact as they talked. It also gave Zeke the pleasurable opportunity to caress Abby's legs. He was doing just that when he noticed a small scar on her left knee.

"Sweetheart," He asked, "How did you get this scar?"

"Oh, that." She looked at him, reached out, took hold of his hand and sighed. "Long story; It's the result of a sports injury…

"I was on my high school cheering squad. In fact, I was captain. We were doing a pyramid during a football game. I was the top—what used to be call the flier. I was just getting into position as the ball was snapped. The quarterback ran the ball up the sideline, and just as we set and were about to dismount, he was knocked out of bounds and plowed right into us. The next thing I knew, I really was the flier, sailing through the air. Then everything went dark.

"I regained consciousness in the hospital several days later with my left leg and left wrist in casts, a bandage on my head and a huge headache. They told me that I had hit the concrete bleachers on my left side, so my knee and wrist took most of the impact. I also hit my head pretty hard, which gave me a concussion and put me in a coma.

"My wrist was broken, and my knee had been shattered, with torn tendons and ligaments, so they had to do emergency orthoscopic surgery while I was still unconscious.

"Not long after I woke up, the quarterback came in with a dozen roses and a box of candy and laid them beside me. He asked me how I was feeling and then began explaining that it was all his fault because a running back was open and he could've thrown a pass, but he chose to run the ball instead.

He took my hand and began apologizing profusely, then fell to his knees, crying like a baby.

"Some of the other girls had also been injured, but not nearly as bad as I was, so I received all of his sympathy and attention. The quarterback continued to pet and pamper me through my whole ordeal, during which we started dating. He was the star, so I became his biggest fan, cheering him on from the sidelines.

It was six months and several more surgeries before I could walk without crutches, and then two more months of intense physical therapy before I could run again. During my final appointment with my orthopedist, he told me that my knee had healed nicely, but that my cheerleading days were over, which only verified what I had already suspected.

"By then our romance had become hot and heavy. One thing led to another and one night in the back seat of his car I found myself naked and about to have sex. I told him that he should be wearing a condom, but he said that was like showering in a raincoat and promised that he would pull out in time. Well, he didn't. Not long after that I was late for my period and about forty weeks later I became the seventeen year old mother of a beautiful, bouncing baby boy."

"The quarterback was Jack," Zeke said sympathetically.

"Yep. And that, as they say, is the rest of the story. Javi has been such a blessing in my life. And now, I have another blessing… you." Then she kissed his hand.

"I love you, Abril Gonzales."

"I love you, too, Ezekiel Sikes."

The moment was tranquil, with the ambience of the flowing river, a light summer breeze and the sounds of birds singing along the riverbank. Far downstream, distant voices and music could faintly be heard.

Zeke looked at Abby, reached out and took both of her hands in his, took a deep breath and said, "Abril, despite the fact that we both feel we've known each other for a very long time, truthfully, we know that it hasn't been very long at all.

"But, in that short time I've come to know what a truly wonderful person you are; you're courageous and compassionate, intelligent and funny, exciting and adventurous, you're drop-dead gorgeous. Your enchanting smile not only lights up your face, it also brightens the world around you. Yet you never use that to get your way; instead, you're modest and unassuming about your beauty. And you're also beautiful on the inside; you have a noble and beautiful soul. You take great pride in your Native American heritage, which makes me even more proud of you.

"You're hard-working and ambitious, and not afraid to tackle anything that needs to be done. You have a ferocious temper, yet your easy-going nature is as gentle as an early morning breeze. You're fiercely patriotic, and you love God and your family with a passionate devotion. And I know that you love me just as much as I love you."

As Abby listened intently to his words, her eyes grew wide and she pulled her hands away from his and covered her mouth as she drew in a deep breath in anticipation of what she felt was about to happen.

"Abril Gonzales, I want to take care of you and Javi. I want to love you and protect you and be there for you always. I need you beside me and I desperately want you in my life. Will you do me the honor of accepting my hand in marriage?"

Abby squealed with delight and screamed, "Are you kidding me?! Yes! Yes, I will marry you, Ezekiel Sikes!" Then she clenched her fists and held them high above her head, looked up at the sky and yelled, "Yes! Yes!! Yeeesss!!!" then she literally jumped from her float tube and into Zeke's arms, smothering him with passionate kisses.

When Zeke and Abby came back to reality, a group of people that had been floating just behind them broke out with whistles and applause. They had realized what was happening, silently watched Zeke's entire proposal and also made videos.

Luís, Bekah and Javi had decided to stop in a shady spot beneath overhanging limbs and wait for Zeke and Abby to catch up, so they were not very far downstream and thus able to witness Zeke's proposal as well.

Abby was a bit embarrassed to discover that so many people had seen her reaction to Zeke's marriage proposal, so she cuddled up to Zeke and hid beneath her large, floppy hat. However, Zeke had come prepared and wasn't quite finished. With the cameras still filming, Zeke reached into the pocket of his swim trunks and pulled out an engagement ring. Abby peeked out from beneath her hat, saw the ring and quickly sat up, then she gasped, looked at Zeke and covered her open mouth with her right hand. Then she silently held out her left hand, which was now trembling with anticipation. Zeke gently took her hand and slipped the ring on her finger just as another round of applause and whistles erupted from the on-lookers.

By that time, they had drifted further downstream, catching up to Luís, Bekah and Javi, all anxiously waiting with tearfully happy cheers and congratulations. Zeke and Abby invited the on-lookers to join them for lunch, during which everyone became acquainted.

The video of Zeke's proposal of marriage to Abby was posted to Facebook and went viral. Within days it had received tens of thousands of likes.

Zeke and Abby's respective families were all delighted to learn of their engagement. They set their wedding date for the 21st of July, one month from their engagement date. Mama insisted on having the wedding in her back yard in Payson. Initially, she was intent on preparing all of the food herself, but Zeke and Abby were able to talk her into having the wedding catered.

***

Back on the border it was a return to the same day-in and day-out routine for Zeke and Luís. But Zeke's idea to tap in to the Minutemen Project as a surveillance resource was beginning to pay off. One morning just after Zeke and Luís started work, Luís opened the emailed Minutemen report waiting in his inbox from the previous evening.

Luís quickly perused the report and said, "Doc, looks like we finally got a nibble."

"Oh? What do you have?"

"There are several reports of Chinese looking people seen yesterday near Puerto Peñasco."

(Puerto Peñasco is also known as Rocky Point)

"The Minutemen Project has people that far into Mexico?" Zeke asked inquisitively.

"The reports are probably coming from Mexican citizens who are paid informants."

"That's not exactly verifiable," Zeke remarked.

"Well, at least this looks like the kind of activity that we've been searching for."

"You're right. Any other details?"

"Just that they were sighted near a marina."

"If not for the turf war, I'd think they were just tourists on a fishing trip." Zeke said. "But Rocky Point is hot right now. Control of ports on the Gulf of California is vital; drug shipments come in through there."

"I can't imagine anyone wanting to fish that badly!"

***

On that particular day, Zeke and Luís had scheduled a Drag Road sweep, during which they spotted tracks crossing the Drag Road and apprehended several illegals, all from Mexico. Otherwise it was another uneventful day.

That evening at dinner Zeke's mind was on Abby, so he wasn't very talkative. After their engagement, being separated from each other wasn't quite so difficult because he and Abby knew that soon they would be together forever. They continued their brief morning text messages and long, intimate late night phone chats, which made them feel closer and helped reduce a lot of stress and worry. But that didn't stop Zeke from thinking about her every waking moment.

Zeke ate only part of his meal, and then sat there with his right elbow on the table, resting his cheek on his fist, staring blankly.

"You appear to be deep in thought, Doc. Thinking about Abby?"

Zeke looked up and smiled, "How'd you guess?"

"I'm an extremely intelligent and very perceptive person. Surely you've noticed."

Zeke sat up and asked, "Are you sure that Bekah is attending NAU? Maybe she's just staying in Flagstaff to limit her exposure to your smartassery."

"Smartassery," Luís repeated the word musingly. "I like that. It sounds like an intellectual occupation."

Just then, the server brought Luís another beer, so he looked up at her, and speaking with a haughty New England accent said, "I have a PhD in Smartassery."

She laughed, rolled her eyes and walked away, slowly shaking

66

her head.

"I wonder if she thinks you're extremely intelligent and perceptive."

Then Luís took a drink of his beer and said, "But seriously, Doc, what's bugging you?"

Zeke took a deep breath and sighed. "When Abril and I were talking last night, I asked her what she thought about moving in with me right away. Javi is on summer break. He'll be going to school here, so I was thinking that living here for a while before he starts school might help him acclimate better to his new surroundings."

"And, you would have Abby here with you," Luís added.

"Well, yeah," Zeke admitted, "Abril is at the very top of my priority list. But she said that she was concerned that we would be too cramped in my motel room. I told her that it would only be temporary and maybe not a problem at all since I'm actively looking for a suitable rental."

"Since you don't know how long you're going to be here, renting might be a problem," Luís pointed out and then added, "but you're all welcome to stay with me. I'm renting a four-bedroom house out on the Five Acres north of town. It sits on five acres, interestingly enough, and is all fenced. I don't have next door neighbors, so it's peaceful and quite. Nothing else was available when I was looking for a place, and now that I've been there for a while, I kinda like it. And the rent is reasonable."

"I wouldn't want to impose," Zeke admitted.

"Not a chance, Doc. Sometimes I feel like I'm living in a warehouse. I'd enjoy the company. Besides, Abby's a good cook – she learned from Mama."

"Well, Amigo, I certainly appreciate your offer. I'll tell Abril tonight. I'm sure she'll be delighted. However, we won't be moving in until after the wedding."

"I thought you wanted Abby here right away?"

"I do," Zeke admitted. "But as we continued discussing it, I sensed that Abril wasn't comfortable with the idea, so I asked and she admitted that she didn't feel right moving in with me before we're married. And she's correct, it isn't appropriate. I realized that I was being selfish and I apologized for putting her in such an embarrassing position. Besides, how would we explain it to Javi? It would give him the impression that it's okay for an unwed couple to live together. And morally, it isn't. So we decided to wait."

"I've said it before, Doc, you have integrity." Then Luís tapped his index finger on the side of his head, and with a cheeky grin, said, "Extremely intelligent and perceptive."

The first week in July came, and with it, Independence Day. Zeke, Abby and Javi, along with Luís, Bekah and the entire Gonzales family spent the day together and then watched the fireworks display at Green Valley Park in Payson.

That week, and the following week in July, were uneventful for Zeke and Luís with respect to their daily surveillance patrols, but the daily Minutemen reports contained more and more sightings of suspected Chinese Nationals in Mexico. Not only around the marinas of Puerto Peñasco, but other cities in the State of Sonora as well, including El Golfo de Santa Clara, Sonoyta, Magdalena, Cananea, Agua Prieta and Nogales.

The information was sketchy, but most of the descriptions provided in the reports suggested that the individuals were businessmen of some form or another. It was feasible that the reports were accurate, because the cartel turf war had slowed down considerably, with only isolated reports of violence. All travel restrictions had been lifted, so life in Northern Mexico was slowly returning to normal, including the industrial business community.

The information compiled by Zeke from the Minutemen reports was accurate enough to compel him to submit a report to his supervisor, Senior Special Agent Alexander. So early on the morning of Friday, July 13, Zeke sent out the coded report.

"Well, here goes," Zeke said to Luís as he hit the send key.

Luís propped his feet on Zeke's desk and asked, "How long do you think before we get a reply?"

"Ray is serious about this and, as he put it, has his 'ear to the ground'. I doubt it'll be very long at all."

Just over one minute later, Zeke's smartphone rang.

As he answered the call, Luís commented, "Ray must be a speed reader."

The phone call didn't last very long, Zeke's part of the conversation consisted of, yes, sir. Thank you, Sir. Yes, Sir. Thank You, Sir. Etc., etc.

Then he ended the call, smiled at Luís and said, "Ray is beside himself. Some of the intel that he's been getting over the past few weeks fills in the blanks of the Minutemen intel, providing the verification that we've been hoping for. He's very impressed with our mission accomplishments. Ray sends you his personal thanks, and said that he will be sending Agent Breen a note informing him of how pleased he is with your support of the mission.

"He also said that the daily directives will cease as of this day. I am to continue pursuing my mission objective at my own discretion, and your liaison support will continue to be required until the mission objective is completed. He also said that I'll be getting a full report shortly.

"Oh, and he also congratulated me and Abril on our engagement and said that the proposal video on Facebook was very touching."

"Did you tell Ray about the video?" Luís asked.

"No."

"Then Ray has a lot more than just his ear to the ground."

"Apparently so."

"Well, Doc, things are looking up."

"Yes they are Amigo, yes they are…"

Then Zeke closed his laptop and said, "It may be Friday the thirteenth, but good things are happening and my wedding is in eight days. Abril and I have plans to make. You and I are outta here!"

And hour later Zeke and Luís were headed to Payson. When they arrived at the Gonzales' house, two police cars were parked in front of the house with emergency lights flashing. Zeke and Luís hurried up the steps and across the porch to find out what was going on. When they walked in, several policemen were talking to Bernie. Abby was sitting on the sofa with Mama beside her.

Zeke rushed to Abby. "Sweetheart! What's wrong? Are you okay?"

Mama answered his questions. "My baby's back is hurt. That pinche bastard pushed her down!"

Abby patted Mama on the knee and said, "I'm okay, Mama, really."

Then she reached out to Zeke. As he took her into his arms, Abby started crying.

"You're okay, Beautiful, I'm here now. I've got you. Everything is okay."

Abby pulled away and looked at Zeke, sniffing, tears still running down her face.

He wiped away her tears and tenderly said, "You're okay now. I'm here. Just tell me what happened."

"The doorbell rang about an hour ago," Abby began, "I answered it and there stood Jack, drunk as a skunk, demanding to see Javi. I told him that Javi was at school. He just cursed me and demanded again to see Javi. I told him to leave and go sober up, and then I told him that he was not allowed to visit Javi when he has been drinking. Then he cursed me again and pushed me really hard. I stumbled backwards and fell across the end table."

Then Mama cut in, "Papa and I saw him push her—the pinche bastard! Papa hit him, then shoved him outside and locked the door. Then I called the police."

Abby continued, "Jack kept banging on the door, yelling and cursing me. Then I guess he heard the sirens and left. I tried to call you, but I guess you were in a dead zone in the mountains."

By then Zeke was so angry that he was shaking and unable to speak. He pulled away from Abby, stood up and headed for the door. Fortunately, one of the policemen stepped in front of him and said, "Hold on, Sir. Settle down. I can see that you're angry. But you won't solve anything like this; you'll just end up being arrested, too. We'll handle this. We're searching for him now. When he's found, he will be arrested and charged with assault and battery. You need to settle down and stay here. That young lady over there needs you right now, and she certainly doesn't need to deal with anymore violence, especially not from her fiancée."

Zeke looked at him in surprise and then turned and looked at Abby. Then the policeman addressed them both, saying, "Your proposal on YouTube is too cool. I'm thinking about proposing to my girlfriend like that." Then he shook Zeke's hand and said, "Congratulations by the way," and then added, "Congratulations to you both."

"Thanks," Zeke replied, somewhat bewildered, then looked back at Abby and said, "YouTube?!"

She looked at Zeke with an equally bewildered expression and said, "I had no idea."

After the police left and things had settled down somewhat, Zeke took Abby's hand and led her to her bedroom. Then he said, "I need to look at your back. Lie down on the bed."

She quietly complied, but she laid down on her back and pulled him on the bed with her. Then she pulled him to her and they kissed passionately.

Then Zeke said, "I get the feeling that you don't want me to look at your back."

She kissed him again.

"I just want to make sure you're okay," he explained.

"Alright," she said relenting, and rolled over. Zeke lifted up her tee shirt to find a long, wide, reddened swath across her lower back, and it was already beginning to show bruising.

"That cowardly son-of-a-bitch!" Zeke uttered angrily.

Abby quickly turned over and grabbed his hands. "Remember what the policeman said; you are to stay here and take care of me." Then she pulled him down to her again.

"He didn't say that," Zeke reminded her and smiled.

"Well, that's what he meant," She coquettishly replied, "I could tell."

"Oh, I see, so you're extremely intelligent and very perceptive, just like Luís."

She threw her head back and laughed out loud, then said, "You do know me really well, don't you!" then she kissed him deeply once more.

Early Sunday morning Zeke was alone, sitting on the front porch, drinking coffee.

Luís came out and asked, "Mind if I join you?"

"Pull up a chair."

"Before we go in to breakfast," Luís began, "I wanted to ask you what you're planning to do about Jack."

"Right now I'm struggling very hard to control the urge to kill 'im." Zeke answered bluntly.

"Well, why don't we go one better?"

Zeke looked at him with interest.

"I doubt seriously the police have found him yet," Luís conjectured. "And I'm pretty sure I know where he is. We can bring him along with us when we head back to Ajo this afternoon. I have a jar of honey at home and I know where a huge desert ant hill is, and it's in a very remote spot…"

"I'm guessing you have a way to convince him to go with us?" Zeke replied, "He sure as hell isn't going voluntarily."

"I think general anesthesia is the best idea," Luís suggested.

"Well, I'll just run down to the drugstore and pick up a couple of syringes full," Zeke replied sarcastically.

"Actually, the anesthesia isn't a problem," Luís informed him.

"Oh? Remember, I am a DEA Special Agent," Zeke warned facetiously.

"I used to be an EMT," Luís explained. "I have a friend in the medical field that owed me a favor, so you'll just have to look the other way, because I picked up the drug and two syringes yesterday."

"I see," Zeke said. "And just how are you planning on injecting the anesthesia into that mad behemoth?"

"You're gonna have to get me close enough to stick a syringe in his ass," Luís said bluntly.

"Amigo, I'm beginning to understand why Agent Jackie Williamson called you a lunatic."

Zeke and Luís left for Ajo early, right after attending mass, using the excuse that they had to be at work before sunrise the next day, which, under normal circumstances would be true. They stopped at a convenience store and bought a six-pack of beer. Then Luís directed Zeke to a winding, dusty gravel road several miles outside of Payson. Several more miles down the gravel road, and up a narrow, deep rutted trail, sat a rundown travel trailer.

"I have it on good authority that he's here," Luís said.

Zeke backed the Raptor up near the trailer and stopped. Then they got out and started walking toward the front door. Just then the door swung open, Zeke and Luís each reached for their weapon, but Jack stopped at the door, stuck his head out from underneath the top of the doorway and yelled, "Well, well, well, if it isn't the big, bad, fed cop boyfriend. You gonna arrest me mister big, bad DEA man?"

"No, Jack, I didn't come to arrest you, I just came to talk, okay?" Zeke replied.

"What the hell is there to talk about?" Jack shot back.

"There's a lot to talk about, Jack," Zeke said as he lowered the tailgate. Then he reached into his ice chest, retrieved a beer and held it out towards Jack.

"Let's have a beer and talk. Anyone else here? Bring 'em out and we'll all have a beer."

"It's just me in here mister DEA man," Jack said as he walked over, accepted the beer, popped the top and took a long drink

Luís positioned himself beside the tailgate with the syringe held behind his back. Zeke patted the tailgate near Luís, and said, "Have a seat and take a load off."

Jack turned around, leaned back on the tailgate and Luís quickly injected him in his right buttock. Jack jumped slightly and looked down at the tailgate.

"Watch out Jack that tailgate can pinch your ass," Luís warned.

Jack looked at Luís, then his eyes rolled back in his head and he fell backwards, hitting the ground with a thud.

Zeke looked at Jack and said, "I thought he was supposed to fall on the tailgate."

Luís looked at Jack and said, "I just shot 'im down, I didn't pick the crash site."

Moments later they were struggling to put Jack in the back seat. Zeke was on the inside pulling and Luís was on the outside pushing.

As Luís strained, he said, "I've pushed cars that weighed less than this guy!"

"I just hope I don't get a hernia," Zeke grunted, "My wedding's in six days."

Just after sunup, Jack opened his eyes and found himself staked to the ground, spread eagle, completely naked, and alone. He looked around as best he could and discovered three things: his body was covered with honey—he could taste it on his lips, he was directly beside a huge ant hill, and he could see nothing except desert.

Jack screamed, "Hey! Get me the hell away from these ants! They're all over me! Untie me you sorry bastards! Help!"

Actually, it was a Desert Harvester Ant hill. These large black ants do not sting, and they eat mostly seeds. They smelled the honey and were crawling around on Jack to determine if the honey was a suitable food source.

From a discrete distance, Zeke and Luís sat on the tailgate of the Raptor, munching on burritos, drinking coffee and watching Jack with binoculars. He was yelling so loud that hearing him wasn't a problem.

After about an hour, Jack began to hallucinate and started screaming, "Help! Help! The ants are starting to eat me! Please! Help me!"

Apparently the ants had decided the honey was edible and were in the process of removing it from Jack's skin and transporting it to the nest.

Luís sighed. "I guess we'd better rescue him before he goes insane."

"Yeah. I suppose," Zeke replied, sounding disappointed. "Although, watching that useless bastard suffer is great therapy. Over the past hour I haven't thought about killing him even once."

They drove over, got out and walked up to him.

Jack said, "Thank God! You're back. Guys please let me loose. Please!" He squirmed around and yelled, "The ants are eating me!"

Zeke squatted down and looked Jack in the face. "I warned you Jack. I warned you that if you laid one finger on Abril this would happen. You shoved her Jack. She fell and hurt her back. That distresses me greatly. I can't stand the thought of Abril getting injured. And you caused it."

"I'm sooo sorry, man. I was drunk. I didn't know what I was doin'. I didn't mean to hurt Abby, honest. Please, don't let the ants eat me. Please!"

Zeke looked at Luís and asked, "What do you think?"

"I say we let the ants have 'im."

"I agree," Zeke said and signaled Luís to inject Jack with the second syringe.

Jack looked at Zeke and yelled, "No, man! Please! Don't leave me to die like this! I don't want…"

"Night, night, Jack," said Luís.

"I hope he has nightmares about this for the rest of his life," Zeke said.

Then they cut Jack loose, dragged him onto a tarpaulin and washed off the ants and honey.

As they were putting Jack's pants back on Zeke commented, "I'm afraid I can't compete with his equipment. I sure hope Abril doesn't have a problem with that."

"Doc," Luís said seriously, "Abby is so much in love with you that she'd still marry you if you were a eunuch."

Later that afternoon, the Payson police responded to a call to Rumsey Park, where they found Jack, bound & gagged, and tied to a tree. A note attached to him read, 'Jack Marristan, wanted by Payson police for assaulting a young girl'.

Around that same time, Zeke and Luís entered the front door of the Gonzalez home.

Bernie was watching TV, looked at them and asked, "What are you boys doing back up here?"

"We had to run an errand, Papa," Luís answered and then headed into the kitchen to look for food.

Abby heard Luís talking and ran into the living room, hugged and kissed Zeke and asked, "Honey, what are you doing here?"

"Luís and I had to run an errand and I wanted to see you. How's your back?"

"Sore," She replied, then lifted her tee shirt to reveal a very dark blue bruise all the way across her lower back.

Zeke said, "Oh, my poor sweetheart." Then kneeled down and began softly kissing the hurt.

She stood there, allowing him to continue, then moaned softly and said, "Can we continue this in my bedroom?"

"I'm not listening to this!" Bernie commented from his recliner.

Zeke stood up, put his arms around her and kissed her, and then said, "I wish we could, but Luís and I have to get back."

"Darn!" said Abby, and stuck out her bottom lip in a pout.

Then Zeke said, "You won't have to worry about Jack any longer."

"Ezekiel!" Abby gasped, "You didn't..."

"No, no, it's nothing like that. We just gave 'im a serious attitude adjustment and left 'im tied to a tree in Rumsey Park. I'm sure he's in police custody by now."

"You tied him to a tree?!" Abby chuckled.

"Way to go Zeke!" Bernie commented.

"Yes. We had to leave him somewhere. But Jack received his attitude adjustment earlier this morning."

Zeke then showed Abby a picture on his smartphone that he had taken of Jack staked out near the ant hill.

Abby covered her mouth, then laughed and said, "You didn't!"

"A picture's worth a 1000 words."

Just then Luís walked into the living room. "Showing your bride-to-be our morning's work?"

"I was just keeping Abril in the loop," Zeke replied and looked Abby in the eyes, "One thing I refuse to do is keep secrets from my sweetheart."

A wide smile brightened Abby's face, then she placed her hands on his cheeks and kissed him.

"As I've said before, Doc," Luís remarked, "You're a man of integrity."

The following day a policeman, who was an old family friend, stopped by to ask Abby some questions.

"Abby, I just wanted to let you know that Jack has been charged with assault and battery for his attack on you on Friday. He also told us a crazy story about ants and honey and being tied to an ant hill out in the desert by Luís and your fiancée. Do you know anything about that?"

"It sounds like Jack was on a binge again and started to hallucinate. It's happened before you know."

"Yeah, I'm aware of that," He replied. "Besides, he didn't have one single ant bite, and he wasn't sun burned either. A man, tied naked over an ant hill like he claims, would've fried beneath that hot July sun and have ant bites all over him as well. I guess you're right, he must've been hallucinating. It's sad to see what he's become. He was a fine quarterback. Could've played in the NFL. Oh, well. Thank you for your time, Abby. And congratulations on your engagement."

"Thank you, Frank." She saw him out, then she closed the door, leaned against it and breathed a sigh of relief.

With Monday over and Jack out of the way. Tuesday and Wednesday trudged by uneventfully for Zeke and Luís on the border. They both left work early on Wednesday. Luís drove his pickup to Payson. Zeke went to Phoenix to meet his parents and paternal grandparents who were arriving at Sky Harbor in the late afternoon. He picked up their luggage and then they followed him up to Payson in their rental car. The wedding was only three days away, and a lot of preparations had to be made.

Thursday and Friday were a hectic blur for everyone as they all worked together to prepare for the early morning wedding in the back yard of the Gonzales' home on Saturday, July 21st.

Saturday dawned clear, calm and beautiful with a slight chill in the pre-dawn air. The back yard was decorated beautifully, with a lovely flower-covered arch beneath which Zeke and Abby exchanged wedding vows that they had each written themselves.

The summer Monsoon season had begun in early July, creating daily thunderstorms in the mountains, but that Saturday the towering cumulonimbus clouds were billowing on the far horizon, with only distant rumbles of thunder heard during the ceremony.

Luís stood as Zeke's best man and Bekah stood as Abby's maid of honor. Javi was the ring bearer, and Bernie gave his youngest daughter away in a picture-perfect, fairytale wedding. Abby called Zeke her knight in shining armor that rescued her from the depths of despair and brought her into the light of a love that she had only imagined in her wildest dreams. Zeke called Abby his fairytale princess that captured his heart and soul the instant that he first saw her. (Zeke and Abby may have collaborated slightly on the knight in shining armor and fairytale princess analogies)

The mid-day reception was perfect, with an outstanding array of delicious food and drink provided by the caterer. The Gonzales family were longtime Payson residents and well-known in the community, so the back yard and house were crowded with guests, all delighted to see Abby finally find happiness.

Abby and Zeke received a lot of wedding gifts, but one of the most precious gifts for Abby was a large, family bible engraved with her and Zeke's names. It had been gifted by her Aunt Antonia, who was anxiously waiting for Abby to open the package.

As Abby was thanking her aunt for the gift, Antonia said, "This is the New American Standard Edition of our Holy Bible. It's much easier to read than that King James thing with all of the flowery Elizabethan English nonsense. Besides, you don't want the King James Version; King James was an evil tyrant that didn't deserve to have a Holy Bible named after him."

Mama immediately scolded her sister by saying, "Antonia! Seriously?!"

Antonia replied, "Well, he was an evil tyrant!"

After the reception was over and the guests had departed, the family gathered in the back yard to spend some precious time with the bride and groom before they departed for their honeymoon.

Suddenly, the doorbell rang. Bernie answered the door to find Jack standing there. Antonia saw him, quickly found Javi and led him out to the back yard.

Jack was well dressed, wearing a coat and tie, and polite for a change as he apologized to Bernie for interrupting the celebration. Then he asked to see Abby and Zeke. They came to the door, along with Luís and Bekah, Abby's older sister, Maria, and her three older brothers. Abby, still clutching her new Bible, stood in front of Bernie. Zeke was standing on her right side, and Luís was standing on her left.

"Abby, I apologize for intruding," Jack began, still standing outside because no one even considered inviting him in.

Abby scowled and asked, "What do you want, Jack."

"I just wanted to congratulate you and your husband, and to offer my deepest apologies for my behavior the other day when I pushed you down and hurt your back. I'm so sorry, I have no excuse except that I was drunk."

"Thank you, Jack," Abby replied. "Now we are still celebrating, so would you please leave?"

Jack turned and began walking away. Everyone continued watching him, all in disbelief of what they had just witnessed. Suddenly he spun around and yelled, then produced a pistol and fired two shots in rapid succession. Abby fell backwards into her father's arms.

The instant Zeke and Luís saw Jack's handgun, they each drew a handgun from their belt holster and fired simultaneously, five rounds from Zeke's .40 caliber Smith & Wesson, and four rounds from Luís' 9mm Glock, all hitting Jack center mass except the fifth round from Zeke's S&W that hit the center of Jack's forehead. He sprawled backwards, dead before he hit the sidewalk. Thankfully, Jack was only able to fire two rounds because his heart and brain had been blown apart before he could squeeze the trigger again.

Zeke and Luís immediately turned their attention to Abby, who was lying on the floor in her father's arms, with Bekah and Maria kneeling beside her.

Mama screamed, "That son-of-a-bitch has killed my baby girl!" and then collapsed.

Her three sons rushed to her aid.

Just as Zeke reached Abby, she coughed, opened her eyes wide and drew in a deep breath.

Maria yelled, "Oh, thank God, she's alive!"

Abby was still holding the Bible against her chest, so Zeke pulled it from her arms, anticipating having to tend to her gunshot wounds, but he found no blood at all and no evidence of any wounds.

Abby looked up at Zeke and asked, "Honey, are you okay?" And the whole room literally erupted into joyful celebration.

Abby looked around, then looked at Zeke once more and asked, "What happened? Did Jack just shoot at me?!"

Without answering, Zeke picked up the Bible lying beside her and inspected the two bullet holes in the cover. The room was silent, with all eyes on him as he flipped through its pages and then turned the Bible up-side-down. Two bullets tumbled out and fell into Abby's lap. She looked down, picked up the bullets and said, "Oh, my God!"

Zeke lifted her up from Bernie's arms, held her tightly and

whispered, "Oh, my God indeed, Beautiful, God has just spared your life."

Luís then helped his father to his feet. Bernie put his arms around Zeke and Abby, kissed her on the cheek and walked through the front door and over to Jack's body, now lying on the sidewalk in a large pool of blood. Bernie stood there staring at the body for a moment, and then looked around to find Luís, and his other three sons, Zeke's father, and Zeke's grandfather, all standing there staring at the body.

Bernie looked back down and said, "Well, I guess we should call the police."

"Aw, to hell with that," Zeke's grandfather remarked without looking up, "let's just throw the bastard in the back of a pickup and take 'im to the dump!"

Bernie looked at Ezzy, smiled and said, "Ezzy, I like the way you think!"

Then Luís and his brothers almost fell on the ground laughing.

Shortly, everyone had seen enough of Jack's dead body, and went back inside to wait for the police. They were all in the living room, looking at the bullet holes in Abby's Bible and marveling over the miracle that they had just witnessed.

Then Abby suddenly posed the question, to no one in particular, "Who shot Jack?"

Bernie replied, "Ezekiel and Luís."

Abby then asked, "How?"

One of her brothers laughed and answered, "With their guns, silly!"

Abby's eyes narrowed as she said, "With their guns!" and looked directly at Zeke and Luís who were standing nearby.

They each opened their tuxedo jackets and revealed a handgun tucked in its holster.

Abby's well-known temper flared as she yelled, "You mean to tell me that you two were armed during my wedding!"

"Mija," Bernie said consolingly, "Jack obviously came here with the intention of killing you. If Ezekiel and Luís had not been armed, Jack could have killed you, Ezekiel, and perhaps several more of us."

Abby thought for a moment and then replied, "You're right, Papa." Then she went to Zeke and Luís, wrapped her arms around them both in a group hug, kissed them on the cheek and said, "Thank you both for saving our lives."

Luís then fell back on the sofa beside Bekah, looked at Zeke and said, "Whew! That was close. For a minute there I was sure we were about to get our asses kicked!"

Zeke looked at him curiously.

"She's beat me up before!"

Abby glared at Luís, then pointed her finger at him and said, "That's because you insulted my cheering squad. And nobody insults my cheering squad!"

"All I said was—"

"Don't even go there!!"

Luís glanced at Zeke, gave him an 'I told you so' look and pointed at Abby.

After a considerable delay dealing with the police investigation, Zeke and Abby were finally ready to depart for their honeymoon.

Zeke had scheduled a stay in a luxury houseboat on Lake Powell at Antelope Point in Page, Arizona. He was very much looking forward to spending time alone with Abby on beautiful Lake Powell, in a houseboat with luxurious furnishings, and a top-deck hot tub.

Zeke had made reservations for a full week on the houseboat, but their parents surprised the newlyweds with a week's stay at the Kahala Hotel and Resort in Honolulu. Bernie revealed that Special Agent Ray Alexander had conceived the Hawaiian honeymoon idea. He pitched it to them, proposing that, if they would be willing to split the bill for the accommodations in Hawaii, he would provide the first class airline tickets.

Zeke and Abby had a wonderfully romantic time on the houseboat on Lake Powell, then departed for their Hawaiian honeymoon from Phoenix Sky Harbor on Wednesday, July 25th, and returned after six amazing days in paradise on Wednesday, August 1st.

Abby had packed up her and Javi's belongings before the wedding, so while the happy couple were on their honeymoon, Luís and his brothers moved her things to his house in Ajo. Zeke's grandfather, Ezzy, arranged and supervised the shipment of Zeke's belongings from his apartment in Arlington, Virginia to Ajo, so when Zeke and Abby returned from their honeymoon, all they had to do was pick up Javi in Payson and head to Ajo.

They arrived in Ajo on August 2nd. Abby and Javi had visited Luís on several occasions and she had a key to his house, so she went directly to the door and started to go inside.

The house was a modern, single-story beige brick home with a shingled roof, a large front porch as well as a large back patio. It sat far off the main road at the end of a long gravel driveway.

As Zeke walked through the gate behind her, he called, "Missus Sikes, just where do you think you're going?"

She turned and said, "I'm going inside of course." Then she whispered anxiously, "And I have to pee!"

"Not yet you're not. This may only be our temporary home, but I'm still going to carry you across the threshold." Then he took her key, unlocked the door and swung it open, and then scooped her up into his arms. As he carried her across the threshold, she smiled, said, "I love you, Husband," and kissed him.

Javi was curiously watching this romantic moment from the steps. As he walked in behind them, he looked at Abby and asked, "Mom, why can't you just walk through the door on your own?"

Abby smiled at him, then knelt down and replied, "I can Mijo. Ezekiel was just carrying me through the door because he loves me."

"Oh. I love you, too, Mom."

She hugged him and said, "And I love you, Mijo. Ezekiel and I both love you." Then she kissed him on the forehead and added, "Just don't you try to carry me, okay?"

"Okay, Mom," he said. As he was walking away he added, "Anyway, I can't carry you, you're way too heavy. You probably weight a ton!"

Abby got a shocked look on her face and looked at Zeke. He was biting his lips to conceal his amusement.

Abby frowned at him and smacked him in the stomach with the back of her hand.

Zeke held out his hands, palms up, shrugged his shoulders and said, "He's your son."

She smacked him again.

Abby immediately set about unpacking and arranging, anxious to make the house feel like a home for her new husband and her son. As Abby unpacked, Zeke went through his things, conferring with Abby to decide what needed to be kept and what should be given way to charity.

As Abby unpacked, she discovered her bathroom scales and called Javi.

"Yes, Mom?"

"Javi, do you remember earlier when I told you not to try to carry me?"

"Yes, Mam."

"And you said that I probably weigh a ton?"

"Yes, Mam. I'll bet you do!"

"How about we weigh you? Step up on the scale and stand very still."

Javi complied. About then Zeke came into the bathroom.

"44 pounds," Abby declared, then said to Javi, "Look down at the scale. You see where the line is? It's just one mark below the middle line, which is 45 pounds, halfway between 40 and 50. Each mark counts as one pound. Since you're just one mark below the 45 pound mark, one minus 45 is 44, which means that you weigh 44 pounds. Does that make sense?"

"Yes, Mam."

"Now, I'm going to step on the scale… 122 pounds. That's not quite three times your weight. Three times your weight would be… let's see… three times four is 12… carry the one… Three times 44 pounds is one 132 pounds. So, I'm ten pounds less than three times your weight, understand?"

"I think so."

"The main thing is, when you said that I probably weigh a ton, a ton is 2000 pounds, and I only weigh 122 pounds. That's a long way from a ton, don't you think?"

"Yes, Mam, a ton is a lot more."

"Alright! Fist bump," Abby declared and held up her fist.

Zeke rubbed Abby's back gently and said, "Nicely done."

"Thank you," Abby said and gave him a peck on the cheek, then she quietly explained, "I'm really not that vain, but I could just picture Javi telling his teacher and classmates that his mom weighs a ton."

Then she said, "Now, let's see what Ezekiel weighs."

Zeke stepped on the scale.

"185 pounds," declared Abby. Then she whispered, "Yum!" and gave him a sexy glance.

"Wow, Mister Zeke!" Exclaimed Javi. "I definitely can't carry you!"

"Okay Mijo," Abby said, "I think you have a pretty good understanding of pounds. And I do not weigh anywhere near a ton, right?"

"Right," he replied.

"Okay! Good job!" She said and smiled.

Finally, Abby stopped unpacking and arranging, sat down and said, "I need to get started preparing dinner."

"Oh, no," Zeke replied, "You're not preparing dinner after working so hard unpacking. We're going out for dinner. And by the way, the place is looking really great." Then he kissed her.

Abby smiled contentedly and said, "Thank you, Husband!"

Zeke took Abby and Javi to Marcella's Café. Abby and Javi had eaten there before while visiting Luís because he rarely ate anywhere else. As they were munching on chips and salsa and perusing the menus, Zeke said to Abby, "I've been wondering something."

"Oh, what's that?"

"When did you know that I was the one for you? I knew the first time I saw you, although I can't really explain why I felt that way. I just knew. And spending time with you only reinforced that feeling.

I had no expectations that you would be mine, but I was certainly praying that, at the very least, you would show some interest. You can't imagine how my heart soared when you treated me with so much courtesy when we were introduced and then flirted with me while getting my coffee. But when did you know for certain that I was the one for you?"

"For me also it was our first meeting. Honestly, fireworks went off when I first saw you. You were so handsome, and sexy. You were very respectful and courteous, not only to me, but also my parents and Javi. And I knew that it wasn't an act just to impress me, because when we went for ice cream, you were also courteous and respectful to other people, even when you didn't think that I was watching.

She giggled. "And you were so handsome and sexy." Then she paused and said, "But, I can't explain why I knew you were the one, either. Until I saw you, I had been avoiding men. Single guys would come to the house with Luís and I would just ignore them completely. But something wondrous happened to me when I saw you for the first time, and I thank God for bringing you into my life."

Suddenly Zeke and Abby looked up to find the waitress standing there, wiping away her tears.

"That was so sweet!" she said, and then hugged Abby. Then she regained her composure and asked,

"Are you ready to order?"

Abby smiled graciously and said, "I think we need a little more time."

"Take all the time you need honey. That was so sweet!"

After they had time to look over the menu, Zeke asked Abby what she was having.

"I think I'm having the chorizo plate." Then she asked, "What are you having?"

"I believe I'll wing it."

When the server came to take their orders, she asked Abby first.

Before she had time to reply, Zeke looked at Abby and said, "My wife will have the chorizo plate, with extra cheese on the beans, shredded lettuce, tomato wedges and sour cream on a separate plate, and a fresh, hot tortilla."

Abby smiled at Zeke and said, "Perfect." Then Zeke ordered, and helped Javi order. Abby placed her elbows on the table, then rested her chin on her laced-together fingers and gazed at her husband with loving adoration.

Just then, Luís came in and walked over to their table. "Hi guys! Welcome back!"

Zeke stood up, shook his hand and said, "Hello brother-in-law. Pull up a chair. We've just ordered. I'll call the server back."

"Don't bother, they already know what I want for dinner."

"And that would be anything they bring you, right?"

"Right." Then Luís looked at Abby, waved his fingers in front of her face and said, "Hellooo."

Without batting an eyelash she replied, "Hello Big Brother," and continued gazing lovingly at her husband.

Luís leaned over toward Zeke and whispered, "Is she in some sort of trance?"

"No," replied Zeke as he returned Abby's blissful gaze, "We're just in love."

Chapter Five
A Very Big Surprise

Monday morning, August 6th. Zeke and Luís were back in the office, catching up from the time off for the wedding. Zeke softly hummed a tune as he checked his email and worked on his event calendar.

"You're in a good mood this morning, Doc."

"You betcha."

"Have anything to do with a certain young lady waiting for you at home?"

"Amigo," Zeke began and propped his cheek on his hand, "I had no idea that it was even possible to be this happy. I've just spent ten wonderful days in paradise with an angel. And that would've been enough to last me several lifetimes, but I had the singular privilege of being allowed to bring that angel home with me to stay forever! Abril is beyond amazing. Maybe one day someone will come up with words suitable enough to describe her and how I feel about her."

"I'm happy for you both, Doc. You already know thrilled I am to see Abby happy again. Thank you for being so good to my sister."

"It's me that should be thanking you; I just can't even begin to know how. I'm a different man today, and all because of Abril. Who knows how much longer I would have been able to keep going before the loneliness and misery that was holding up the prison walls that I had built around myself would have collapsed and simply crushed me. Granted, she is the one who pulled me out of that dark hole that I was living in, but had you not invited me to your parents' house…"

"I see where you're coming from, Doc. So, let me put it like this; consider the gift of happiness that you've given my sister, to be the greatest gift that you could ever give to me."

"You're a good man, Luís."

Luís smiled, tapped his head with his index finger and repeated in an I-told-you-so tone, "Extremely intelligent and very perceptive

85

person…"

"Arrrahh!" Zeke groaned and rolled his eyes. "I set myself up for that."

Just as Zeke and Luís returned their attention to the tasks at hand, Assistant Patrol Agent in Charge Ron Addison arrived, coffee cup in hand, and leaned against the doorjamb.

"Well, well, the A-team is back at the controls. And the team leader came back with a ring in his nose! How long before she'll be leading you around with it, Special Agent Sikes?"

Without looking up from his computer Zeke asked, "Don't you have someone else you're supposed to be annoying right now?"

Ignoring Zeke's comeback, Addison said, "I understand you're forwarding your daily assignments to Agent Breen. I need to be cc'd on those."

"That protocol was ended last month, Agent Addison," Zeke replied, still looking at his computer. "Agent Gonzales and I will be giving Agent Breen a personal weekly briefing every Monday morning starting next week. You'll need to check with him, but I'm certain that he'll include you in the briefing."

Then, Zeke looked up at Addison. "And one more thing; you insult my wife and my marriage one more time and you'll have to drink that coffee through a soda straw."

Luís looked at Zeke and raised an eyebrow.

Addison turned abruptly and walked out without a word.

Zeke looked in the direction that Addison had just gone and said, "That guy is about as abrasive and annoying as anyone I've ever met." Then he looked at Luís and asked, "What is his problem?"

"I think you nailed it awhile back when you said that you were getting the distinct vibe of interagency rivalry and mistrust. He's normally abrasive and condescending, but it looks to me like he resents you because you're DEA and you're in his house. He doesn't trust you, or the DEA. Come to think of it, he doesn't trust anyone."

"Well, I'll give him the benefit of the doubt on that. He has good reason to mistrust the DEA, and by extension, me. The environment between the alphabet agencies in DC is replete with mistrust and rivalry. And since his condescending abrasiveness is part of his nature, I can deal with that I suppose, but I won't tolerate insults directed at Abril."

"Ahmm… I'm pretty sure he received your message about that,

loud and clear."

During the next two weeks, Zeke and Luís concentrated on collecting data on unusual border activity across all of Northern Mexico, including ports of entry, the Minutemen Project, local law enforcement, the military and even civilians living and traveling along the border.

Since it was the middle of summer, foot traffic crossing illegally into remote desert areas had slowed down considerably. Also, very little unusual activity had been sighted, except for the continuing reports of men appearing to be of Chinese nationality in cities all over Northern Mexico, with one particular exception; an unusual number of heavy haulers carrying large earth moving equipment had been seen coming from the US and Southern Mexico, all headed for Northern Mexico. At the same time, rumors were spreading about a large construction project about to start in the San Luis area. No additional information was available.

At the beginning of the fourth week in August, Zeke and Luís received word that the heavy haulers had been seen arriving at an area near the small farming village of Cerro Colorado Numero Dos, only 13 miles west of Lukeville.

Zeke sat at his desk, looking at the report and wondering aloud, "What reason would anyone have to park construction equipment there? It's in the middle of nowhere, and over 100 miles from San Luís where the construction project is rumored to be."

"That's true, Doc." Luís replied, "But it's not really in the middle of nowhere, it's just an out of the way place, and I have a hunch. Check out this map."

Luís brought up a satellite map of the Southwest on his laptop, searched Lukeville and then zoomed out.

"The construction equipment is coming from Southern Mexico, from Texas, and from California through San Luís—that city was named after me by the way…"

"San Luís? Sure it was. That city's a bit older than you. I'm thinking it's more likely your parents named you Luís because maybe you were conceived there while they were vacationing on the lower Colorado River."

"Nah. I was there just once and they were so impressed that they changed the name in my honor."

"What was the former name?"

"Los Yuma."

"The map," Zeke pointed at the computer screen. "Cerro Colorado Numero Dos. Your hunch, remember?"

"Oh, yeah. Well, the equipment is all converging on that little farming village. It would be a great place to stage equipment for a big construction project if you wanted to stay away from cities and avoid drawing attention to it."

"But who would care if people saw their earth-moving machines? And staged to go where? Certainly not San Luís. Some of the equipment just came through there."

"I've been thinking about that," Luís said, "There's no reason to build another highway near San Luís. And there's already an airport. The Altar Desert lies to the southeast of San Luís, and it's protected by the Pinacate and great desert of Altar Biosphere Reserve."

"Well then, where?"

"What about south?"

"South?"

"Yeah, toward Puerto Peñasco, which is only thirty five miles straight south from Cerro Colorado Numero Dos. The next village is El Pinacate, on the way to Puerto Peñasco, just twenty two miles south of the border, and there's a small farm there, so you know there's water."

"Amigo, I'm not following you. There's already a highway, so what would they be doing that needs that much earth moving equipment?"

"That area is on the southeastern edge of the Altar Desert. It might not be part of the Biosphere Reserve." Then Luís brought up the measuring tool. "You can easily plot a seventy square mile rectangular area in between El Pinacate and Puerto Peñasco, and, it's all flat sand…"

Zeke studied the map and muttered to himself, "Heavy construction in a flat sandy desert area just thirteen miles north of seaports on the Gulf of California… What would someone want to build there that needs mega earth moving equipment?" Then he looked at Luís and asked, "Runways?"

"Man, it could be really long runways. Ten miles long for a north-south runway and twenty miles long for an east-west runway. That could be a spaceport for space shuttle landings."

"Let's speculate that the Chinese are up to something—."

"Doc, at this point I think that qualifies as a wild ass guess."

Zeke chuckled. "You're probably right, but let's run with it anyway. Why would they want to build a spaceport in Mexico? China has a lot of territory for things like that, and in-country, where it's much more secure."

Then Luís said, "But, running with your theory as far as I can go, it sure would be a handy place to launch a military attack on the US."

"I don't know why China would be stupid enough to do that," Zeke replied, "but you know, you're right! But it would really take some doing. They'd have to sneak assault troops and support equipment in little by little, and find some way to keep everything out of sight."

"Equipment and Troops could be hidden in large warehouses," Luís offered. "And airports have big hangars."

"Good point," Zeke replied. "We really need to find out who's behind this construction project and get some details about it. We may be barking up the wrong tree."

Then Luís said, "We need someone in Mexico that's connected with the project, but friendly to us. And we're not even sure that the rumor of the project is true, so who could we turn to?"

"I'll toss our idea to Ray and see what he thinks."

That weekend, Zeke, Abby, Javi and Luís went to Payson. Bekah came down from Flagstaff and met Luís there.

On Saturday morning, Bernie loaded everyone into his Suburban and took them to breakfast at Crosswinds Restaurant at Payson Municipal Airport, also known as Rich Henry Field. Crosswinds Restaurant had long been a favorite of the Gonzales family because of the excellent food and the grand view of the Mogollon Rim from its location on the high mesa where the airport is located.

As Bernie pulled out of the parking lot after breakfast, he said to Mama, "I think I'd like to show my new son-in-law my favorite toy."

She smiled and said, "I was wondering when you were going to get around to that."

Bernie pulled up to the security gate, punched in the code and drove toward one of the hangars.

"Where are we going?" Zeke asked Abby.

"This is my dad's way of saying that you are now officially part of our family. This is the home of his favorite toy. Jack was never allowed to see it."

Bernie parked near a hangar, unlocked the hangar door, and

opened it to reveal a beautiful high-wing, taildragger single engine aircraft. It was white with yellow trim, had a three-blade polished chrome prop, and the aircraft was immaculate.

As Zeke walked up to get a closer look, Bernie said, "Ezekiel, this is my favorite toy. She's a '97 Maule M-7-235C with a 235 horsepower Lycoming IO540 engine. I used to fly to work at Sky Harbor and this was my commuter. Before this one, I had a '47 Stinson 108-2, and before that, a '55 Cessna 180. I've always been fond of taildraggers."

Zeke looked at Abby in amazement, then looked back at Bernie and said, "Sir, this is awesome!"

Bernie put his arm around Zeke's shoulder, grabbed him by the back of the neck and shook him ever so slightly, then looked at Abby and said, "Abril, we're going to have to get this 'sir' business out of your husband's system."

"Yes, Papa," She replied.

Then he spoke to Zeke, "I was a 'sir' when I was in the Air Force, and I was a 'sir' when I was an airline captain. I was even a 'sir' when Jack-ass addressed me, but you're my son now, so I'm just Papa, okay?"

"Okay, Sss—Papa."

"There you go. Now how about let's take my toy for a spin? What 'da ya' say?"

"That would be cool... Papa."

Abby smiled happily, grabbed Zeke's face and gave him a big kiss.

"Since my little bird seats five, Mama and Javi are going to head back to the house. They've both flown with me many times. You four lovebirds and I will fly up to Lake Powell, and we can all see where you and Abril honeymooned from the air. Now, gentlemen, after you get your ladies onboard and comfortable, we will roll this little bird out of the hangar, get her preflighted and head north."

In no time the preflight was done. Luís climbed in and Zeke started to get in the right front seat.

Bernie said, "Ezekiel, you take left seat."

Zeke looked at him with surprise and said, "But, Papa, I've never flown a taildragger, or a high-performance aircraft like this before."

"Well, son, it just so happens that I'm a certified flight instructor, so consider this your introduction to conventional landing gear, variable pitch props and some serious short field performance."

As Zeke climbed into the left seat, he looked at Abby, seated directly behind him, with the excited expression of a teenager about to drive a car for the first time.

Bernie walked Zeke through the operating checklist; before starting, starting, after starting and engine check. Then he instructed Zeke to taxi to runway six. As he taxied, Bernie explained the finer points of taxiing a taildragger, the relationship between the prop pitch control and the throttle, and some of the aspects of the advanced avionics in the Maule.

Zeke taxied the Maule to the hold line and stopped. Bernie walked him through the before takeoff checklist and then operated the radio, clearing Zeke onto runway six for takeoff.

Then he instructed Zeke to taxi out onto the runway, get lined up and hold. Zeke applied the brakes and listened as Bernie explained how, with a taildragger, it is important to come up on the power while keeping the tailwheel on the ground, which increases airflow from the prop over the rudder to maintain steering control of the aircraft after the tailwheel lifts off the runway and tailwheel steering is lost.

Bernie also warned him that the Maule will want to lift off before you're ready to fly, so you have to stay ahead of the aircraft and be prepared to fly it off the runway.

"Okay," Bernie said, "advance the throttle and release the brakes."

There was an immediate sensation of being shoved back into the seat from the acceleration.

"She will lift off in about 450 feet. That's just one and a half football fields. Put some back pressure on the yoke and be ready. It's going to feel like a rocket ride compared to the 172 you've flown before."

Suddenly the Maule seemed to almost leap into the air.

"Holy shi…!" Zeke exclaimed.

Bernie chuckled and said, "Okay, trim the elevator for best angle of climb at 75 mph."

Zeke looked back to see the runway quickly shrinking behind him and said, "I see what you mean about the rocket ride. This is awesome!"

"Okay, there's a noise abatement departure procedure here at

Payson. You're over the numbers and passing a thousand feet, so start making a standard rate turn to thirty degrees. When you get wings level, the Beeline Highway should be right below you. Continue climbing to 9200 feet to clear the Rim, then level out and steer 358 degrees. Set the throttle for seventy five percent power. It's about 180 miles to Lake Powell. We should be over the lake in just over an hour."

Below them lay the Mogollon Rim, the southwestern edge of the Colorado Plateau, with its sprawling emerald green carpet of the largest ponderosa pine forest in world. They could see lakes, rivers and streams all across the plateau, rushing life-giving water toward the reservoirs and valleys to the south.

Over Lake Powell, Bernie took the controls, slowed the Maule down to just above the stall speed of forty five mph, and gave the two couples a grand view of Lake Powell, the second largest man-made reservoir in the US, with its crystal blue water filling the deep canyons of the sprawling red rock desert. Bernie made it a point to circle over Antelope Canyon, where Zeke and Abby honeymooned on the houseboat.

By then it was midmorning. Bernie directed everyone's attention to the mountains to the south. "See the thunder bumpers starting to build over the mountain peaks? We'd better get back before it gets too bumpy."

Zeke took over the controls again and steered the Maule toward Payson and home. By the time they had the Maule secured in the hangar, Mama and Javi arrived to take them home.

Late that afternoon, a thunderstorm rumbled across the Payson area bringing a welcomed, refreshing summer shower. Zeke and Abby snuggled beneath a blanket on the front porch swing, watching it rain and smooching.

Back at Ajo Station on Monday morning of the last week in August, Zeke received a reply from Agent Alexander concerning his and Luís' theory about the arrival of construction equipment at Cerro Colorado Numero Dos: Good work. Good theory. Plan in works. Continue surveillance.

Zeke sighed and read the message aloud.

"Short and sweet as usual," Luís observed.

"Continue surveillance," Zeke repeated and drummed his fingers on his desk. "The only place that we have left to surveil is Cerro Colorado Numero Dos. And how are we supposed to do that? It's in

Mexico. And why would we want to?"

"Well…"

Zeke looked suspiciously at Luís. "You're about to come up with another one of your crazy ideas aren't you?"

Luís just pointed at his laptop and said, "Look at the map. There's a unique geological formation about thirteen miles west of Lukeville on the Drag Road, just south of the base of the Sierra Pinta Mountains, called the Pinta Sands. The sand is like talcum powder and it's a great place to get stuck. I've gotten stuck there twice. The Pinta Sands surrounds the Pinacate lava field, and there's a number of extinct cinder cones and small calderas there. One of the calderas is a natural rainwater catchment right near the Drag Road and the mesquite around it is really thick."

"And you're telling me this because…"

"The mesquite around the caldera is the only concealment along that stretch of the border, and we should have an unobstructed view of Cerro Colorado Numero Dos right across the border, no more than two miles away."

"Okay, that sounds promising. Let's load up our gear and be there at daybreak tomorrow morning."

"How 'bout we take along a camera drone?" Luís suggested.

"Where can we get one of those?"

"From my bedroom. It's hanging on the wall."

"Amigo, you are full of surprises."

Luís tapped his head with his index finger and said, "Extremely intelligent and very perceptive person…"

Zeke sighed and rolled his eyes.

Early the following morning Zeke and Luís concealed the truck behind the mesquite trees near the caldera and set up their equipment, a digital camera with a powerful telephoto lens, and an audio telescope. Zeke searched the area with the camera, taking pictures of objects of interest and Luís scanned the area with the audio telescope, searching for voices to record.

"The reports of heavy equipment certainly wasn't an exaggeration," Zeke commented as he pressed the camera's shutter. "There is every description of construction equipment parked over there."

"Are you seeing anyone?" Luís asked. "I'm not seeing a soul."

"I haven't seen anyone yet. Maybe the equipment is just being stored."

"But if that's the case, shouldn't there be security guards?"

"Good point. Why don't you run your drone over there and let's see what happens."

As Luís piloted his drone over the area, both men watched the computer screen.

"Doesn't look like there's a soul there," Luís observed.

"Good. Let's get some video of the equipment and get your drone out of there. We're probably violating a half-dozen international laws by doing this."

Shortly Luís landed the drone, stowed it in its carrying case in the back of his vehicle and then smiled and said, "I haven't seen any drones down here on the border. Have you?"

Zeke shrugged his shoulders and replied, "Not a one."

Throughout the remainder of the week several more shipments of heavy equipment arrived and were unloaded, but only the drivers and crews were seen. Zeke took pictures nevertheless, and Luís recorded several conversations, but both were essentially useless.

On Friday afternoon just before leaving for the weekend, Zeke uploaded the pictures and audio files to Agent Alexander.

On Saturday morning, Luís and Javi were at the Ajo swimming pool, so Zeke and Abby were alone in the house. Zeke was relaxing on the sofa, wearing shorts and a tee shirt, reading a book.

Abby put some Smooth Latin Jazz on the stereo on low volume, and was swaying gently to the rhythm. She was wearing an above-the-knee length light blue print sleeveless sun dress, in her bare feet, with her hair pinned back slightly so that it hung down her back and off of her shoulders.

Then, she walked over to where Zeke was sitting. He looked up and said, "Um, um, um, you sure do look good in that dress."

"Thank you," She said, smiling shyly, then she lifted each side of her skirt slightly and waved it as she turned all the way around, modeling it for him.

"Oh, yeah... very sexy."

He reached out, took her hand, pulled her to him and kissed her. She sat by him and wrapped her arms around his right arm. Then she wrapped her right leg over his right leg, laid her head on his shoulder and snuggled comfortably against him.

He laid his book aside, gently stroked her exposed thigh, then kissed her softly on the forehead, smiled and said, "Hi, Beautiful."

She returned his smile and said, "Hi, My Love."

Then he continued reading as he gently stroked her thigh.

Abby snuggled against Zeke, quietly listening to the music and absorbing the presence of her husband; feeling his warmth, breathing in the smell of his skin, watching his chest rise and fall as he breathed, and basking contentedly in the secure comfort of his strength and love.

Then she looked at him and whispered, "Husband, I love you."

"I love you too, Beautiful." He replied as he put down his book.

"Do you remember telling me about the advice that your Grandpa Ezzy offered you the day that he gave you the Raptor?"

"Sure."

"Have you ever told him that you're following his advice?"

"No, not really. But then, I shouldn't have to; he's aware that, thanks to you, I'm happy and having the time of my life. He certainly knows that I found the girl of my dreams and that we were married; he attended our wedding."

"I forget, what exactly did he tell you that day?"

"Well, he told me that I had been too serious for far too long, and that I had been alone too long. He said that he was proud of my accomplishments. Then he said that it was time for me to live a little, kick up some dust and stretch my legs. And to get out there and have some fun. Then he said that he wanted me to find a nice girl, get married and start making babies because he wants more great grandkids."

"I remember that," Abby smiled, "It made me laugh." Then she changed her tone, "So, you haven't done everything that he wants you to do."

"Well, you and I haven't made any babies yet, but Javi certainly qualifies as a new great grandchild."

"True, but I still think that you might want to let him know that you're really trying to do everything that he asked."

Zeke looked at Abby with a raised eyebrow and asked, "Do you really think that telling him that you and I are making love every night is necessary? Don't you suppose he's already assumed something like that?"

Abby began slowly and playfully running her index finger up and down his arm and said in a sultry voice, "Well, what we've been doing every night is certainly the best way that I know of to make a baby..."

"Well then..." Zeke kissed her very tenderly and quietly suggested, "Why don't I carry you to our bed and let's try to make a baby right now?"

"That's not necessary," Abby replied rather matter-of-factly.

"What do you mean it's not necessary?"

"We already have."

"We already have what?"

"Made a baby."

"When?"

Then she took his right hand and gently placed his palm against her belly and said innocently, "About a month ago."

He looked at his hand on her belly, then looked into her sparkling eyes, and gasped, "You're pregnant!"

"Yes!" She replied as a beautiful smile lit up her face.

"We're pregnant!" Zeke shouted as he jumped up, then scooped her up into his arms and twirled her around. "We're going to have a baby!"

"Yes, Husband, we are…"

Zeke kissed Abby passionately and carried her to their bed.

Chapter Six
No Choice But One

For lack of a better idea while they waited for a response from Special Agent Alexander about his "plan in the works" reply, Zeke and Luís continued their daily surveillance of the heavy equipment stored at Cerro Colorado Numero Dos. Their schedule was still covering the morning half of the day due to the afternoon heat. The Monsoon season was also on-going, so afternoon thunderstorms were still an unpredictable daily occurrence.

The first weekend in September Zeke and Abby went to Payson to surprise her parents with the good news that she was expecting, with an approximate due date during the last week in April. On September 7th they flew out to Cambridge to surprise Zeke's parents and grandparents with the good news.

One day during the second week in September, around 10:00 a.m., Zeke took a break from peering through the camera's telephoto lens to wipe the sweat from his face and said, "You know, Amigo, when you said, back in April, that May would only be warm, I honestly thought that you were just trying to tiptoe around the grim reality of the inevitable blistering hot desert temperatures.

"As it turned out, you were right, May was only a bit warm. During June, just as you predicted, it was hot, but I had no concept of what it was going to feel like in July when the Monsoon season cranked up and humidity was added to the mix. The past two months out here on this desert floor have been bloody miserable."

"Doc, there's a saying around here that summertime in the desert is what sends the Snowbirds north and separates the men from the boys."

"Amigo, it's also about to separate me from my sanity. You say the Monsoon ends in early October?"

"Usually."

"I hope that I can hold out that long; come on October!"

Just then the sound of an approaching helicopter drew their attention.

"I hear a helicopter," Luís said, "must be the airborne patrol out of Yuma running the border."

"I don't think so," Zeke said, "the sound's coming from the south."

In the distance, a fast moving, sleek, black helicopter suddenly appeared just above the mountains behind Cerro Colorado and quickly descended toward the area where the construction equipment was stored. Zeke followed the helicopter with his camera, snapping pictures as it circled the area once and then hovered briefly before it landed in a cloud of dust.

"See if you can capture some audio," Zeke said to Luís as he reattached the camera to the tripod and focused on the helicopter, which was now shutting down its engines.

Luís put on the headsets and aimed the audio telescope at the passengers as they began to exit the aircraft.

"Two males exited the right rear door," Luís said. "One is speaking to one of the crewmen—something about time because he looked at his watch."

"Both are in business suits," Zeke added as he clicked the shutter. "A female just exited from the rear door. She's in business attire as well, carrying a portfolio."

"The female is speaking to one of the males. His back is toward me, but she said something about a queasy stomach. He put his arm around her and kissed her cheek."

"I saw that," Zeke said, "If she's his secretary, they have a close working relationship."

"I wonder if his wife knows," Luís quipped. "Sounds like they're talking about the construction equipment. I'm getting bits and pieces about numbers and types of machinery."

"I'm getting some good shots of all three passengers, and the crew," Zeke said.

After about twenty minutes everyone boarded the helicopter, it started up and lifted off. The pilot circled the area once more, then turned and approached Highway 2, coming to hover directly over the highway with the nose of the aircraft pointing directly at Zeke and Luís' position.

"I think they've spotted us," Zeke said.

"I don't see how they can make us out beneath this camouflage netting," Luís replied.

"Maybe they just spotted the netting and are suspicious," Zeke speculated.

Then the pilot turned the helicopter perpendicular to their position so the passengers could get a better look. They hovered there for a few moments and then the pilot turned and headed back toward the south, climbed toward the top of the mountain and disappeared on the other side.

"Well, that was interesting," Zeke said as he stood and watched the helicopter fade from sight. "Let's pack up and get these pictures and sound files back to Ajo Station."

As they were driving toward Ajo Station, dark, billowing cumulonimbus clouds were towering high on the eastern horizon and lightning flashes could be seen arcing from cloud to cloud.

"Looks like thunderstorms are making a serious effort to dump some rain this afternoon," Luís remarked.

"I hope so," Zeke replied. "Javi has been wanting to see Ten Mile Wash flowing again. I told him we'd try to run out there if the opportunity presented itself. Maybe today's the day."

"That would be cool."

"I'll get these video and audio files uploaded to Ray as soon as we get to the office, and then text Abril to pack up an ice chest so we can just pick them up on the way and go straight out there."

"Sounds like a plan…"

Back at the office, Zeke quickly looked over the pictures that he had taken before sending a copy of the file to his boss, Senior Agent Ray Alexander.

"Amigo, I think we should do some investigating ourselves."

"Oh?" Luís replied.

"Yea. We can run the aircraft registration number and, depending on who owns it, might be able to dig deeper."

"No reason that Ray should have all the fun."

"Well, if he's working on his own like he said, then I'm sure he'd appreciate some help with analysis of this data. I wish we had access to facial recognition software."

"Let's see what we get back on the registration number," Luís suggested, "Who knows, we might not need it."

As Luís turned onto the long driveway to his house, Zeke asked, "Do you want to take the Raptor?"

"Nah, we'll take my truck."

"Okay, I'll grab the ice chest. Otherwise Abril will be trying to lug it out here by herself. That girl is so stubborn—I keep fussing at her about lifting and straining and she always says the same thing,

'I'm just pregnant, I'm not recovering from spinal surgery.'"

"Welcome to Abby's world, Doc. You should've heard her and Mama going at it on that subject when she was pregnant with Javi."

Luís drove them to the Picnic Grounds, which is located five miles north of town and about 1.5 miles east of the airport, near the small community of Childs, locally known as "The Well" because the water source for Ajo is there.

In the distance, east of the Picnic Grounds, which is on the banks of Ten Mile Wash, the thunderstorms had built into a massive, menacing wall of dark grey clouds and mist dominating the eastern horizon above the Pozo Redondo Mountain Range, making it impossible to distinguish mountain from sky.

The thunderstorm tops, now reaching to the upper levels of the atmosphere, were painted in highlights of bronze and gold from the rays of the setting sun, bathing the scene in a surreal, greenish glow.

"Wow! Look at that!" Javi said and pointed to a dark dust cloud sweeping toward them just as they stepped out of the truck

Before anyone could react, the moist, chilly gust front hit, carrying with it dust, sand and debris.

Abby squealed and turned away from the stinging sand, covering her face with her hands. Zeke quickly wrapped her in the blanket that he was carrying and sheltered her from the wind as the thunder rumbled in the distance.

The gust front disappeared as quickly as it came, leaving a chilly breeze carrying the refreshing fragrances of greasewood and ozone, compelling the brain to command the lungs to take a deep breath through the nose, inhaling as much of the energized air as possible.

Abby held the blanket like a cape, spread her arms wide and threw her head back, her long silky hair flying in the breeze as she exclaimed, "Ummmm greasewood! I love the smell of a desert thunderstorm!"

Not far away, Javi and Luís had gone down into Ten Mile Wash.

Abby suddenly realized where they had gone and ran toward the wash yelling at the top of her very healthy lungs, "Luís Reginaldo! Javier Bernado! Get your asses on high ground now!!"

Two heads quickly popped up from down in the wash.

Abby slowed to a walk and yelled, "You heard me! Move!!"

They were both climbing out of the wash like two puppies with their tails between their legs as Abby and Zeke made it to the bank of the wash.

Abby pointed her finger accusingly at Javi and said, "You know better than that young man!" Then she turned to Luís, her eyes flared as she started to launch into him, "And you...!"

Just then a roar, carried on the wind, made its presence known. They all looked down the wash toward the east with anticipation. Suddenly, a wall of mud, water, driftwood, trees and other debris came roaring around the bend of the wash, quickly making its way toward them as they stood on the bank.

Within minutes, the wash, which is fifty feet wide and eight to ten feet deep near the Picnic Grounds, was filled to its banks with fast-flowing muddy water, overflowing in several places.

Javi started to get closer to the edge. Abby grabbed his arm and said, "We can see fine from here, Mijo."

Luís was busy taking video and snapshots with his smart phone as they watched large trees, a storage shed, and other jetsam float by, carried quickly along by the raging flood. By then the storm had moved closer, as did the lightning, so they loaded into the truck to leave just as large rain drops began falling.

That evening, Ajo received a rare and much-welcomed, soaking summer rain.

The following day dawned crisp, clean, and cool from the effects of the over-night rainfall. Before breakfast, as Abby and Zeke watched, Javi and Luís carefully observed a giant Sonoran Desert Toad (poisonous) that had responded to the soaked earth and emerged from its hibernation in the back yard to feast on bugs and breed.

"This is a smart toad," Luís observed.

"And how do you know that?" Abby asked.

"Ajo was recently named a Certified Wildlife Habitat Community by the National Wildlife Federation. It's the second community in Arizona and the sixty fifth in the nation to earn that certification. The toad knows that."

"And how, pray tell, did the toad learn that?" Abby asked as she played along.

"He heard it on the Toad Report. You know, on the Froggy network."

Javi cracked up laughing.

***

Later that morning at the office, Zeke and Luís began researching the model and registration number of the helicopter that Zeke had photographed the day before. Luís researched the model of the helicopter and Zeke researched the aircraft registration.

Luís sat with his feet propped on the desk, sipping coffee and searching the internet on his laptop.

"I think I've found the helicopter," Luís announced. "It's a McDonnell Douglas MD 902 Explorer, a fast and powerful twin-engine workhorse that's used for law enforcement, air ambulance and exec service. It performs well in hot climates and at high elevations, which probably explains why they're using it. Whoever owns it has a fat budget for aircraft acquisitions."

"It's a sharp looking aircraft, I'll give 'em that," Zeke replied as he concentrated on his computer screen, and then said, "The registration prefix is 'XC'. ...that's the Mexican government... Here we go... Holey buckets!"

Zeke looked up from his computer, then looked Luís square in the eyes and said, "The aircraft is registered to the US consulate in Hermosillo."

"Caramba!"

"Amigo, I think we've just waded into the swamp up to our necks. I wonder how this will affect Ray's 'plan in the works'?"

Zeke forwarded the new information to Agent Alexander, and included a question; "How do we proceed?"

An hour later came the reply: Stand down. Will contact 1 Oct.

Zeke sighed, leaned back in his chair and said, "Well, Amigo, I got my answer. And you're not going to believe it."

Luís looked at Zeke's laptop and then said, "Looks like we've been shifted to neutral. What now, Doc?"

Zeke rubbed his eyes with both hands and said, "I don't know. When Ray says 'stand down' that's precisely what he means. We're dead in the water until we hear from him. But I'll go nuts sitting in this office doing nothing day after day for two weeks. School's back in session, so all we have is the weekends to get away."

"How 'bout we go fishin'?"

"Fishing."

"Sure. Fishin'. Don't you like to fish?"

"Of course. It's been a while, but—"

"Well?"

"And just where are we supposed to go fishing in the desert?"

"There's nothing out here since the Painted Rock Reservoir was emptied, but the Lower Salt River below Saguaro Lake, north of the stretch of the river where you proposed to Abby is a good area to fish."

"I fish there all the time. You, Abby and I can go scope out the good fishing holes while Javi's in school, and then we can take him fishing on Saturday. Whaddya say?"

"Sounds like a good idea, especially taking Javi fishing. I'll discuss it with Abril during our walk after work."

"Cool! Then it's a cinch—she's great at fly fishing. I know she'd love to go."

"Fly fishing? Huh. I had no idea."

"My little sister is full of surprises, Doc."

"That makes me look forward to our future together even more."

That afternoon after work, Zeke and Abby were walking hand in hand around the half-mile circumference of Bud Walker Park, Ajo's green oasis and Ajo Community Center, getting Abby's daily brisk walking exercise. Javi was playing on the playground.

"This morning Ray ordered us to stand down until October first."

"Oh? What was his reasoning for that?"

"It has to do with the helicopter that we saw on the border yesterday."

"Well, what are you two miscreants going doing to do with yourselves for the next two weeks?"

"Anything but sitting in the office doing nothing."

"What about Luís' boss? He's bound to want to put Luís out patrolling the border."

"Luís is assigned to my mission until it's complete. I'm not going to allow Agent Breen to coopt my liaison. We'll still give Agent Breen the Monday morning briefing, but just not include the stand down status, and continue, business as usual. Luís and I report to Ray."

"So, what's your plan?"

"Luís suggested fishing on the Lower Salt River, north of where we were engaged."

"Oh, that would be nice. If Game and Fish is still stocking trout it could be pretty productive, not to mention just wading the river—I love to do that."

"Luís said that you like to fly fish."

"Yes, I do. What about you?"

"Dad and I used to fly fish on Lake Erie for Muskie, but I've never fly fished in a stream for trout. Maybe you could teach me."

"Teaching my husband to fly fish for trout. Humm…" Abby replied reflectively, then looked at him and smiled, "I'd like that."

"Luís reminded me today that there's a lot of things that I don't know about you, like… fly fishing, for example. And I suppose there's a lot that you don't know about me. I'm finding that learning about you is very enjoyable. Each day you become even more amazing to me."

Abby pulled Zeke's hand up to her face, kissed his palm and said, "Husband, you are such a charmer. I think if I died you could actually charm me back to life."

"Just keep in mind that I wasn't charming until I met you."

Abby looked at him with a raised eyebrow and said, "I seriously doubt that, but I'll take it under consideration."

"Not trying to change the subject," Zeke said, "but we haven't talked about religion very much. I know that you are a devout Catholic, and I'm honored to attend mass with you and Javi. You know that I'm not Catholic, but I'm surprised that you haven't asked more questions about my faith, especially before we were married."

"Asking questions like that makes me uncomfortable. It feels like I'm prying. I know I shouldn't feel that way; you and I have no secrets and I love that about our relationship. I trust you and I have faith in you. It's just that religion is such an intensely personal thing, I guess I've just assumed that we would eventually discuss it."

"I suppose that I didn't bring it up because your family made me feel so welcomed. I didn't sense any prejudice or racism, nor any issues about religion. My family is also very open minded; but still, for generations we have dealt with prejudice on a very personal and emotional level. We are very sensitive and cautious, because we know what it's like to be hated."

"I don't understand."

"We are Jews."

"Oh, I see. Your great grandfather. You said that he was a doctor in Germany that fled to America.

It just never occurred to me he was a German Jew."

"Yes. He fled Germany in 1940 with his family, including my grandfather, who was four years old at the time, to escape persecution by the Nazis. He knew that the Nazis could force him into medical service with the German Army and possibly send his wife and children to a concentration camp. Although some Jews did serve voluntarily in the German Army, my great grandfather refused to even consider it. He was devout and refused to serve Hitler—the 'insane monster that is raping and pillaging Europe' as he described him.

"According to my great grandmother's diary, he became conflicted about his faith due to his friendship with Christians at the hospital where he practiced in Dresden. When he came to America, he was introduced to, and embraced, Messianic Judaism, which he believed kept him faithful to his Jewish heritage while allowing him and his family to accept Yeshua—Jesus, as the Messiah and Savior, just as his Christian friends believed and taught. Thus began a family religious legacy that continues to this day."

"Ezekiel, you have a very rich and interesting family history. I also understand prejudice, racism and hatred all too well. As American Indians, my family, each one of us, has dealt with irrational, racial hatred at some point in our lives, my Papa especially.

"So, Husband, we're not so different after all, you and I. And, just so you know, I wouldn't care if you were a Druid, I'd still love you."

"Funny that you chose Druid. I've studied Druidism. I find their devotion to peace, the spirituality of nature, and their goals of wisdom, creativity and love quite compelling."

Abby stopped and turned to face Zeke, then she put her arms around his neck, kissed him and said, "You are a fascinating man."

Off and on for the next two weeks, Zeke, Abby, Javi and Luís played and fished on the picturesque and peaceful Lower Salt River. Abby taught Zeke how to fly fish in a shallow stream for trout, which is not as easy as it might seem. Fishing was fair, and the time spent together as a family was priceless.

Back at the office, on Monday morning, October 1st, Zeke and Luís sat drinking coffee and waiting for a message from Special Agent Alexander. Luís read every newspaper available from headlines to obituaries, and Zeke surfed the internet news for anything happening in Mexico that could possibly lend itself to what they had seen on the border.

Suddenly they heard voices coming down the hall. Zeke and Luís looked up just as Agent Breen knocked on the doorjamb and said, "Is anyone home?" and walked in. Directly behind him was

Senior Special Agent Ray Alexander.

Both Zeke and Luís were instantly on their feet.

"Here you are, Ray," Agent Breen said, "Your team has been anxiously awaiting your… message, so I'll leave you to deliver it in person."

Then Agent Breen and Special Agent Alexander shook hands and Agent Breen said, "If you need me, you know where to find me. Good morning gentlemen." And departed for his office.

"Greetings, gentlemen," Ray Alexander said, and shook their hands. "It's good to finally meet you, Agent Gonzales. Needless to say I've heard a lot of good things about you."

"Thank you. Sir. It's good to meet you as well. Somewhat of a surprise…"

"I apologize for the ambush. At the moment, four people know I'm here; you, Agent Breen and Kathy." Then he turned to Luís, "Kathy's my administrative assistant, or more accurately, my Girl Friday."

"Here, have a seat," Zeke said as he pulled out his chair, and then asked, "How was your flight, Sir?"

"It's Ray. And that goes for you as well, Agent Gonzales."

"Then I'm Luís."

"Good, Luís. And welcome to the team by the way."

"Thank you, Ray."

"How was my flight?" Ray repeated as he sat down. "Non-stop first class from DC. I got in just before nine last evening, stayed overnight in Phoenix and drove down early this morning. Saw a beautiful sunrise. I had forgotten how grand this desert landscape is."

"Welcome to Ajo and the Sonoran Desert," Luís said.

"Thanks, it's good to be here. We have a lot to discuss gentlemen. Zeke your office leaves a bit to be desired. All I've had is coffee this morning, how about we get some breakfast and talk."

"I know just the place," Luís said.

As the men were waiting for their breakfast to be brought to the table at Marcella's Café and Bakery, Zeke asked, "Ray, do you mind if I text my wife to let her know that you're in town? I know Abril will want to meet you, and I'm equally certain that she will want to invite you for dinner. Probably tonight."

"As long as it's just between you and Abril. But, as far as dinner, I wouldn't want to impose—."

"It's no imposition, believe me. On the contrary, she will insist. I'm certain of it," Zeke replied.

"He's right, Ray. I would strongly suggest surrender. It's the best option," Luís added.

"I see… I get the impression that the new Missus Sikes is somewhat, ah, strong willed."

"Very perceptive," Zeke replied.

"You nailed it," Said Luís.

Zeke sent the following text to Abby: Ray here as of this morning! Just between you and I. Dinner out is fine, but your choice as always. Love you much, Z.

Abby's reply: Dinner here. Enjoy your surprise meeting. Love you more, A.

After breakfast, Ray bragged about the food to the entire staff and then asked Zeke, "Is there a park or somewhere we can go to talk privately?"

"How about the mine overlook?" Luís suggested.

"Good idea," Zeke replied. "The Mine Lookout on Indian Village Road. There's also a visitors center that's open October through May, so it should open today, in fact. Abril and I have been waiting for it to open so that we can take Javi."

The three men stood at the mine overlook, taking in the grand view of the massive terraced cone and multi-colored strata of rock and stone that is the New Cornelia Open Pit Mine, which is over a mile across and over eight hundred feet deep.

"That is one seriously big hole in the ground," Ray commented, and then began.

"Gentlemen, the data that you've been sending, plus the pictures and audio that you uploaded to me added some major parts to the puzzle that I've been piecing together. So much so that we're going to have to shift gears.

"The construction equipment that you photographed—the drone video was outstanding, by the way. And worth the risk."

"What kind of risk?" Luís asked.

"Had you been caught, it would probably have been escalated into an international incident. We would have faced numerous federal charges and heavy fines, and probably termination."

"Oh, is that all," Luís replied and made an 'oh, crap' expression.

Zeke smiled mischievously at Luís and said, "Extremely intelligent and perceptive…"

Then Ray continued. "But what your drone video showed was some of the newest and largest earth moving equipment manufactured today. It's too expensive for most construction companies to own, so it's typically leased. However, sales personnel from the US dealers report the equipment was purchased for cash—around $20 million, by a Chinese company known as G^2 (pronounced Gee Squared) International.

"When the sales people inquired why the equipment was being shipped to Mexico, they were given different answers; 'G^{2}I is about to start a very large construction project in Northern Mexico' or 'the equipment is going into temporary storage in preparation for building the wall on the U.S, and Mexico border'. Obviously, something's fishy; the big construction project is only a rumor, and no contract bids have been let for the wall. Besides, it's unlikely that a Chinese company would be included in the bidding, considering the ration of shit that DHS caught for buying Chinese-made steel fence posts for a section of border fence near Nogales."

"So, what is G^{2}I?" Zeke asked.

"This will blow your mind," said Ray, "G^{2}I appeared on the scene about eight months ago when the company bought an underground mine in Central America for $30 million. Before that G^{2}I didn't exist in any form. The headquarters are in Shanghai. The CEO is Quan Ji Zhang, a retired Chinese Army General, controlling an estimated 850 billion dollars in liquid assets. There are only 29 countries on the planet that are richer than G^{2}I. Where the money came from is anyone's guess.

Quan Ji Zhang is a Taoist. China just built a monument to the Taoist God of War; Guan Yu, in Jingzhou. It was made from 4000 strips of dense bronze placed over a steel skeleton of the statue. It stands 190 feet tall and weighs 1320 tons. The thing is, Guan Yu was actually a general that lived in the third century, during the Eastern Han Dynasty. He is worshiped as the Taoist God of War, and referred to as 'Lord Guan'. That's the English translation. In Chinese it's pronounced Guan Gong.

"Notice the similarity; Guan Gong, GG, or, "G" times "G"—"G" squared. The full name of General Zhang's 850 billion dollar company is Guan Gong International. The God of War International."

"Aye Caramba!" Luís exclaimed.

"Caramba, indeed," Ray replied.

"Guan Gong, the God of War," Ray continued, "doesn't bless

those who go into battle. He blesses those who observe the code of brotherhood and righteousness. If Quan Ji Zhang believes that his mission is to uphold the righteousness of the brotherhood of Red China, and believes that the U.S. is a threat to that mission, he has the resources to attack and destroy the threat."

Then Luís suggested, "Why don't we get some refreshment, and maybe some snacks, and go to Ajo Regional Park. We can have privacy to talk there."

"Great idea," Ray said.

At the park, they sat on a large concrete and stone bench encircling a giant mesquite tree and Ray continued; "Gentlemen, we have but one choice. We need to know exactly what Quan Ji Zhang plans to do in Mexico. The only way to find out is to go there."

Luís looked at Ray and said, "I get the distinct feeling we're about to go to Mexico."

"We? You have a mouse in your pocket?"

"I'm not going to Mexico, you are going to Mexico. You and Zeke. He speaks only formal Spanish, so you're his official interpreter. We must find out what's going on down there. We have no choice."

"Where are we going, exactly?" Zeke asked.

"To the source. The Consulate General in Hermosillo. That's the key. And I quote, 'the officers and staff work to ensure that American citizens visiting and residing in the area are provided courteous and expeditious service when they visit the Consulate.' So, we'll ask them for help.

"Zeke, you'll be Ralph Williams, chief representative for Bright Star Technical, one of the leading engineering services in North America. They provide outstanding industrial and civil engineering for every conceivable construction project, from sky scrapers to domed stadiums and from super highways to seaports, airports and oil refineries. BST does it all. I sound like a commercial don't I?

"Luís, you'll be Alex Alvarez, Mr. Williams' personal assistant and interpreter. I have a dossier for each of you, which will provide your life history, education and job history, passports and identification. The people that you'll be meeting are the helicopter passengers that you photographed and recorded. Their info is also in your dossiers.

"The main target will be Emilio Velazquez. He is CEO of Desoto Construcción, based in Monterey, and the one who was

109

flown to Cerro Colorado to inspect the construction equipment. He is also the head of the Serpiente Cartel, now the largest and most ruthless drug cartel in Mexico."

"The serpent. The head of the snake. How appropriate," Luís commented.

"I'm sure the inference wasn't accidental," said Zeke.

"Gentlemen, I can't begin to tell you how vital your mission is or how dangerous. Velazquez, the head of the snake, was flown to Cerro Colorado in a U.S. government aircraft to inspect construction equipment owned by a Red Chinese company with more financial resources than eighty percent of the governments on Earth. And that company is controlled by a former Chinese Army general that is most likely a religious, nationalist fanatic. Whatever they're up to does not bode well for America, and there are strings tied directly between the Consulate in Hermosillo and Washington DC. We are in deep shit. Let's try to dig us out."

Later that afternoon, as Luís, Zeke and Ray walked across the front porch, Abby opened the front door. She was wearing a stunning, floor-length, flowing white maxi dress with a modestly plunging bodice. Her hair was done up loosely with a white silk ribbon, allowing her long, silky chestnut-brown locks to flow over her shoulders and down her back. As she opened the door, a light breeze blew past her and into the house, causing her dress and her hair to flow with the wind, creating the image of a royal princess from a scene in a fantasy movie. All three men froze and stared at her in breathless awe.

Then Zeke sputtered to awareness and said, "Uh, Abril, I would like to introduce Ray. Ray, this is my wife, Abril."

"Oh, my…" Ray began and approached to take Abby's hand in greeting. "Young lady, you take my breath away! When your unworthy husband told me that you were beautiful, he conveniently left out the part about you being a goddess. Missus Sikes, you are stunningly beautiful, and it is my humble honor to meet you."

A lovely red blush blossomed across Abby's cheeks as she smiled and said, "Thank you, Ray, you are too kind. It is an honor to meet you as well. Please, come in. Welcome to our home."

Then she put her arm in his, escorted him into the house and said, "So, tell me, Ray, are all DEA Special Agents such adept charmers as you and my husband?"

"Ahhh, that is a closely guarded secret," He replied with an air of tongue-in-cheek humor, then winked at Zeke. "Perhaps you might be able to coax your husband into revealing some of our secrets."

Abby gave Zeke a playful glance and said, "Humm, I'll have to consider that."

Then Javi dashed in from playing in the back yard. Zeke corralled him long enough to introduce him to Ray. Then he got a drink and a snack from Mom and out into the back yard he went.

"Ray, what can I get you to drink?" Abby asked.

"I could go for a cold beer about now," Ray replied, then walked over to Zeke, grabbed his bicep and whispered, "You lucky dog! Abby is adorable!"

Zeke smiled and replied, "Thank you, Ray; she's my dream girl."

Abby brought Ray a chilled glass filled with beer.

"Thank you, Mam. And what is that delicious aroma?"

Abby led him into the kitchen and showed him what she was preparing for dinner – a pork shoulder, baked sweet potatoes, assorted steamed vegetables, a green salad, fresh-baked sourdough rolls and a multi-layer chocolate and vanilla cake.

"Young lady, you are preparing a feast!"

"I hope it will all be good," She replied

"Of that, I have no doubt."

Abby then showed him into the dining room. "The munchies are on the table—I'm sure Luís is already well into those. There's soda and beer in the fridge, or Luís will prepare a mixed drink to your order. I'll be serving wine with dinner, and iced tea if you prefer. That will be my dinner beverage. Or you can have a glass of milk with Javi!"

"I think I'll go with this cold beer for now, and wine sounds excellent with dinner."

"Good. Then, please, make yourself at home. Dinner should be ready in about thirty minutes."

Then Abby returned to the kitchen.

Just then Zeke walked into the kitchen. "Honey," Abby said, "the wine is chilling. Could you please set out the wine glasses and—"

Zeke walked up to her, slid his arms around her waist and gave her a very passionate kiss. Then he looked into her eyes and played with her hair as he said, "You are so incredibly amazing. You simply blow me away; you are so beautiful."

She kissed him tenderly and whispered, "Thank you."

Then he dropped to his knees, placed his hands on her waist and gently kissed her pregnant belly that was just beginning to show. Then he hugged her around her bottom and laid his face against her belly as she looked down at him and stroked his hair.

At that point Ray walked into the kitchen. "Excuse me for interrupting, but I have neglected to congratulate you two love birds on your pregnancy."

Abby smiled and said, "Thank you, Ray."

"So, what are you hoping for, boy or girl?"

Zeke looked up at Abby and said, "It doesn't really matter to us, as long as the baby's healthy."

"That's what we're praying for," Abby added.

"I'll light a candle for you," Ray said.

"You're Catholic," Abby commented.

"Yes, Mam. Catechism, parochial school, the whole lot."

Abby and Ray talked about their mutual experiences growing up Catholic as she continued tending to dinner. Shortly she announced, "Gentlemen, dinner is ready. Luís, would you please call Javi in to wash up."

Javi said the blessing, and then Ray proposed a toast. "Here's to Abril, our hostess and beautiful mother-to-be. May all of your days be blessed with joy and love, and may the saddest day of your future be no worse than the happiest day of your past."

Abby's dinner was excellent. Everyone enjoyed themselves and the evening went swimmingly. After dinner they all relaxed on the patio, talking and sipping wine, except Abby, who drank ice tea.

Abby had arranged for Ray to stay in the extra bedroom, so he announced that he was exhausted, bid everyone goodnight and turned in early.

Luís went to his room to call Bekah, and Javi went to bed, so Zeke and Abby had the patio to themselves.

The evening was peaceful and cool, with a quiet serenade of crickets and toads. Zeke fetched Abby a blanket, and they cuddled up on a large wicker sofa with overstuffed cushions underneath a crystal-clear moonless sky filled with sparkling stars.

"The dinner was delicious tonight, Sweetheart."

"You think so?"

"I know so. I think you're the only one that didn't have seconds."

"Thank you. I was afraid that the pork was going to be too dry."

"Everything was perfect, Sweetheart," Then he kissed her cheek.

They lay quietly for a while, watching for satellites and shooting stars, as Zeke gently caressed Abby's belly. Then he said, "I'm looking forward to feeling our baby kicking."

"Me, too... sort of."

"Why 'sort of'?"

"Babies seem to want to be awake kicking in the middle of the night when it's time to sleep. And then they sometimes kick you in the kidneys, which is kinda painful. But still, I'm looking forward to feeling our little bundle growing in my belly. I'm only nine weeks, so right now our little one is really a little one; between two and three inches long and weighs about as much as a peapod."

Zeke slid his hand underneath her dress and pressed his palm against her bare belly and said, "Our itty bitty little one."

Then he looked at her and said, "Again, I'm sorry that I've not been able to be there for all of your appointments with your obstetrician."

"That's okay, Honey. I've told you not to worry. You'll have plenty of opportunities. In fact, I have an ultrasound scheduled this Thursday morning. And besides, Mama is always there with me. She's so excited; it's simply adorable."

Then Abby paused and grew serious. "Honey, we have no secrets, right?"

"That's right. No secrets."

"Ezekiel, something is wrong. Ray isn't just down here on a lark. He's here for something serious. What is it?"

"This teasing we've been doing about you and Luís being 'extremely intelligent and very perceptive' isn't just teasing. I know you're both extremely intelligent, but you're also extremely perceptive."

"Something just doesn't feel right. I'm not certain why. Please, tell me what's going on."

"I apologize, Sweetheart. I honestly wasn't trying to keep anything from you, I just wasn't certain how and when to tell you. Ray came down to brief us on our new orders. Luís and I have to go undercover into Mexico. We're traveling by car to Hermosillo, which is only a one hundred fifty miles straight south of Nogales. We'll be

acting as representatives of an engineering firm, trying to get information about a big construction project that is supposedly going to
start soon near Puerto Peñasco, and there is a lot that's fishy about
it. We need to know what's going on."

"Will it be dangerous?"

"You know I can't lie to you. It could be. We don't expect any
problems, but Mexico is unstable right now, so we'll just need to
watch our backs. We've both been well trained, and we'll be armed,
so there's no need for you to worry. We'll be fine."

Abby didn't say anything else, she just snuggled as close to him
as she could, and held on tightly.

***

Over the course of the next two days, Ray reviewed the plans
and their fake identities, making certain that the personal and professional data associated with the characters that Zeke and Luís were
assuming became second nature.

Before they concluded on Wednesday afternoon, Ray said,
"And the last thing gentlemen; the website for Bright Star Technical
went active just before I—Rex Tillman, called Emilio Velazquez. I
built the site with a lot of flash, BS and impressive pictures, but I
conveniently left out the physical address. No doubt he's looked at
the site and could be considering sending one of his people to find
BST.

"I've had the BST sign and logo placed in the kiosk of one of
the big office buildings in Dallas that requires a security badge to
enter the elevator. I'm hoping that will keep them in the dark in the
short term.

"Pictures associated with your on-line identities have been re-
placed with photo-shopped pictures of non-existent people, so as
long as this meeting isn't dragged out, and you can get in and out
of Mexico with no snafus, we should be okay. Just do your best to
get Velazquez to brag about the project and the investors, maybe
his boasting will cause him to slip up and reveal something about
General Zhang.

"Good luck gentlemen. Godspeed."

***

Ray returned to DC on Thursday. Zeke went with Abby to her
appointment and marveled over the ultrasound pictures of their
baby—after the obstetrician censored the sexual organ because they
decided they wanted the sex of the baby to be a surprise. Luís headed

to Payson to spend the weekend with Bekah. Zeke, Abby and Javi spent family time in Ajo.

In the pre-dawn hours of Monday, October 8th, Zeke and Abby lay in bed, silently holding each other, unable to sleep.

Then Abby crawled partially on top of Zeke, so that they were face to face, close enough to feel each other's breath, and said, "I don't want to be that wife who lays a guilt trip on her husband because he has to leave her side and go into harm's way.

"I trust in you and I believe in you. I think your choice to be a DEA Special Agent was courageous and selfless. I'm proud of who and what you are, and I love you with all of my heart and soul. All that I ask is that you do your best to come back to me. It's all that I can ask."

"Beautiful, you are the reason I'm alive. Yes, I had a heartbeat before I met you, but I wasn't living, I was only existing. You are my world and everything in it. I live to be with you, and until God takes me from you, I will be with you, loving you, always."

Abby gently caressed his face and kissed him ever so tenderly.

Then she whispered, "Make love to me…"

At 10:17 a.m. on October 8th, Ralph Williams and Alex Alvarez, unarmed, and leaping into a potential pit of evil, crossed the U.S. border into Mexico.

Chapter Seven
Into the Serpent's Den

Ralph Williams and Alex Alvarez cleared Mexican Customs and slowly cruised through downtown Nogales. Alex was driving.

"I hate the name, Ralph," Zeke complained.

"Can't blame you. But at least I'm not Norton."

"The Honeymooner's we're not."

"I kinda like the name Alex. I had a buddy at ASU named Alejandro and we called him 'Alex'."

"You have a masters in criminology and criminal justice from ASU, right?"

"Yep. A Sun Devil to the core."

"I hope we spot that street vendor soon. I feel naked down here without a weapon."

"No kidding."

Luís drove slowly, periodically pulling over to avoid holding up traffic as they searched both sides of the street for the street vendor.

Finally, Luís said, "Here we go. On the right, just ahead." He parked and said, "I'll be right back."

Shortly, he returned with two plastic grocery bags. Zeke put both bags on the floor at his feet. One bag was filled with tortas (Mexican sandwiches), burritos, and sodas. The other bag contained two Glock G43 9mm pistols wrapped in newspaper, along with belt holsters, eight loaded clips and two boxes of ammo.

Zeke looked into the bag filled with the food. "Apparently, you're already hungry."

"Well, it's almost 11," Luís said, "and it's almost a 150 miles to Hermosillo. We might as well keep up our strength."

"That's what I love about you, Amigo, your survival instincts are always so keen."

"Hey, first order of survival…"

Zeke emptied the contents of the bag with the weapons on the seat between them and said, "Well, I sure as hell hope we won't need this much ammo."

Luís looked down and said, "Yeah, me, too."

Then Luís merged their rental car onto Federal Highway 15 headed south toward Hermosillo.

"Say, how 'bout hand me one of those tortas... and a soda... and a burrito, too."

"Why don't I just sit the bag beside you?"

"Good idea."

They arrived at the U.S. consulate in Hermosillo in the early afternoon. Mr. Williams and Mr. Alvarez were expected, and received a warm welcome at the reception desk. They were immediately taken to the office of the U.S. Ambassador, Willamina Samuels. Deputy Chief of Mission, Alfred Chase, was also present to greet them.

"Gentlemen," Ambassador Samuels began, "I have reviewed your paperwork, and I must say that I am impressed."

"Thank you, Madam Ambassador." Ralph replied. "Our contracts people will be pleased to hear that. At Bright Star Technical we pride ourselves on attention to detail, not only in our engineering endeavors, but our administrative functions as well."

Then, Mr. Chase commented, "We found that your contractor ID number was assigned in record time. I see your DUNS and SAM registration has been approved, but we need some clarification on the SAM action. We realize that SAM is required for actions in excess of 25,000 dollars, but the value provided on your documentation was 2 million dollars. Was that a typographical error?"

"Oh, no sir. Actually, that is a conservative estimate; our larger engineering contracts routinely exceeded that figure, and based on our knowledge of the project, we estimated our bid accordingly."

The ambassador and the deputy chief looked at each other and then the ambassador said, "So we understand that you have coordinated with Mr. Velazquez of Desoto Construcción?"

"Actually, Rex Tillman, CEO of BST, initiated contact with Desoto Construcción and called Mr. Velazquez directly to make the initial offer and coordinate our first meeting. But based on our research, we feel that the scope of this project will affect Mexico and the United States in a very big way, so we felt that it was prudent to meet with you first.

"We certainly appreciate your consideration, Mr. Williams., The ambassador said. "Mr. Velazquez has also contacted us. Apparently Mr. Tillman and he think alike. We understand that Mr. Velazquez has arranged the meeting on his private yacht near Tiburón Island in the Sea of Cortez—pardon me, Gulf of California; I prefer the traditional name."

"Yes, we're scheduled to meet his helicopter at the airport in the morning."

"Well, it has been good meeting you gentlemen. I'm sure you'd like to get settled in. I trust you have comfortable accommodations?"

"Yes, we're all set."

"Good. I think you will find the residents of Hermosillo to be friendly and gracious. And good luck with your meeting tomorrow."

"Thank you madam ambassador, it has been a pleasure meeting you and Mr. Chase."

Just after Zeke and Luís let the room, the deputy chief said, "I think we should tail them."

"That won't be necessary," the ambassador said, "You can bet that Velazquez is already watching them."

As Luís and Zeke drove away, Luís asked, "Did you get the bug planted okay?"

"Yeah, I placed it underneath my chair in the ambassador's office," Zeke replied as he pulled his laptop out of his briefcase and powered it up. "Where's the relay?"

"I put it underneath a table in the lobby when I tied my shoe," Luís replied.

"Well, let's see if that overpriced gadgetry is working." Zeke brought up the monitoring program. "Uplink shows strong and solid. Assuming the data is being sent to the crypto-cloud, Ray should have access now."

"How often do you think they sweep for bugs?"

"Depends on how overconfident and sloppy they are."

The following morning Zeke and Luís waited in the car for the Desoto Construcción helicopter at Hermosillo airport.

"We'd better check these glasses," Luís said as he put on a special pair of glasses that looked like typical prescription glasses but had a built-in video camera.

Zeke opened his briefcase, turned on his laptop and configured it to receive the video. "Clear as crystal." He said, and closed the computer.

"I wonder how many people are watching us right now," Luís

said.

"Who knows?" Zeke replied. "The two last night at dinner were pretty obvious. And the two that tailed us here might as well have a flashing beacon marking them."

"Do you think they're Serpiente, or do you suppose they were sent from the Consulate?"

"It's hard to say. I would guess that Velazquez has a small army, and deeper pockets, but if General Zhang's tentacles already reach to this level then money is inconsequential."

They were suddenly aware of the sound of a helicopter coming from a westerly direction, and then it came into view and set up an approach to land. As it swung around to point toward the west before touching down, the Sikorsky S-92 Executive Helicopter displayed its pearl-white paint scheme with 'Desoto Construcción' in large gold letters emblazoned along the full length of the fuselage.

The door opened and the pilot exited the aircraft and came to greet them.

"Mr. Williams and Mr. Alvarez? Good morning, gentlemen. I'm your pilot. Will you please follow me?"

Zeke and Luís boarded the aircraft and were greeted by two lovely young Hispanic girls dressed in airline attendant-like uniforms, only much more revealing. The girls escorted them to their seats, buckled them in and served them champagne. The helicopter lifted off shortly thereafter and headed west toward the coast. The girls sat directly across from them. It became readily apparent that neither of the girls were wearing underwear beneath their very short skirts.

Soon the azure blue Gulf of California came into view, with the mountainous, rocky Tiburón Island looming just off shore directly ahead. Several other smaller, but similar, rocky islands were also visible nearby.

The helicopter flew over the small fishing village of Bahia de Kino, then passed by the south end of Tiburón Island, turned north and quickly descended toward a large, bright blue, majestic yacht anchored in a small cove on the southwest side of the island. The helicopter pilot set up an approach and landed on the helipad located on the bow.

As Zeke and Luís exited the aircraft, they were greeted by Emilio Velazquez, stocky, athletic and darkly tanned, in his late-40s. He was wearing a custom white silk sport suit, a red graphic tee with a green marijuana leaf on the front, and Balenciaga Speed High Slip-Ons. He sported a well-trimmed grey beard, medium-length grey hair, and had green eyes. He was wearing an Omega wrist watch on his left wrist, a diamond-encrusted gold bracelet on his right, and a long, thick gold necklace hung from his neck.

Velazquez was well educated, and spoke with only a slight Hispanic accent.

"Gentlemen! We bid you welcome to my yacht, *The Flying Lady*." Then he shook their hands in greeting and said, "Come, join me for some champagne and fresh steamed seafood."

Six armed guards in white attire were stationed as strategic positions around the yacht. Two on the stern, one with an M4 Carbine with a grenade launcher, the other with an MP5K. Two guards on the bow were armed the same. On the starboard and the port side amidships, two guards each manned a M134 7.62mm Minigun mounted on a turret.

As they walked across the helipad toward the portside of the yacht, Velazquez turned to them and said, "Please excuse my guards. These waters are known to pirates and other unpleasant entities."

They walked along the teak deck and then followed him along the portside railing. Below, there were several bikini-clad young girls riding jet skis and swimming from a platform at water-level. One of the girls waved at Velazquez and he waved back. The crystal-clear water looked deceptively shallow from the shore to the open-water port side of the yacht where it gradually faded into a deep azure blue into the depths below. On the stern, several other bikini-clad young girls were playing in a large swimming pool.

"This way gentlemen," he said as he ran ahead, taking two steps at a time, leading them up a teak stairway to the open-air bridge deck, shaded by a large awning, where he offered them a seat in plush leather, hi-back lounge chairs, paired with small, elegant, round, glass-top tables.

"You are in excellent physical shape, Mr. Velazquez." Zeke observed.

"Thank you," he replied. "But I have to be…" and smiled as he patted the bare bottom of one of the two lovely young, bikini-clad girls that were just serving chilled champagne and fresh steamed scallops and shrimp, along with bite size pieces of lobster and conch, all on bamboo toothpicks cut into the shape of daggers.

Then he said, "Please, gentlemen, join me for my mid-morning snack."

As the exceptionally attractive girl who was serving him finished pouring his champagne, he took the bottle from her hand and sat it on the table beside his chair, then he pulled her into his lap. He then fed her a bite of lobster and handed her his champagne glass. She ate the lobster bite, sipped the champagne, then fed him a shrimp and held the glass for him to take a sip.

Then he patted her bare bottom again and said, "Vámonos, Meja." He kissed her hand as she stood up and then said, "You and the other girls help yourselves my love." Then he kissed her hand again.

As he watched her walk away he said, "They take such good care of me; I'm completely spoiled."

Then he looked at Zeke and Luís and said, "Please, eat as much as you like. It is delicious, no?

My chef is outstanding. And the seafood was delivered fresh from Bahia de Kino just this morning."

"Yes, indeed, Mr. Velazquez, this is very delicious. My compliments to you and your chef," Zeke said.

"Yumm!" Luís mumbled and nodded as he ate.

All was quiet since the girls had parked their jet skis to eat. A light breeze swept across the deck. Above, on the flying bridge, the flags fluttering in the breeze mixed with the sound of the waves rolling onto shore.

Velazquez stretched and leaned back in his chair. "*The Flying Lady* is beautiful, is she not?"

"Oh yes, she is very impressive," Zeke replied.

"I flew all the way to Greece with my crew to sail her back to Mexico. She is my pride and joy, all 110 meters (almost 361 feet) of her."

"Very understandable. Do you live on *The Flying Lady* year round?"

"Yes, I do. I had intended to live at my home in Monterey part time, and aboard *The Flying Lady* the rest, but I can't bring myself to leave her. I go to the office on business when I must, and then return here to my grand lady and my beautiful lovelies as soon as I can."

"I can see why," Zeke said.

"Gentlemen, I had a very compelling discussion with your CEO, Rex Tillman, recently. I regret that his time is so limited, I would have liked to talk more with him, but I tend to agree that a face-to-face meeting with his top representatives is a wise choice. So, gentlemen, what can Bright Star Technical offer Desoto Construcción that we cannot find right here in Mexico (his pronunciation: Meh-he-ko)?"

"We have no doubt that engineering firms here in Mexico are up to the task, but BST can offer world-class engineering from a hand-picked team that has no equal. Not only are our engineers, designers and drafting specialists from the top three percent of their class, 90% of our team were the top of their graduating class.

"They must also be in the top one percent of engineering exam scores for professional organizations like I-triple-E. We are, by design, leaders in our field. If you can imagine it, we can design and engineer it. If you only have a basic concept, our imaginative and innovative team will expand on that basic concept. And we excel at that as well.

"We also provide on-site, hands-on engineering expertise to enable you to get the job done on-time and under-budget in many cases."

"Impressive," Velazquez said.

"Now that we have explained the advantages of BST, we need a more specific idea of the scope of your impending project. We've only heard rumor, certainly substantial enough for me and my colleague to travel here to meet with you; however, do you have drawings or plans that we might look over today?"

"Come with me gentlemen."

Velazquez walked down the corridor in the direction that the girls had gone earlier, stopped at the door to an elevator, opened the door and said, "After you, gentlemen."

Velazquez pressed 'c,' the doors closed, and the elevator descended to the cargo hold. Then he led them to a small room, opened the door and turned on the lights. Before them was a detailed scale model of the complex that Desoto Construcción intended to build. It was a massive airport complex, located north of Puerto Peñasco in the exact location that Luís had speculated it would be built.

"Gentlemen, this is the Sonoran Logistics Hub and Space Port. Impressive, is it not?"

"Most impressive," Zeke said.

"This design was conceived by General Quan Ji Zhang of G2 International, Desoto Construcción's senior partner in this enterprise."

Zeke and Luís exchanged glances.

Velazquez picked up a laser pointer and said, "Here, centrally located between Asia and Europe, North America and South America, we will bring in shipments from all over the world, and redirect them to their intended destinations, not only utilizing the largest cargo aircraft in the world, but also supersonic cargo aircraft for far distant locations. These high-speed cargo aircraft are now being designed, tested and flown at an advanced aircraft design firm in China as we speak.

"This logistics port will be bigger and more efficient than any other in the world. Within the first year we will dominate the logistics industries worldwide. There will be 80 solar powered climate-controlled hangars—each roof will be covered with high-efficiency solar panels. Some hangars will be dedicated to logistics and some to maintenance. Each hangar, 280 meters by 90 meters, will be large enough to accommodate three Airbus A380 aircraft. That will be a total hangar space of over two square kilometers."

"This is a most ambitious endeavor," Zeke said.

"There will be four 6500 meter runways, with taxiways running underneath the runways to avoid congestion. Elevators will raise and lower the aircraft from taxiway level to runway level, similar to an aircraft carrier. Our facility will also have missile launch facilities 32 kilometers from the main site, to accommodate launch and recovery of space vehicles similar to the retired space shuttle. As technology advances, and low earth orbit hypersonic aircraft emerge, our runways and facilities will be able to accommodate them. And finally, an employee housing village will be constructed near Puerto Peñasco."

"Mr. Velazquez, I must say that this is the largest, most ambitious facility and construction project that I have ever seen," Zeke said.

"I was hoping that you would be impressed. And quite frankly, this is well beyond the engineering capabilities of Desoto Construcción."

Then Zeke said, "I've no intentions of being indelicate, but this is the first we've heard of General Zhang and G² International. Since he is your principal investor…"

"Ah, I see. Perfectly understandable under the circumstances," he replied and then opened a file drawer, pulled out a document and handed it to Zeke. "This is a certificate of deposit from Banamex for 55.8 billion pesos. Three billion American. The living Chinese God of War himself, General Zhang flew it in personally and made a cash deposit. Created quite a stir at the bank that day. He liked my *Flying Lady*, too. And my girls. He stayed for three days. I think he had each one of them at least twice."

"Apparently the general is very serious," Zeke said as he showed the document to Luís, and then said, "Well, Mr. Velazquez—"

"Please, call me Emilio."

"Very well Emilio, I'm Ralph and this is Alex. We have only two more questions; do you have a formal proposal that I can submit to our team?"

"I can fax a copy today."

"Excellent, the team can begin reviewing it right away. And how soon do you require our bid?"

"There's no hard date. How does three weeks sound?"

"That should be more than enough time."

"Good. Good. How about a delicious lunch and then a swim and dessert. My girls love an afternoon delight."

Zeke looked sheepishly at Luís and then replied, "As generous as your offer is Emilio, I'm married and Alex is in a relationship…"

"Forgive me gentlemen, it was not my intention to put you on the spot. Although the girls will be disappointed. That just leaves more for me, so no offense taken. But surely you can join me for lunch?"

"Yes, Emilio," Luís said, and looked at Zeke, "that sounds great."

"Certainly," Zeke said.

"Well then, Ralph, Alex, please join me in the grand dining room. Right this way."

Velazquez escorted them to the elevator and up to the elegant, glass enclosed, zebrawood trimmed dining room, where, sitting on a large oval glass table, they found chilled champagne, along with baked grouper, broiled sea trout, steamed lobster, shrimp scampi, and sushi, all fresh caught, freshly prepared and waiting for them to be served on silver dinnerware.

The girls began serving right away so Velazquez held up his champagne glass and said, "Ralph, Alex, salute. And enjoy!"

Zeke and Luís held up their glasses and Zeke said, "May all your of journeys be on friendly and following seas."

After they had been eating for a short time, one of the girls walked in the room and Luís froze in mid-bite. Zeke looked at Luís and then looked at the girl and also froze. She approached Velazquez, leaned over and whispered in his ear. She was tall and quite lovely, with long, straight golden hair, light blue eyes and a creamy complexion, no tan lines. It was apparent that she worked out daily, because she had the figure of a super model but with much more muscular definition. It was also apparent that, unlike supermodels, she understood the importance of proper daily nutrition. And she was wearing a white thong bikini, but no top.

Velazquez smiled, bit his lip, then looked at Zeke and Luís and said, "My friends, I would like to introduce Daniella. She joined me during one of my visits to Denmark. She is somewhat forward and knows what she wants most of the time. Right now she wants you. Both. At the same time. And she is very disappointed that you two 'pretty boys' as she calls you are not staying to enjoy her attentions. Toward that end, she has asked if she can bid you a proper farewell."

"We wouldn't want to offend Daniella for anything in the world," Zeke said.

"Very well," Velazquez replied, then patted Daniella's behind and said, "Go on, Love; tell them goodbye."

Daniella walked up to Zeke first, and stood behind his right shoulder, and leaned over, pressing her breasts against him. She put two fingers underneath his chin, and lifted his face up so that she could look into his eyes, and then gave him a lingering deep wet kiss. While she was kissing him, she slid her hand into his slacks and thoroughly checked out his package, then took his hand and slid it underneath her thong and pressed his fingers deep inside her, with no hurry to stop. Then she finally pulled away, kissed the tips of his wet fingers and whispered through pouty lips, "Goodbye pretty boy."

Then she turned to Luís and gave him the exact same parting gift, including the pouty "goodbye".

Then she went back to Velazquez and whispered in his ear again. He reached up and wiped a tear from her cheek and said, "It's alright, Love. I'll make it all better." Then he rubbed her bottom and said, "Vámonos now, I'll see you in just a little bit."

All three men watched her walk away. Just as Daniella got to the door, she turned and blew Zeke and Luís a kiss. They both waved and she disappeared through the door.

Zeke cleared his throat and said, "I see what you mean about dessert. I'm certain we'll never forget Daniella's farewell gift."

"As I said, she is a bit forward. And she usually gets what she wants, for obvious reasons. But don't worry, I'll make it up to her."

They finished eating and Velazquez escorted them back to the helipad.

"Ralph, Alex." Velazquez shook their hand in turn, "Gentlemen, meeting you has been a pleasure."

"The pleasure was all ours, Emilio. *The Flying Lady* is beautiful and so are your girls,"

Velazquez said, "Safe travels gentlemen." And walked away.

The helicopter began to spool up. The young attendants escorted Zeke and Luís onboard, buckled them in and poured two glasses of chilled champagne. Just before the aircraft lifted off, each girl brought the filled glass. One sat on Zeke's lap and the other sat on Luís' lap.

Luís looked at Zeke and said, "I get the feeling that Velazquez is insisting that we have dessert."

"This dessert looks a bit fresh to me," Zeke said as he looked at the young girl sitting on his lap and moved the long, black strands of her hair with his finger and straightened them. She ran both of her thumbs under her long hair, bundled it into a ponytail and shook it to get it to lay straight down her back.

Zeke then said, "Young lady, you have very lovely hair."

She looked at him but didn't answer.

"Amigo, I don't think this one can speak English."

Luís asked his girl, "Habla inglés?"

"No." She replied.

Luís then spoke to her in Spanish, flirted a bit and made her feel at ease. Then he spoke to the girl on Zeke's lap in the same manner and got them both to giggling and talking. Then he hinted at their ages, suggesting that he liked young girls and that the girls on the yacht were not young enough for him.

Finally the girl on Zeke's lap, whose name was Camila, admitted that she was fifteen. Luís' girl, whose name was Valerie, said she was sixteen.

About that time the helicopter was coming in for a landing at Hermosillo airport. Luís asked the girls if they would like to go with them to their hotel. The girls agreed. Zeke told the pilot that the girls would be going with them and they exited the aircraft.

Luís drove while Zeke watched to see if they were being tailed. Luís asked the girls if they were hungry and they both said they were very hungry. Then Luís asked them how they liked the seafood that had been served on the yacht earlier. They told him that they weren't allowed to eat with the other girls and that they had shared a sandwich.

Zeke said to Luís, "This isn't sounding very kosher, Amigo. These little girls are sex slaves. Let's get them a really good dinner." Then he looked at their clothes, reached over and tugged on the hem of Camila's skirt to inch it down some and said, "But first, we stop at a clothing store."

Luís asked the girls if they would like to go shopping. They were excited at the idea and naturally chose the trendiest shop in a nearby mall. When they arrived, Zeke asked Luís to tell each girl to buy three pairs of undies, three bras, three pairs of jeans, two nice tops and a sweater. The girls were happy to oblige.

After the shopping spree and the $600+ credit card charge, they went to dinner.

As they got out of the car to go into the restaurant, Zeke asked Luís to tell the girls that they looked very nice.

Camila stepped in front of Zeke on her tiptoes, smiled sweetly and said, "Gracias." And kissed him on the cheek.

"De nada." Zeke replied and smiled.

***

On *The Flying Lady,* the helicopter pilot reported to Velazquez that Mr. Williams and Mr. Alvarez had taken the two girls with them.

"They turned down my Daniella for those two little putas!"

Then he picked up his phone and dialed; "Valerie and Camila are with the two from Dallas. I want them back. Now!"

Then he dialed another number, "I want to know exactly who Ralph Williams and Alex Alvarez is. Everything. Their life story. Find out, now."

Then he walked over to the starboard side of the yacht, pushed the guard away from the M134 Minigun and fired it into the side of the mountain, shredding the rock with the glowing string of tracer rounds exiting the barrel at 6000 rounds per minute until the ammo can was empty.

***

In the restaurant the girls ate like they had not eaten in a week. During the dinner conversation, Zeke asked Luís to bring up Velazquez, but they were very reluctant to say anything about him at all. Then Luís asked about their parents and family. At that point they began to become suspicious.

Zeke said, "Remember that they're probably not wanted by their families any longer because of the life they've been living."

So, Luís asked them directly, "Do you want to go to America?"

"Yes, but we belong to Emilio," Camila blurted out, then quickly put her hand over her mouth. Valerie scolded and glared at her, although she knew that it was too late to take back what Camila had said.

Zeke said, "Tell them that we know and we're going to fix it."

Valerie said to Luís, "No! Emilio will kill us!"

Zeke looked at her and said, "No," and shook his head. "No, he won't."

Then he asked, "Can you drive a car?"

Luís translated.

"Si." She replied.

Zeke smiled and said, "That's it. Keep them here. I'm going to put the hardware in the hotel room. I'll be right back."

A short time later he returned and said, "They're watching the place. I had to stash the hardware in a park. We'll have to take separate taxis back to the hotel and enter separately. That way they'll probably never notice since they're expecting us to return in the rental car."

"Amigo, call your friend at Nogales, and tell him the situation and to be expecting Valeria and Camila in about three hours in our rental car."

Then Zeke wrote his name, badge number and phone number on two pieces of paper and gave them to Camila and Valerie.

As soon as Luis was done on the phone, Zeke said, "Amigo, write your name, badge number, and phone number on those two pieces of paper and tell them to put them in their pocket and show them to the border guards when they get to the border. If they're caught before they reach the border, eat the notes. Explain to them not to stop for anything until they get to the US Customs check point. And tell them that we'll see them in the morning at the border."

Then they drove the girls to a service station, fueled the car, and explained that they simply had to stay on Federal Highway 15 North until they reached the border, and then sent them on their way.

As they sat on a bench waiting for their taxi rides back to the hotel, Luís said, "I wonder what Ray's gonna think when he sees that credit card charge at a women's boutique?"

"I'll just tell him we needed some clothes for a really wild party."

Zeke and Luís arrived separately by taxi after picking up the weapons and ammo that Zeke had stashed in the park, and went directly into the hotel, so the Serpiente watchers were none the wiser.

Later they were sitting on the balcony in Zeke's room, drinking beer and discussing the day's happenings.

"It's strange that we weren't frisked," Zeke commented. "He's awfully confident. He had to know that we were armed and just didn't care."

"Velazquez wasn't at all what I expected," Luís said. "He seemed to be a fairly decent guy, just too rich, oversexed and spoiled. I may never be able to eat normal, frozen seafood again. And Daniella. Wow. That is one beautiful, wild woman. You know we could sell that video we made with the spy camera glasses."

"Ray might have something to say about that."

"I'm not talking about Velazquez and his little mockup, I mean the girls. I've never seen that many gorgeous, almost-naked girls in one place before."

"You gonna tell Bekah?"

"You gonna tell Abby?"

"Of course. We have no secrets. But she doesn't need to see that video. If a picture is worth a thousand words, then that video is worth a million. Abril would chew my ass for a month!"

"You got that right."

"Well?"

"Well, what?"

"Are you going to tell Bekah?"

Luís sighed. "Yes."

"Good. Just don't mention the video."

They sat in silence for a while, then Zeke said, "You know, there's more to the head of the snake than meets the eye. Why, with that bevy of willing paid courtesans pleasing his every whim does he need sex slaves like those two beautiful little girls that we just sent to freedom. I just don't get it. I think behind the façade of that lovey-dovey, accommodating playboy lies a monster. You know he didn't rise to the top of the Serpiente Cartel by being a nice guy."

"So you think he's a loose cannon?"

"Anyone who thinks that General Zhang is the living Chinese God of War, and controls the kind of power that the Serpiente Cartel wields, is a time bomb with a screwy clock. And you know something else?"

"What's that?"

"We're fighting the wrong war."

"What do you mean?"

"I've spent a big chunk of my life preparing to be a soldier in the Drug War. We were just aboard the yacht of one of the most power drug lords in Mexico and, aside from the picture of the pot plant on his tee shirt, I never thought about illegal drugs once. We saw the plans for a base from which an attack on America could be launched that couldn't be stopped. Aircraft, missiles, tanks, and God knows what else. The weapons of a fierce enemy thirty five miles from our southern border. Potentially thousands of Red Chinese soldiers only minutes from American soil. The Drug War is a joke compared to that."

***

Valerie and Camila's trip went smoothly until they were spotted about a mile from the border checkpoint.

"There they go!" The passenger of a black Chevy Tahoe said.

The driver gunned the SUV, cut off traffic and fell in behind Valerie and Camila. Valerie saw the SUV in the rearview mirror and floored the accelerator.

Camila said, "What are you doing? Are you crazy?!"

"They're behind us," Valerie said.

Camila turned around, saw the SUV getting closer and said, "Hurry!"

"I am hurrying, Meja."

As Valerie quickly approached the border, one of the U.S. Customs Agents pointed to a car that was coming too fast and said, "Hey, that's the car we've been waiting on. Wave them through! Wave them through!"

Another guard stepped out and started waving his arms, trying to attract Valerie's attention. Behind her, the black Tahoe was almost on her bumper. She slammed on the brakes and the driver swerved trying to avoid hitting her car. Then she floored the accelerator once again. The border guard was signaling the cars in line to move over and waving at Valerie, signaling her to move into his lane.

The Tahoe accelerated again and was just a few feet from her rear bumper. It was obvious that he was going to try to tip her bumper and cause her to lose control and roll over. She saw the Tahoe getting closer and swerved to the right, went around two cars in an adjacent lane and then veered left and shot through a gap in that line and back into the cleared lane she was aiming for. The Tahoe driver tried to head her off, over-steered and hit the back corner of a car in line, the Tahoe pitched up and rolled over on its side.

Just ahead of him, Valerie flew through the open border gate into the U.S. and slammed on the brakes. The Tahoe, still sliding on its side, slid through the gate right behind her and, as it slid to a stop, was met by six armed guards.

***

On the balcony, Luís' phone rang. "Hello. … Hey, thanks man, that's great news. We'll see you in the morning." Then Luís looked at Zeke and said, "They made it."

Zeke made a fist, swung an uppercut punch and exclaimed, "Yyyesss!"

On the bridge deck of *The Flying Lady* with his girls, Emilio Velazquez received the news a bit differently; he screamed and then threw his smartphone into the gulf. Shocked at his outburst, his girls looked at him in fearful surprise.

He yelled, "Vámonos! Get out! Go!" And then proceeded to trash the bridge deck.

Early the following morning Zeke called Alfred Chase at the U.S. Consulate.

"I'm sorry to bother you at this hour, Mr. Chase; in fact, I'm a bit embarrassed. … Well, we had intended to head to Nogales early this morning. We need to catch an air taxi to Dallas for a very important meeting. Unfortunately, it seems that our car was stolen last night, and we don't have time to arrange for another rental to get to Nogales in time for the flight. I know it's asking a lot, but if the consulate's helicopter is available, I wonder if I we might get a quick ride to Nogales? My company will be happy to reimburse you for the fuel and aircraft costs. … Excellent, Mr. Chase, excellent. We'll call a taxi and be with your shortly. … The meeting? Oh, yes. The meeting went quite well. We are very impressed with the project. And hopeful that we will get the bid. … We'll see you momentarily. … Thank you, Sir."

131

Zeke and Luís smiled at each other and bumped fists.

"Let's remove ourselves from this place!" Zeke said.

Thirty minutes later they were airborne, heading to Nogales.

Luís had arranged for transportation, so just as soon as the helicopter dropped them off, a Border Patrol vehicle picked them up and took them to the border station. The moment Zeke and Luís walked in, Valerie and Camila saw them and came running. Camila hugged Zeke and Valerie hugged Luís. Then they met with Luís' friend, who had been supervising the girls since they arrived.

"Both girls got a good night's sleep after they settled down. They were a bit wound up when they arrived. That was quite an arrival show. They had a good breakfast and have been talking with one of our counselors this morning."

"Where do they go from here?" Zeke asked.

"We've arranged for them to stay in a safe house in Tucson. They'll get a complete physical exam, intense counseling, an educational assessment, language tutoring, and begin attending in-house private school. Mostly they're going to be allowed to just be themselves, mix with other girls their age and begin the process of being deprogrammed. It will take a while until they realize that they are no longer someone's property and that their bodies are their own again. Then comes the hard part; rebuilding their pride and self-worth. That takes the longest because that's the first thing that the human traffickers break.

"Depending upon the dangers they face, at some point they may have to receive new identities and be relocated. That's very difficult to do for a child that doesn't have a family. Hopefully, these girls will be 18 by then, so at least they can start a new life as a young adult."

Zeke looked down at Camila and stroked her hair. "Tell them that I said they are going to be okay, and that my wife and I will be back to visit with them very soon."

Luís told them, and both girls hugged Zeke.

Luís and Zeke said farewell to Valerie and Camila and then arranged to get a lift to Ajo Station onboard a Border Patrol helicopter.

Just before 11a.m. on October 10th, Zeke unlocked the door and walked into the living room. Abby heard the door and came from the kitchen to see who it was.

A big, beautiful smile lit up her face as she said, "Hello, Husband," and ran to him with open arms.

"Hello, Beautiful." Zeke replied and held her close in a long and loving embrace.

Upon receiving word from Zeke on the morning of October 10th that he and Luís were back in the U.S., Ray caught a flight to Phoenix that day. By midmorning on the 11th, Ray was sitting at the breakfast table with Zeke, Abby and Luís having coffee.

"Guys, I can't begin to tell you how pleased I am with your mission," Ray said, "and I know that Abby is pleased to get you both back safely."

"Every time I think about it, I thank God again," Abby said.

"How about I buy everyone breakfast?" Ray offered, "And then we'll debrief and I'll take the data back with me."

"I like the breakfast part the most," Luís said, then smiled and added, "and I know just the place."

"I'll bet you do," Zeke said, "And they probably already know what you're going to have before you even get there."

Later that afternoon, Ray concluded the meeting.

"Guys, tomorrow it's back to the usual boring routine. Continue business as usual, just like nothing has happened. As soon as I put all of this together in a comprehensive report, we're going to have to go out on a limb and try to convince the right people that this is all real. Since it sounds like something from a spy movie, it's going to be an uphill battle. At some point very soon I'll need you both to come to DC.

Until then, as much as it sucks, pretend to be busy. I'll be in touch."

***

Two weeks later, onboard *The Flying Lady*, Emilio Velazquez was on the phone and growing impatient.

"What do you mean you don't have anything? … How long can it take to run simple facial recognition on two men? … I'm not interested in your excuses. I don't give a damn about your problems. Get it done. Now!"

Velazquez paced the deck, shot skeet, paced the deck, played cards with the captain of the yacht, and paced the deck some more. Finally his phone rang.

Velazquez recognized the number, answered and said, "You'd better have something for me or I'm using you for target practice. … Facebook? And I care about Facebook, why? … A proposal video? … What in the hell are you talking about? … You're shitting me.

… I am in no mood to be screwed with. … They're what?! … If you're screwing with me I swear you're a dead man. … Seriously. You're serious. I allowed feds on my lady? I showed feds the general's plans. I faxed them the plans! … You and the ambassador need to pull your heads out of your asses. … They were in your office! … And you didn't think it would be prudent to check them out? … Have you swept for bugs? … Naturally. They're probably listening to our conversation at this moment. … You damn right you'll do it. This very minute. And I want them dead. Do you understand me? Dead!"

Then he screamed into the phone, "NOW! NOW! NOW!" and threw his phone up against a bulkhead and shattered it. He walked away mumbling to himself, "The general will have my head on a pike."

***

On Monday morning October 29th, Luís sat with his feet propped up, reading the paper and drinking coffee. Zeke sat at his desk, looking bored, his chin propped on his left hand, a computer mouse in his right, looking at his computer screen.

Luís looked up from his paper and said, "So, what do you want to do today, Doc?"

Zeke just sighed. Then looked at Luís and said, "I don't know."

Suddenly he perked up and said, "This doesn't look right. I think there's something screwy with my email."

"When is there not something screwy going on with a computer?"

Zeke tapped on several keys and said, "What is going on with this thing?"

"What's the problem, Doc?"

"There's something odd about my email program. It's acting weird."

"Get Bekah's mother to look at it. She'll find something wrong."

"I gather she's a computer whizz?"

"No, she can just find something wrong with anything."

"I'll be right back," Zeke said and left the room. Shortly he came back with the IT guy.

"Let's take a look," The IT guy said.

Zeke sat on the corner of his desk drinking coffee and watching him work.

About ten minutes later he looked at Zeke and said, "You've been hacked."

"Hacked?!" Zeke and Luís said simultaneously.

"Hacked. And it will take some time to dig in here and find the problem, plus I also need to debug our server before you hook up to the network again, otherwise it may cause bigger problems."

"Will you be able to do a back-trace and find who hacked me?"

"Maybe. I'll have more to tell you by this afternoon."

Zeke looked at Luís and said, "What do I want to do today? Shoot a hacker."

"Why don't we go cruise the Drag Road instead?"

"You drive. I'll gripe."

As they walked out of the office Luís said, "Let's take your equipment case. Maybe we'll spot some quail or something."

"Sure."

Just as Luís pulled onto Highway 85, Zeke said, "Pull into the casino, I think I'll get a soda. What'll you have?"

"Pepsi."

"You got it."

While Zeke was getting the sodas, a black Tahoe with blacked windows drove slowly behind Luís' Border Patrol truck. Luís saw the vehicle in the rearview mirror and watched as the Tahoe pulled into a parking space on the opposite side of the parking lot.

Zeke returned, hesitated briefly before opening the door, then climbed in and handed Luís his soda.

"Did you notice that black Tahoe over there?"

"Yeah. We saw one just like it in Mexico. It was following us."

"I think this one is, too," Luís said.

"Well, let's find out. Head to the border and don't let any grass grow under you."

"You got it, Doc."

Luís pulled out on Highway 85 and floored it. At 90 mph he let up and held that speed.

In the rearview mirror he could see the Tahoe. But it was far behind them.

"Maybe not. They're not keeping up anyway," Luís said.

"We're probably being paranoid. Let's see if we can find some quail."

***

At the Washington DC offices of U.S. Senate Armed Services Committee ranking member, Senator Roland Martel, the secretary said, "Agent Alexander, the senator will see you now."

Ray smiled, "Thank you."

"Right this way," She said and walked down a short hallway, opened the door and then said, "Senator, Agent Alexander."

Ray walked in and the secretary closed the large oak door behind her. He found himself standing in a large stately room furnished with antique furniture. He was facing a massive oak bookcase filled with law books and classic novels. There was a cozy fire in the large fireplace, and even the hardwood window frames and trim were relics from a by-gone era, creating an atmosphere that made him feel as though he had just stepped through a time portal into the era of Benjamin Franklin.

"Welcome!" the senator said. He was short and rotund, in his sixties, with white hair and dark-rimmed glasses, wearing a dark blue pinstriped suit with a vest, and suspenders. His coat hung on a hall tree near his desk.

He crossed the room to meet Ray and offered his hand. "What can I do for the DEA today? Please, have a seat."

Ray sat on a plush leather sofa and the senator returned to his massive oak desk with matching leather upholstered high-back chair.

"Well senator, first I would like to thank you for giving me this opportunity to speak with you. And second, I'm not here on the behalf of the DEA specifically."

"Oh? Your request for a meeting was quite compelling. I just assumed it was an official request."

"It was official, certainly. But this is presently a behind-the-scenes issue. My team and I have collected a considerable amount of data. I've just finished this report and I felt compelled to bring it directly to you because it concerns the security of the United States."

"That's quite a bold statement coming from a DEA supervisor. I would expect, at the very least, this report would have been vetted up the chain of command and presented by, perhaps, the deputy administrator."

"Quite frankly sir, this report is too critical and time sensitive to wait. I would be happy to brief you on the highlights of the report, or, if you prefer, read it yourself. The important thing is that you see this information ASAP. It is crucial that you be made aware of it immediately."

The senator got up and took the report from Ray. "I sense the sincere urgency of your request, Agent Alexander. I'll review this report right away and deal with it appropriately."

"Thank you senator, that's all I could ask."

"My pleasure. Good day, Agent Alexander."

***

Luís drove west along the Drag Road from the Lukeville border crossing for about 2.5 miles. There the Drag Road climbed about 450 feet above the desert floor over the crest of a three-mile rib of mountains that extended from Sonoyta, Mexico into the Organ Pipe Cactus National Monument. He stopped just below the crest and pulled off of the Drag Road.

"How's this, Doc? We should be able to spot a lot of wildlife from up here. Whaddaya think?"

"This works. Good view. Let's set up the spotter scope."

Zeke pulled his equipment case out of the back of the camper shell-covered pickup just far enough to reach in and get his spotter scope. Then he shoved the case back in the truck and closed the tailgate and the camper lift door. Then they walked toward the west for about 200 feet up to the crest of the ridge.

The driver of the black Tahoe had hung back, but the passenger had kept track of Luís' vehicle with binoculars. The passenger looked at a map and said, "Turn here."

The driver turned west onto a pig-trail road about a mile north of the border. The trail meandered west for about a mile, and then turned south for about a quarter of a mile and ended at the Drag Road.

Zeke and Luís were setting up just one-half mile west of that intersection.

The driver stopped so that the passenger could get their weapons ready, then he slowly eased along the Drag Road toward Zeke and Luís and stopped about 200 feet from them.

Luís heard something and turned to look. "Our friends are back. I wonder what they want."

Zeke looked just as both doors opened, they stepped out, and using their doors as cover, opened fire on full automatic; the passenger with an AK47, the driver with a M4 Carbine Commando, with a grenade launcher.

As Zeke and Luís dove for the ground, Luís yelled, "I think I know what they want!"

Zeke pulled his pistol and fired several rounds at the assassins.

Luís reached for his pistol and winced. "I think I'm hit in the shoulder."

As Zeke fired several more rounds, he saw blood running down the sleeve of Luís' right arm from his shoulder toward his elbow.

Luís tried to move his arm again but couldn't. "I don't think the bullet hit bone, but it hit nerves 'cause this hurts like hell."

Zeke fired again, then pulled out his knife and cut the sleeve so that he could determine the severity of the bleeding. Then he took his red bandana out of his back pocket, placed it over the wound, then took Luís' left hand and placed it over the bandana.

"Keep pressure on it. I'm going for my rifle."

He started to go and Luís grabbed his arm. "You be careful. You're gonna be a dad soon."

Zeke smiled. "Yes, I know." Then he put Luís' hand back over the profusely bleeding gunshot wound and repeated, "Keep pressure on it." And then began crawling down the face of the ridge.

He fired several more rounds, then loaded another clip and crawled around rocks and stones through creosote bushes and cacti toward the truck. He fired several more rounds as the machine gun rounds peppered the ground around him, shattering rocks, the shards tearing into his skin.

The driver launched a grenade at Zeke, but overshot. The resultant explosion blew rocks, dirt and dust in all directions, showering Zeke with the debris. He winced as a large rock landed with a thud in the center of his back.

About a mile east of Zeke's position, Agent Jackie Williamson was heading west, patrolling the Drag Road when she heard the explosion. She drew her weapon and sped up, heading toward the trouble.

The black Tahoe came into view, but before she could assess the situation, the driver turned and fired at her. The bullets ripped up the grill and hood of her GMC Yukon and shattered the windshield. She dived into the passenger floorboard, opened the passenger door, and began returning fire through the gap between the door and the fender.

That gave Zeke the opportunity he was looking for. He ran to the truck, grabbed a rock, opened the passenger door, and smashed the rear window out of the pickup. Then he reached in, pulled his equipment case to him, opened it and grabbed his LAR-15 Carbine and two clips of armor piercing rounds. He put one clip in the side pocket of his jumpsuit, shoved the other one in the rifle and pulled back the bolt.

Then he crawled along the front of the truck, leaned against the bumper and took aim at the driver, who was still taking cover behind his door and spraying the Yukon with bullets to keep Agent Williamson pinned down. Zeke fired three rounds, piercing the door and killing the driver.

The passenger had crawled underneath the Tahoe to take himself out of Agent Williamson's line of fire, but that position made it impossible for him to shoot anything but the front of the Yukon, so he was waiting for a shooting opportunity. Then he saw the driver fall to the ground and crawled toward him underneath the Tahoe, attempting to get to the driver's side and escape. He continued firing randomly, spraying bullets toward Agent Williamson and then toward Zeke.

Zeke saw movement underneath the Tahoe and lay down on the ground in front of the tire to get a better shooting position. The passenger reached out and grabbed the bottom of the doorjamb to pull himself along, providing a clear view of his torso. Zeke fired one shot and the man went limp.

Agent Williamson carefully climbed out of the Yukon and cautiously approached the Tahoe. Zeke kept his weapon trained on the passenger. She carefully peaked around the driver's side, then slowly approached the two men on the ground, verified that they were dead and signaled all clear.

Zeke yelled, "Luís has a shoulder wound." He threw her the first aid kit from the truck as she ran by. Then he called Ajo Station Com Center and reported an officer down and two assailants dead

Agent Williamson ran to Luís' side and began to tend to his gunshot wound.

"Hi, Jackie. What's up?"

"Hi yourself, you lunatic. Geez, you guys get to have all the fun."

"I was having fun up the point where I got shot. After that, not so much."

Luís was transported by helicopter to an urgent care facility in the Phoenix area. Zeke was treated at the scene for minor cuts and abrasions.

Zeke arrived home before noon and received some very attentive petting and pampering from Abby. Then they picked up Javi after school and went to visit Luís at the hospital.

Luís was released from the hospital the following day and told to go home and take it easy.

Zeke took the opportunity to buy Abby a pistol while they were in the Phoenix area. He chose between several pistols small enough for Abby to hold and then let her decide which one was the most comfortable. She chose the Glock 26 Gen 4 9mm semi-automatic. It holds 10 rounds in the magazine and one in the chamber. The following day he and Abby went to the Ajo shooting range and he helped her get familiar with the new Glock. She had been raised shooting pistols with her brothers and sisters, so she was a good marksman, Zeke just used torso targets and water-filled milk jugs to get her confident with hitting an intruder, either center mass, or in the head, based on the situation.

Luís made it all the way through the weekend following the doctor's orders, but come Monday morning, November 5th, he was back at work.

"I still think you should stay home another week. Abril was so aggravated with you this morning at breakfast that I thought she was going to beat you up again."

"Look, Ray told us to pretend to be busy, right?"

"Yes."

"Well? I can pretend to be busy with one arm just as easily as I can with two. I can read an e-book on my laptop and turn the pages with my left index finger just as easily as I can with my right."

"Point taken. Just take it easy with that arm until it heals."

"Will do."

Just then Zeke's phone rang. "Good morning, Ben. How are things from the captain's chair?" Zeke chuckled. "It never ends, does it? … Well that's good news, who were they? … That's what we figured. … Thanks for letting us know. … Yep, see ya' later."

Having heard Zeke's end of the conversation, Luís was looking at him and waiting.

"It's just as we suspected, it was the Serpiente Cartel."

"I guess Emilio is really serious about his girls, even the sex slaves."

"I wonder. I'm sure he's possessive of his property, especially property as special as Valerie and Camila. But they're out of his reach. It would serve little purpose to kill us for setting them free."

"Maybe it was a show of revenge; 'mess with my girls and you die'."

"I think anyone who knows Velazquez, knows that. No, there was another reason for the hit. I'm thinking he, or they, assuming that the consulate is involved, found out we're feds, and that's how they found us. It has to be."

"I wonder what General Zhang will have to say about that."

"I'll bet he won't be happy."

***

Senator Roland Martel finished reviewing Ray's report and then called Senator Jake Spade, Chairman of the Senate Armed Services Committee.

"Jake, Roland. You're not going to believe the report that I have here on my desk. Come to my office. You need to see this right away, and we need to discuss it. Okay, see you in 30 minutes."

Senator Spade, a staunch member of the Congressional Old Guard, was a living example of the need for Congressional term limits. At 81, he was in his eleventh term as the Democratic US senator from Vermont. He walked in to Senator Martel's office and said, "Okay Roland, what is this report that I must see?"

After their meeting, Senator Spade returned to his office and made a call; "Did you take care of the problem? ... I see. ... We have another problem now; Alexander has just released a report with a lot of incriminating evidence. If a congressional investigation is launched I won't be able to keep it in check. ... No witnesses. ... You heard me. ... Sikes, Alexander, Gonzales, Breen, and everyone they've had contact with. ... Yes, everyone. ... And no bombs. I don't want chemicals and device fragments that can be traced. I want this clean. ... Exactly what part of everyone do you not understand? ... Good. ... No, the general will take care of Velazquez."

Then he hung up.

***

A week later, just after dawn, Emilio Velazquez awoke to find himself handcuffed to a flagpole on the flying bridge of *The Flying Lady* in his pajamas. He heard his helicopter and looked up just as it lifted off from the bow of the yacht. His girls were looking at him through the windows with shocked expressions.

He yelled, "What the hell is going on? Who did this to me?

Bring my helicopter back! Now!"

His entire crew had abandoned ship in the early morning hours and, beyond the stern of the yacht, he could see his security guards departing in his two speedboats that were stowed in the stern dry docks.

"You bastards will pay for turning your backs on me!" He screamed. "I will use you all for target practice!"

In the distance, two F-16 Fighting Falcons with Panamanian markings approached from the south, flying fast and low over the Gulf of California. Then they suddenly popped up to an altitude of 500 feet and one dropped back in trail of the other.

Velazquez saw the fighters approaching. "What the hell are you doing? General, no! Not my *Flying Lady*! Nooooo!"

The pilots were coordinating their attack via radio:

Red One, Red Two, target is acquired and locked.

Copy Red Two, arm now. Drop on my mark, 3, 2, 1, drop, drop, drop.

Instantaneously, two Mark-82 Snake Eye 500 pound drag bombs dropped away from each F-16.

Two bombs impacted the yacht near the stern. Simultaneously, two bombs impacted amidships.

The F-16s pulled up and broke hard left to avoid Tiburón Island as the beautiful, majestic yacht's hull opened upward and outward, erupting into a ball of fire from bow to stern.

Chapter Eight
Ordeal

On the afternoon of November 19th, Zeke was scheduled to testify before the Senate Armed Services Subcommittee on the investigation into corruption allegations and collusion by the U.S. Consulate in Hermosillo, Mexico with Chinese General Quan Ji Zhang.

Agent Ben Breen arranged for Zeke to catch a hop on a U.S. Customs & Border Patrol Cessna C-550 Citation jet on its way back from a reconnaissance mission in Panama. It was due for an equipment modification to be performed at a maintenance facility at Dulles International Airport. The crew consisted of the pilot and copilot. The sensor operator had remained in Panama.

Abby drove Zeke to the Eric Marcus Municipal Airport just north of Ajo. The Citation's engines were already running when they arrived.

Zeke reached over the back of the seat, gave Javi a fist bump and said, "Take care of your mom for me okay?"

"Okay, Dad," he replied.

Zeke paused and then looked at Abby and smiled. She gasped, covered her mouth with her hand and whispered, "Awww."

"Have you—?"

"No, I thought it might be too soon," Abby replied. "He's made that decision all on his own."

"Our son is growing up," Zeke said and kissed Abby. She returned his kiss very tenderly.

Then he said, "You and Javi take care and be safe. I'll be back in a few days. I love you, Beautiful."

Then he leaned over and kissed her pregnant belly.

She looked down, ran her fingers through his hair and said, "I love you, Husband."

Abby and Javi watched and waved goodbye as the jet taxied to the runway and took off immediately, then made a graceful turn to the east, climbing toward the rising sun.

Then she looked at Javi and said, "So, how about you and I get some breakfast and then I'll take you to school?"

"Okay, Mom. Can we go to Marcella's?"

"We sure can—you sound just like your Tio Luís."

Nearby, parked in a secluded spot, two suspicious looking men, both dressed in casual business attire, sat in a black Chevy Tahoe watching the airport.

As they watched the twin-engine executive jet disappear into the distance, the driver said, "Farewell, Special Agent Sikes," with flippant contempt, then pointed to the Raptor as Abby drove away from the airport. "There she goes. She's takin' the kid to school. We'll wait 'till she gets back home."

"I'll take her out just as she walks in the front door, then we can get the hell outta here, this town creeps me out," The passenger said.

"What's your rush?" The driver asked, "Let's have some fun before we off the bitch. She is fine! I want to tap that. You can have sloppy seconds."

"She's pregnant you perverted bastard."

"What difference does that make? You mean you'll kill her but you won't screw her?"

"We're gettin' paid to kill 'er," The passenger replied, "We don't get this done, we're dead men. These people don't play."

"You worry too much. This bitch is a piece of cake and I'm gonna have a slice."

***

Zeke looked out the window of the jet, watching the eastern Arizona mountainous desert terrain slowly pass by far below, but his thoughts were on Abby and Javi. He closed his eyes and said a prayer of thanks to God for being blessed with the gift of Abby, Javi and her family in his life, and asked that God keep her safe until his return.

Just then the pilot entered the cabin from the cockpit, shook Zeke's hand and said, "Welcome aboard, Agent Sikes. We're at our cruise altitude and on schedule for Dulles. We should have a smooth ride. Feel free to help yourself to snacks and drinks in the galley. There are magazines, or DVD's if you'd like to watch a movie. Just make yourself comfortable and enjoy the flight."

"Thank you, captain, I will."

Meanwhile, a classic Sukhoi SU-15 Russian fighter roared skyward from a private airstrip in western New Mexico, its two afterburning engines quickly pushing the sleek jet up and westward toward its deadly rendezvous.

Periodically seen at airshows around the U.S. and Canada, the fighter's hard-points had recently been illegally restored to operational status, and modified to accept AIM-9 Sidewinder heat-seeking missiles. Two were now slung underneath its wings. It was also armed with a 23mm twin-barrel machinegun pod originally used with this fighter during its operational status as an interceptor with the Soviet Air Defense Force during the 1960s.

As the pilot reached 25,000 feet at just over Mach 1, he crossed the state line into Arizona, leveled out, throttled back and carefully monitored a modern tracking receiver that had been installed in the aircraft. He also watched his weapons radar screen closely.

One hundred-fifty miles away at the FAA Air Route Traffic Control Center in Albuquerque, New Mexico, a radar controller signaled to his supervisor; "We have an unidentified aircraft running west at flight level 25 in my sector. He's ballistic, with no transponder, no IFF, and no response to radio calls. He has to be military. What the hell is he doing?"

"A military jock wouldn't be that stupid. It's probably some rich prick with an over-priced toy. Russia's sold a shitload of old trainers and fighters since the USSR went south. Looks like the radar track is intermittent. We'll try to track his landing destination and notify Flight Standards. They should pull the bastard's ticket, but he probably has his own private strip on a ranch out there somewhere."

Suddenly a readout appeared on the SU-15's tracking device. The pilot adjusted his heading and altitude and correlated the tracking data with the blip on his weapons radar screen. Minutes later, below and left he could see the Citation going in the opposite direction about five miles away. He rolled left, pulled back on the stick, and dove inverted toward his target. As he lined up in trail, below and left of the Citation, he applied throttle and eased up closer to verify the tail number.

"Gotcha!" he said.

Then he throttled back to get some separation, and flipped the switches to activate a Sidewinder. Almost immediately he received the growl in the headset as the missile locked on to the heat from the Citation's engines. He opened the safety on the pickle switch and fired.

The Sidewinder sprinted away from his aircraft and, seconds later, blew the Citation's starboard engine completely off the pylon. The jet immediately pitched nose down, trailing fire and smoke. The fighter pilot broke high and right, then rolled inverted and dove, following the Citation as it plummeted toward the rugged mountainous terrain below.

Zeke felt the thud and heard the explosion as the right engine separated from the fuselage. The fasten seatbelt sign came on, but he was already buckled. Smoke began to seep into the cabin as he tightened his belt and looked around to see if he could see any visible fire that he might be able to fight with the cabin fire extinguisher.

Then the captain came on the intercom and said, *"We've lost number two, literally, and we're going down. When I say, 'brace, brace, brace,' assume the position."*

Zeke watched through the window as the earth rushed up to meet the doomed Citation. Then the aircrew managed to control the descent and level the aircraft out slightly.

"You're looking good," The copilot said. "That high plateau straight ahead is your best bet. The chart shows 6000 feet elevation. Looks like mostly grassland with scattered shrubs."

"Let's hope they're friendly shrubs," The pilot replied.

Then the copilot called over the radio. *"Mayday! Mayday! Mayday! Omaha four one foxtrot. Mayday! Mayday! Mayday! We're going down 25 miles northwest of St. Johns, Arizona. I repeat, Mayday! Mayday! Mayday! Omaha four one foxtrot is going down 25 miles northwest of St. Johns."*

Then the pilot called over the intercom, *"Brace! Brace! Brace!"*

Zeke leaned forward, put his head between his knees, wrapped his arms over his head and stretched his legs forward. Seconds later the Citation hit the ground.

***

Abby returned home from dropping Javi off at school, put some up-tempo tunes on the stereo, turned up the volume and started vacuuming.

She smiled when she thought of Zeke, fussing at her for doing what he considered strenuous housework. He would immediately switch off the vacuum cleaner and say, "What do you think you're doing, young lady?! You shouldn't be doing things like this; I can do it."

And she would always reply, "I'm not recovering from spinal surgery, I'm just pregnant!"

But, he would ignore her comment, take her by the hand and sit her down on the sofa, and then continue doing the vacuuming himself.

Abby noticed the sun illuminating the blinds on the east side of the house, and decided to let some of the morning light in. So, she turned off the vacuum, walked over to one of the windows and started to open the blind. Suddenly a shadow moved passed the window. She carefully peaked through the blind and saw a man dressed in grey slacks and a dark sports jacket heading toward the back of the house. She quickly ran to the bedroom and retrieved her Glock 26 from the gun safe.

Abby intended to get her weapon and hide in the closet, but just as she turned toward the closet, the driver, who had already gained access to the house, came up from behind her and knocked the gun out of her hand and onto the floor.

She punched him in the mouth and tried to kick him, but he shoved her onto the bed.

Then she started to scramble off of the other side of the bed, but he pointed the gun at her and said, "Move and you're dead."

Then he walked up to the bed, looking at the blood on his fingers that he had just wiped from his mouth. "Damn! You're a little spitfire, and one fine filly."

Then he climbed onto the bed on his knees, and positioned himself at her feet. He held the gun on her with his right hand, began undoing his pants with his left and said, "Baby, you and me are gonna have some fun."

Abby bent her knees, raised her legs against her stomach and then reached her arms out to her sides and grabbed hold of the bed covers with both hands.

He laughed and said, "Honey, you ain't gonna keep me from getting' to that sweet thing like that."

Just then Abby yelled, "I!" as she kicked him in the groin as hard as she could with both feet.

He grunted loudly and tried to reach for her as she yelled, "am!" and kicked him in the groin again.

He moaned louder and dropped his gun onto the floor as he grabbed his groin with both hands and fell face-forward on the bed.

She raised her legs for a third time and yelled, "pregnant!" as she kicked him in the head. He sailed backwards off the bed, stumbled and hit the wall, then slid down the wall into a squatting position.

She quickly got off the bed and yelled, "Pervert!" as she stomped his groin as hard as she could and then kicked him in the face, knocking him over onto his side.

Abby picked up his pistol and shoved it underneath the mattress, then she retrieved her pistol from the floor and quickly hid in the closet.

A moment later the passenger cautiously entered the bedroom with his gun ready and saw his partner on the floor. His partner weakly pointed toward the closet. He eased over to the closet, snatched open the door and fired once. Simultaneously, Abby fired three shots. His shot barely missed her, but blood, skull and brain matter sprayed outward behind him as two rounds from Abby's Glock hit their mark.

As he fell backwards onto the floor, Abby saw the first man reaching toward the bed where she had stashed his pistol. She aimed and fired three more rounds in rapid succession. The man slumped onto the floor.

Abby pointed her pistol at the men as she cautiously checked their carotid artery to make certain there was no pulse. Then she went into the living room, pulled her smart phone out of the back pocket of her slacks, and steadied herself on the arm of the sofa as she dialed 911 and said, "Help. I need help, I've shot two men…" and collapsed unconscious on the floor in front of the sofa.

***

All hell broke loose as the Citation plowed into the ground, and then bounced, roared and shook to its core. Debris flew about the cabin as it filled with smoke. Suddenly Zeke was thrown sideways as the left wing hit a large clump of trees and part of the wing ripped away from the fuselage. The aircraft slid sideways, plowing up more trees and dirt and fire erupted on the left side of the aircraft at the wing root just as the tail section was torn away. Dust, dirt and debris poured into the cabin through the gaping hole where the tail section had been.

After what seemed like an eternity, the Citation finally lurched to a stop. Zeke unbuckled and rushed to the cockpit to check on the flight crew. The fire on the left side of the aircraft continued to grow more intense and Zeke could feel the heat as he reached the cockpit door.

The pilot and copilot, covered with glass, dirt and debris were just climbing out of their seats as Zeke opened the door.

"You two okay?"

"Yeah, I think so," The Pilot replied, somewhat dazed, and then said, "The fire is blocking the exit door. We need to climb out through the cockpit windows."

"The tail section is gone," Zeke said, "We can exit through the rear. Come on, this way! Hurry!"

Zeke started crawling through the mangled rear fuselage and turned around to help the copilot, who was right behind him, just as the SU-15 roared overhead. He pulled the copilot out and then helped the pilot out. The pilot looked in the direction that the SU-15 had gone but the dense, acrid, black smoke obscured his view. He coughed and asked, "What the hell was that?!"

Zeke was also coughing as he said, "It looked like an old Soviet fighter, but I only got a glimpse. What it's doing out here I have no idea but at least we've been spotted."

"He's coming back around," The copilot said. "Let's get out of this smoke and away from this thing before it blows—."

Just then the SU-15 rolled wings level and opened up with machineguns. The bullets ripped up the ground as they plowed a line directly toward them.

"Holy shit!" the copilot yelled, "He's shooting at us!"

All three men dived away from the aircraft just as the bullets ripped by, riddling what was left of the fuselage of the Citation, which then exploded in a yellow and gold ball of fire.

The SU-15 pulled up and made a hard right turn, setting up for another pass.

Zeke yelled, "This way!" And ran for a clump of juniper trees nearby. Both pilots were right behind him.

"Get into the trees," Zeke told them, "Maybe the pilot won't see us."

The SU-15 rolled wings level and opened up with his machine guns once more, this time kicking his rudder pedals right and left to sweep the area on both sides of the burning Citation with the deadly bullets. Some of the rounds ripped through the limbs around the three men as they crouched inside the cover of the trees.

Then the Sukhoi pilot pulled up, turned hard right, leveled his wings and extended his outward run before he began turning to set up for another pass.

"Wait a minute," The copilot said, "Why is he setting up so far out?"

Just as the fighter rolled wings-level the remaining Sidewinder left the missile rail and roared toward the heat of the burning aircraft.

The pilot yelled, "Grab your ass and hang on!"

The concussion of the explosion blew Zeke and the copilot out of the trees and sent them tumbling as shrapnel and burning debris flew in every direction.

The jet roared overhead as they scrambled back into the shelter of the trees and watched the fighter make a wide 180 degree turn and fly slowly over the wreckage. Then the afterburners lit and the jet accelerated into a victory roll as it departed toward the east.

The pilot watched the jet fade into the distance and said, "That arrogant son-of-a-bitch!"

Then he looked at Zeke and asked, "And just what the hell was that all about?!"

"It's a long story, Sir."

"I can just imagine," The copilot said, then sat down on the ground and continued, "I fly a zillion combat missions in Afghanistan and where do I get shot down? Arizona. Un-freakin'-believable!"

"Agent Sikes, meet former F-16 pilot, Max Ellison."

Zeke offered his hand, and said, "Glad to meet you Max, call me Zeke."

Max shook his hand and said, "It was a pleasure getting shot down with you, Zeke."

"I'm afraid that was my fault, apparently."

"Zeke, I'm Carl Williamson, by the way."

They shook hands and then Carl said, "Zeke, somebody wants you dead very badly."

"Yeah. It's not the first time they've tried either, but this is a bit much. I'm afraid I've underestimated their resolve."

"And just exactly who are 'they'?" Max asked.

"Well, as I said, it's a long story, which I'll be glad to tell you, but I think we need to get the hell out of here before someone else shows up to kill me."

"I think you're right," Max agreed.

Then Carl said, "Now that our adrenalin has wound down some and we've stopped shaking, we need to do an injury assessment.

Anyone in pain or bleeding?"

They inspected themselves and each other.

"Well," Carl said, "with the exception of some cuts, scratches and bruises, we all seem to have survived this man-made disaster intact."

"Thanks to God," Zeke added.

"Yes, thank God," Carl agreed.

"If we are to disappear from this crash site, we're going to have to cover our tracks." Max observed.

"Well, let's get to it," Carl said.

They found juniper limbs that had been broken off by the crash and began to sweep away their tracks from around the crash site and then erased their tracks as they left the scene.

"We might as well head north," Carl said, "and follow along this ridge. There's a railroad and a road running parallel about a quarter of a mile to the east. These roads looked like grids carved out on this plateau as I lined up for our slightly bumpy landing. Must be fire lanes for wildfire control. We need to keep away from those trails, stay sharp and keep out of sight."

***

At the Ajo Station communications center, the radio call from Pima County Sheriff Department, dispatching deputies to the scene of the shooting was heard by the Border Patrol dispatcher. She turned to another member of the staff and asked, "Say, isn't that address Agent Gonzales' place?"

"Hang on, I'll call him. … Hey, Luís. Yeah, maybe a problem. Say, isn't your place at 31 North Rosser Road? We've just heard a call on the PCSD net. There's been a shooting… copy. Got it." Then he hung up, quickly dialed an internal number and said, "Agent Breen, com center. Agent Gonzales wants you to meet him at his place ASAP. Yes, Sir, it's an emergency, PCSD is responding to a reported shooting."

Gravel and dust flew as Luís slid his Border Patrol truck sideways turning off North Rosser Road and onto his driveway. As he flew toward his house, he could see that a sheriff's patrol vehicle was already there with emergency lights flashing. Luís slid to a stop, bailed out of the truck and dashed across the porch and through the front door.

Abby was sitting on the sofa, leaning on a deputy as she helped her drink from a water bottle.

"Abby! Are you okay?!" Luís excitedly asked as he quickly went to her side.

Abby nodded and took his hand as the deputy said, "She's okay. Just a bit rattled and dehydrated. She's a very courageous young woman."

Just then a second deputy rushed in. The female deputy said, "The place is secure." Then motioned him toward the back of the house and said, "They're in the master bedroom."

"Who's in the master bedroom?" Luís asked.

"Two dead bastards who just tried to rape and kill your sister, Agent Gonzales." The deputy replied.

Luís hugged Abby and kissed her on her forehead and then followed the male deputy into the bedroom. The deputy checked the one sprawled out on the floor and Luís checked the one slumped by the bed.

"This one has an ID," The deputy said.

"This one, too," Luís said. "Connie De Campo. He's from Chicago. Sounds like a mob guy."

"This one's from Chicago, too. Bettino Scavo. I think Bettino means 'blessed' in Italian. This guy sure as hell wasn't blessed; his brain's all over the carpet."

Just then Agent Breen walked into the house, went to the bedroom and spoke to Luís and the deputy briefly, then came back to Abby and sat down beside her. "Are you okay, dear?"

"I think so. I'm still a bit shaky."

"She's quickly getting her strength back," The female deputy said. "Her pulse is normal now, and she's getting her color back. But you need to drink more water, sweetie."

Abby took another drink and then said, "They were going to… and then kill me, Ben. My God! Who are they?"

"Apparently, they were hired killers, but thanks to you they won't be killing anyone else."

Abby dropped the bottle of water, covered her face with her hands and began to cry.

The female deputy frowned at Agent Breen, put her arm around Abby and softly said, "Shhhh, you're good. It's okay. You were just defending yourself. Those bastards were going to rape and murder you. You had every right to stop them any way that you could. Thank God you were armed and knew how to shoot. You saved your life. You should be proud of that."

Abby wiped the tears from her eyes and looked at the deputy. The deputy just smiled and nodded her head in reassuring encouragement.

"She's right, Abby. What you did took amazing courage. We're proud of you, and thank God that you're unharmed."

Ben put his arm around Abby and hugged her, then dropped to his knees in front of her, took her hands in his and said, "Listen, Abby, I need you to tell me honestly, how do you feel right now?"

"I'm okay."

"Are you strong enough to drive?"

"I think so."

"Okay. I need you to go get Javi from school and go straight to Payson. Tell your folks what has happened. Is there enough fuel in the Raptor?"

"Yes, Ezekiel filled it up before he left."

"Good. Do you need to pack anything?"

"Yes, I need to pack our overnight bags."

"Then you'll need to go into the bedroom…"

"Oh…" Abby hesitated.

"We can cover the bodies," the female deputy offered, "if that's acceptable."

Abby thought for a minute. "If Luís will go with me."

"I'm right here, Abby."

Abby looked at him and smiled weakly.

"Well, Luís," Ben began, "Why don't you help Abby get ready to go and I'll talk to the deputies."

Luís went with Abby, and Ben said to the deputies; "I assume you have a crime scene investigation team in route?"

"Yes," the male deputy replied, "they should be here in about two hours. But we need Mrs. Sikes to remain here, I haven't interviewed her yet."

"No. She's done here. This isn't the first encounter with assassins. She's in serious jeopardy."

"We can protect her."

Ben chuckled. "No, you can't. These guys appear to be mafia hit men."

"Why is the mafia going after Mrs. Sikes?" The female deputy asked.

"It's a long story, but rest assured, you may think you can protect her, but this situation has just gone out of control. We had no idea. And she's not leaving the country, she's just going to a safe haven. Trust me, she's not culpable in this. But she is in danger, and we can't protect her. She and her son have to go, now."

***

The men slowly made their way north across the high plateau of level grassland spotted with short, thick clumps of juniper trees. The plateau sat atop a rugged, rocky mountainous area at an elevation just above 6000 feet. There were scattered drifts of snow, and the temperature was near freezing.

Max said, "I don't know if either of you have noticed, but it's a bit chilly up here. Come nightfall we're going to freeze our asses off without a fire. And just speaking for myself, I'd rather not have a bomb dropped on me while I'm sitting by our campfire."

"I think I have a solution to that problem if I can get cell service up here," Zeke said.

"I had a phone," Max said as he looked back toward the still-smoking crash site, "Before it got blown up and melted along with my jacket."

"I have mine," Carl said, then paused and said, "Listen… I hear a helicopter."

"All I hear is ringing since that missile blast knocked me out of the tree," Max said.

"It's probably the Navajo County Sheriff's Department Search and Rescue," Zeke said.

"Let's keep low until we determine who it is," Carl suggested.

In a few moments the helicopter reached the crash site and began circling. Then it landed.

They all looked at each other.

"Well, it's rescue," Max sighed.

"And if I get on that helicopter, how do I know that someone won't try to shoot it down? They found us doing 500 knots at cruise altitude in the middle of nowhere. I've jeopardized enough lives today."

"You want your enemies to think you're dead," Carl said.

"I have no choice. These people are deadly serious. I need time to regroup and think. But you guys can go. Get out of here. I've got this."

"No," Carl said, "we're not leaving you here. We're with you."

"Well," Max began, "since we need to lay low until the rescue team has cleared out, we have plenty of time on our hands, which is a good opportunity for you to tell us just what the hell is going on."

Zeke said, "Well, it all began in April, when I received orders to report to Ajo Station…"

As Zeke finished his story, he said, "You know, DEA and Customs, we're in the same business in a sense. Although the scope of your job is wider than mine, we're all three soldiers in the Drug War.

"The Drug War took my fiancée. I saw classmates dying of heroin and cocaine overdoses. That's why I applied with DEA. I wanted to fight in the Drug War. That's what I trained for.

"And here we sit, on this high plateau in the Arizona Mountains, after being shot down by some mercenary pilot, who was likely paid by a crazy, Chinese God of War, to keep me from telling U.S. government officials that I have compelling evidence that America is about to be attacked. And it has absolutely nothing to do with illegal drugs; they're completely irrelevant. I think we've been fighting the wrong war.

"The economic force behind Quan Ji Zhang isn't new money. You don't amass almost a trillion dollars overnight. This has been planned for a very long time, maybe decades. Hundreds, maybe thousands, of people all working toward the goal of taking down America.

"There could be conspirators in China, Mexico, Central America, Russia, the United States, and God knows where else. And they're damn close to pulling the trigger. The last step is building that massive airport complex in Mexico. Once it's finished and the military assets are ready to move, all they have to do is create political unrest in the US, then initiate a coups d'état to throw command of the military off balance and then attack."

***

As soon as Abby had packed the bags she needed, Ben talked to her and Luís.

"I wish that I could send Luís to drive you, but I need him here for something very important right now. Abby, I want you to keep your phone within reach, and call me if you have any problems at all. Also, call me as soon as you get to your parent's house, okay?"

"Okay, Ben."

"Good. Now go get Javi and get to Payson as fast as you can—within reason, not as fast as the Raptor can get you there."

Abby smiled and said, "Okay."

As Ben and Luís watched Abby drive away, Ben sighed and said, "This has not been a day for good news."

"What do you mean?" Luís asked.

"Zeke was supposed to call me this morning at 8 a.m. We had something important to discuss, but he didn't call. You know how prompt he is about things like that. So I called him and got his voice-mail. Then I called the DOJ flight center to find out if his flight was on schedule. They reported that ATC flight following lost contact with the aircraft just after 7:30 over Navajo County near Show Low, and the Navajo County Sheriff's Department had reports about that time of a jet trailing smoke and going down in that area."

Luís sighed, rubbed his forehead and said, "Son-of-a-bitch!"

Ben put his hand on Luís' shoulder. "They're bound to be coming after you next. They've tried once and failed. It's obvious they intend to take all of you out. You know they're going to try again. We can only hope that they don't know these two assholes failed to get Abby, and that will give her a fighting chance to get away. And when she gets to Payson, your dad will know what to do. Meanwhile, I have an idea; follow me to my place."

In the distance, two men in a dark grey sedan watched with binoculars as Abby pulled out of the driveway and turned south on North Rosser Road, heading toward town to pick up Javi from school.

Inside the sedan, the passenger said, "Something went south. They blew it. There she goes. Follow her."

Abby parked at the school and went in to get Javi. The dark grey sedan pulled up a minute later, stopped nearby and the passenger started to get out of the car.

The driver asked, "Where the hell are you goin'?"

"I need to stretch my legs," He replied, then got out and leaned against the car.

"Why don't you attract attention, asshole," The driver said, mumbling to himself. "We already stick out like a sore thumb in this town."

Abby came out of the school, walking hand in hand with Javi. As she walked up to the Raptor she spotted the car and the suspicious guy leaning against it, but avoided looking directly at him. Then she helped Javi into the back, got him secured in his booster seat, and cautiously looked through the dark-tented back window at the sedan just as the passenger opened the door and got back into the car.

"I think she made you," The driver said.

"Nah, she was dealin' with her kid. Follow her. She's probably goin' to her folks place in Payson. We'll hit 'er out on the highway."

Abby watched her rearview mirror as she headed north on highway 85. Behind her, in the distance, she saw the dark grey sedan and pushed the accelerator down on the Raptor. Quickly the speedometer went past 120 mph, and left the sedan far behind.

The passenger saw the Raptor accelerating away and told the driver, "Punch it!"

"I am punchin' it, moron!"

As Abby roared into the check station, the Border Patrol Agent inspecting traffic motioned to Abby to slow down, but she ignored him and quickly pulled up and squealed the tires to stop, then rolled down her window.

"Mam, we need you to slow down. You're driving too fast through the inspection lane."

"I'm sorry," Abby replied, "I need your help."

"What's the problem, mam?"

"I'm Abby Sikes. My brother is Agent Luís Gonzales, he works with my husband. I'm being followed by two men in a late-model dark-grey Ford Crown Vic. They're right behind me... well, they're behind me anyway. And I'm certain that they're armed and dangerous."

Then she motioned for the agent to come closer and she whispered to keep Javi from overhearing, "Two men just tried to kill me about an hour ago in my house and I'm sure these men intend to finish the job."

The agent motioned for another agent to approach, "We have a problem. Two armed men are inbound in a dark grey Crown Vic. They're suspected to be assassins. We need to detain them. They're armed. Spread the word."

"Missus Sikes, you need to go now. Just please slow down a bit, drive carefully and stay safe."

"Thank you. Thank you so much."

Abby hit the accelerator and burned rubber as she exited the inspection station.

All of the agents watched her depart and then looked at the agent that had just let her proceed.

He shrugged his shoulders and said, "I asked her to slow down and drive safe. If that's what she calls slowing down, I'd hate to see getting in a hurry."

Approximately two minutes later the dark-grey Crown Vic quickly approached the inspection station. The agent signaled to the driver to slow down. As the car approached, the driver lowered the window, smiled and said, "Sorry officer, we're in a bit of a hurry."

"Sir, could you please pull to the right and stop? The agents will direct you." Just then he saw the passenger pull out his pistol and yelled, "Gun! Passenger!"

The passenger started firing out of his window at the agents as the driver hit the accelerator and crashed through a barrier in the lane where he had been directed to stop. Several of the agents returned fire and killed the passenger. The driver was hit during the exchange of gunfire, lost control of the car and crashed into one of the Border Patrol vehicles.

The report of the incident made its way immediately to the Ajo Station Com Center and then to Agent-in-Charge Ben Breen, who happened to be at his home with Luís.

Ben got off the phone and said, "Two more followed Abby out of town. She outran them and they were stopped at the check station. One was killed, the other was wounded and is in custody."

"Thank, God. I don't know how much more of this Abby can take. Not to mention me."

"I have the feeling that those two were for us, but went to finish Abby first. You can bet there's more thugs in the area, so it's just a matter of time before they come after us."

"Don't remind me. But I like your decoy idea. This is clever."

"Well, I missed breakfast. Let's go fishing for some hitmen," Ben said.

"I don't like to be the bait, but I'm with you. Marcella's?"

"Me neither. Marcella's it is."

***

Several hours later, Abby's parents were waiting on the porch for her as she pulled into the driveway. Javi jumped out and ran to his grandmother.

"Hello Mejo! How's my Javi?"

Bernie opened the door for Abby, helped her out of the Raptor and hugged her tightly.

"How are you doing, Meja?"

"I'm still shaking, Papa."

"Let's get you inside." He put his arm around her and walked her into the house.

Then he looked at Mama and silently nodded.

She said to Javi, "I'll bet you're starved after than long trip. Let's see if we have something for you to eat."

"Meja," Bernie said, "Why don't you sit down and relax for a moment."

"I will, but right now this pregnant lady really has to pee."

Abby came back into the living room momentarily and said, "That's better!" and then sat on the sofa near her dad who was sitting in his recliner.

"Oh! I need to call Ben," she said and reached for her phone.

"Ben just called. I hung up with him just as you turned into the driveway, so he knows you made it here safe."

"Good. I guess he told you what happened."

"Yes, Meja. It scared your Mama and me to death. I can't imagine what you've gone through. We're so thankful that you weren't harmed."

"Me, too, Papa. I've been thanking God since I left the house. The bullet just barely missed me; it cut some of the strands of my hair."

Bernie stared at the floor and tried to collect his courage.

"I'm okay, Papa. Really."

"I know Meja. But when I talked to Ben he told me something else. Something that you need to know."

"What is it, Papa?"

He took a deep breath and said, "Meja, Ezekiel's plane has gone down."

Abby went pale. "Papa?" she whispered.

"I'm so sorry, Meja. It went down this morning east of Show Low. The Navajo County Sheriff's Department arrived at the crash site about two hours ago. The aircraft was totally destroyed. There were no survivors."

Abby slowly slid from the sofa and onto her knees. "No…" She whispered. "That can't be. It just cannot be. No, no, no, no, no, no, no, no…" Then she collapsed onto the floor weeping hysterically. "Nooooooooo!" She screamed. "Not my Husband! Ezekiel is not dead!" Then she slammed her fists into the floor as she screamed, "God, please, no, no, no, no, no, no, no, no!"

Bernie knelt beside her, held her to him and rocked her gently as she wept uncontrollably.

Mama knelt in the hallway, keeping Javi with her, watching the heartbreaking scene and crying.

***

"Zeke, that's an amazing story," Carl said. "And there's just the four of you?"

"That's right; my boss and I, and Luís and his boss."

"If you go public with this," Max said, "without some serious political horsepower on your side in Congress, you're going to be crushed like four bugs."

"Maybe, but we have to try. The security of our republic depends on it."

"Well, I understand why you need everyone to believe that you're dead," Carl said.

"I just hate what it will do to Abril. She's just entered her second trimester. I just hope to God the shock doesn't cause her to have a miscarriage."

Then Zeke paused, "What am I saying?! The crash has rattled my brain. I have a phone. I'll call her now!"

Zeke pulled his phone out of his jacket pocket and activated the screen. No service. "Dammit!"

"Let me try mine," Carl said, then he touched the screen of his phone and handed it to Zeke.

"Call your wife."

Presently, Abby's phone rang. She ignored it.

"Meja, your phone is ringing." Bernie said.

"I don't care," She said in a muffled voice, still curled up on the floor, leaning against him.

"It could be important."

She ignored him.

"Abby…"

"Okay!" She said disgustedly, and looked at the screen. "Carl Williamson, U.S. Customs. Who is that? I don't know any one by that name."

"Just answer it!" Mama said impatiently as she sat beside her.

"Hello… Who? Ezekiel?!" Abby screamed. "Oh, my God! Honey, is it really you? You're alive! They said that you were killed in the crash. Oh, thank God, you're alive!"

Then she started crying and hugged Mama.

160

Bernie took the phone and said, "Ezekiel? … Yes, Abril's okay; she just a bit overjoyed at the moment. Young man, you gave us quite a scare, and we've had enough of that today … I'll tell you later. … Yes, Ben called. … What's going on with you?"

Bernie listened as Zeke explained his situation.

"Copy that. Just get me the coordinates. There are several dirt strips up there, but if you can find me about 900 feet of reasonably smooth turf, or any level road. … Okay, I'll talk to you then. Now I think a certain young, expectant mother wants to speak with you."

"Honey? Thank God you're alive! I was just praying here on the living room floor, just before my phone rang. I didn't realize God answered our prayers quite that quickly. … Are you okay? … I love you so much! Where are you? ... You're where?! … Oh. … Okay. … I understand. … I'm fine Honey, so is Javi. … Ezekiel, they tried to kill me. … This morning, after I dropped Javi off at school. … Two men. … I got my Glock from the safe and did just like you taught me."

Then she started to cry, "Husband, I need you. Please come home." Then she looked at her dad. "Okay, I understand. … We'll be waiting for your call. … It's so wonderful to hear your voice. … I love you, too, Husband. … Bye."

Abby jumped up and danced across the living room floor singing, "He's alive, he's alive, he's alive, he's alive…" then grabbed Javi and sang and danced with him.

Zeke hung up the phone, wiped the tears from his eyes, sniffed and said, "God I love that little girl."

Then he handed the phone back to Carl. "Thank you. You guys need to call your loved ones, too, and before they receive the news that my wife and family just received. And your official report is that I didn't survive the crash."

***

Ben and Luís drove their Border Patrol vehicles to Marcella's Café and Bakery and parked nose to tail so that the driver's sides would be next to each other.

"Well," Ben began, "Good sign. I don't see any suspicious looking vehicles."

"No suspicious vehicles is good," Luís replied, "Let's eat." and they went in for breakfast.

After breakfast Luís and Ben cautiously exited the restaurant and went to their trucks, climbed in and started them. They both rolled down their windows and Luís said, "What now, boss?"

"We watch our backs and, otherwise, it's business as usual. The thugs may not think we know they plan to hit us. When they're ordered to hit someone, they're given minimal details. That may give us some advantage."

"I gotta tell ya', Ben, I hate this."

"Me too. My wife is frightened out of her wits. I've arranged for off-duty deputies and agents in unmarked vehicles to watch my house and yours. My kids are thrilled because we pulled them out of school. Thank God they don't know the truth. If you're uncomfortable staying at your house alone, we can cut half of the guards by you staying with us. You know my family's crazy about you."

"I think I'll take you up on that."

"Good. Now let's head to Ajo station and pretend to be happy campers."

"Whoopee."

***

After the rescue crew had departed the crash site, Zeke called Abby on Carl's phone.

"Hi, Honey! … Yes, Papa's right here. … Okay. I love you!"

Abby handed her dad the phone. "Yes, go ahead. … Got it. Hang on, I'll bring up the coordinates on Google Earth. … Okay, straight north of you about a mile is a straight stretch of road running east and west. It looks perfect. Check it out for big potholes and such, and let me know how it looks. I'm heading for the airport now. I'll be there in about an hour. … Okay, see you there."

"You mean we'll be there in about an hour." Abby corrected him.

"There's no chance that you could wait here is there?"

Abby just glared at him.

He nodded. "Didn't think so."

Bernie dropped the rugged Maule gently onto the road with expert skill and grace. Before the aircraft stopped rolling, Abby was out the door and running to Zeke. Beaming that gorgeous smile, she jumped into his open arms, wrapping her arms around his neck and her legs around his waist.

Abby was still kissing Zeke when Bernie greeted Carl and Max, both shivering from the cold.

"Bernie Gonzales," he said as he shook their hands. "Helluva way to visit Arizona high country! Climb in, the cockpit's warm and

Mama has a veritable feast waiting to celebrate your survival."

Max and Carl looked back at Zeke and Abby just before they climbed in.

"They'll come along eventually," Bernie said, and climbed in himself.

Bernie came up on the throttle and Zeke and Abby came running, but she held onto him all the way back to Payson as though he might float away if she let go. And for some reason, couldn't stop kissing him. Not that he minded.

After eating generous portions of Mama's delicious Mexican food, everyone sat back and stayed at the table as if they had eaten too much to lift themselves out of their chair.

"Missus Gonzales—" Carl started to say.

"Please, call me Mama."

"Mama, this meal was simply delicious. My stomach says to stop eating but my taste buds are screaming for more food."

"Well, thank you young man. We're just so thankful that you all survived that horrible crash."

"Unofficially, yes, Mama," Zeke said, "But officially, I didn't survive."

"For heaven sakes, why?"

Zeke looked at Max and Carl, sighed, and said, "I might as well tell you; we were shot down."

Abby quickly turned to look at Zeke, "What?!"

"You're not serious," Mama said.

"I'm afraid so. And I suspect who's behind it, but I'm not certain. I need to investigate and I need them to believe that I'm dead. Maybe they'll get sloppy and reveal something. Also, the same group of assassins that tried twice to kill Abril will inevitably try again. I believe they intend to kill our whole family. I alerted my dad and grandpa just before dinner."

"What is going on, Ezekiel?" Mama asked.

"I was going to Washington to testify before the Senate Armed Services Committee. What I know may incriminate high level people within our own government. The people who tried to kill Abril, and me, twice, are not taking any chances that I may have told my family what I know. These people are ruthless. You're all in danger. Papa already knows."

"Yes," Bernie said, "I have the alarm system activated. Any movement on the perimeter of our property and the alarm sounds and the spotlights come on."

"Oh, my goodness! Papa, did you call Luís and let him know that Ezekiel is safe?"

"Yes, Mama. I called him on the way home from the airport. Oh, by the way," then he looked at Zeke, "he said that he owed you one for scaring him to death. And to tell you, 'welcome back to the land of the living'."

Zeke smiled. "I'll be sure to thank him," and then grew serious. "I guess I need to plan my next step, whatever that may be, and be ready to move."

"All of this is very confusing, and very troubling, Ezekiel," Mama said, "but I'm thankful that you're here with us."

"Thank you, Mama," Zeke replied as Abby kissed his cheek and said, "Me, too."

"Well, I wish that we could stay and help," Carl said. "Max and I have some serious issues with whoever shot our Citation out from under us."

"You got that right," Max said.

"But," Carl continued and glanced at his watch, "Our ride is already en route. They'll arrive in just under two hours. We have to be in DC by 9 a.m. DHS gets a bit concerned when one of their aircraft goes down, and I imagine the search and rescue team saw the evidence and reported that we didn't just crash, so our debriefing may take a while."

"Don't remind me," Max lamented.

After dinner Javi went to play video games and Abby pulled Zeke into their bedroom. "Honey, what's really going on?"

"This is very serious, Sweetheart. The security of the U.S. may be threatened. If I don't act, along with Ray, Luís and Ben, this situation could quickly get out of hand and be unstoppable."

"I understand, Honey, but after dinner you said that you'll be planning your next step and getting ready to move. I don't like the sound of that."

"Me either, frankly. What I'd like to do…" he slid his arms around her, pulled her close, kissed her, and then continued, "is stay right here cuddled up on the sofa with you. But I have no choice. I must act."

Abby sighed and laid her head on his shoulder. "I thought I had lost you today. My world was ending almost before it began. I love you so much. I feel so safe when I'm with you, but I'm scared Ezekiel. What kind of monsters are these people?"

"The worst kind, Abril; evil, greedy and power hungry. But they have an Achilles' heel, and I'm it. Along with Luís, Ray and Ben. If we can just stay alive long enough to testify before congress…"

Abby lifted her head from his chest, looked him in the eyes and said, "If you don't mind, Mister, I'd prefer that you stay alive a whole lot longer. I'm planning on growing old with you."

Zeke smiled "And you'll be just as beautiful at 80 as you are this very minute."

Abby walked to the bedroom door and locked it. Then she pulled him onto the bed and turned off the lamp.

The following day dawned uneventfully, both in Ajo and Payson. There were no signs of suspicious strangers, just a tense, nameless fear; not knowing when the next assassination attempt would come, and from whom, and wondering what their next move should be.

Zeke sat at the dining table beside Abby, staring into his coffee cup. She stood up, caressed his shoulders and then peeked into this cup. "Can I warm up your coffee, Honey?"

Zeke broke from his deep thought, looked at her and smiled, then kissed her on the tip of her nose. "You are such a sweetheart. I understand why Luís calls you his little ray of sunshine."

She smiled and blushed, and then replied, "Thank you, but all I did was ask if you wanted more coffee."

Zeke turned his chair to face her, pulled her onto his lap, took her into his arms and held her to him. "You're just as worried as I am, but you don't show it. You're so filled with love and kindness that it just overpowers everything. You give me strength and hope. There's a goodness in you that just radiates happiness. I'm so blessed to have you as my wife."

"I'm blessed to have such a wonderful husband," She whispered, "And if you keep this up, I'm taking you back to bed…"

"I see you two lovebirds are at it again," Mama said as she walked into the kitchen. "I remember when your papa and I were like that. My papa threatened to throw a bucket of water on us a time or two."

"That's right!" Bernie said as he walked in, "And Mama still sparks my fire." Then took her into a warm embrace for a long, wet kiss.

Afterward Mama straightened her hair and apron, then smiled

and said to no one in particular, "Papa's probably up there filling the bucket right now..."

Bernie poured himself a cup of coffee then sat down across from Zeke and Abby. "Good morning, lovebirds."

Still sitting in Zeke's lap, Abby smiled shyly, "Good morning, Papa."

Then he looked at Zeke. "I talked with the chief-of-police last night, they've been running stepped-up patrols through the neighborhood. I talked with one of the officers earlier this morning and they haven't seen anything unusual. I hope that's a sign they're done with us."

"I'm afraid this is just the calm before the storm," Zeke regretfully replied. "Even though the testimony of my family would be hearsay evidence, before congress it would also be public record and damning to the politicians and bureaucrats involved. The repercussions could be career-ending. So, they've dropped the hammer and they're committed."

Zeke kissed Abby on the cheek and then continued, "But they grossly underestimated our ferocious and beautiful Abril."

Mama applauded and said, "Hooray!"

"But they won't underestimate us again. They're monitoring police reports and probably have some inside information sources as well. I'm really worried about Luís, Ben and Ray. I've sent Ray a coded message, but there's been no answer as of yet. That's troubling. He should've answered right away.

"I can't really help Luís and Ben, but I need to know what's happening with Ray."

"That's a quandary; you can't call his office, and there's no one else to turn to," Bernie said.

Zeke suddenly looked at Bernie thoughtfully and said, "That's not exactly true."

"Oh?" Bernie replied.

"No. It isn't…" Then Zeke looked at Abby. "There's someone that we know who has a lot of friends in high places, and he's particularly interested in our sex life…"

"What?!" Bernie said.

Abby smiled at her dad and said, "Grandpa Ezzy. He wants more great grandchildren."

"What does that have to do with this?" Mama asked.

"He's retired Army intelligence," Zeke replied. "He's also a

Medal of Honor recipient, the personal friend of several high-ranking generals, including the commanding general of INSCOM. Excuse me for a moment."

Zeke left the kitchen and went to call his grandpa.

"INSCOM?" Bernie asked.

"U.S. Army Intelligence and Security Command," Abby replied.

Just before Zeke finished his phone conversation with his grandpa, Ezzy said, "Z, do me a favor and don't tell your dad until tomorrow, okay?"

"Sure Grandpa, no problem. Love ya'."

"Love you too, Z. Watch your six."

"Will do."

Just moments later Ezzy called an old friend; "John, Ezzy. … Yeah, great. … You? … Good. Listen, there's something serious going down. We're getting the band back together. Call the guys. I have a few more calls to make, and something to take care of here at home. I'll call you."

Chapter Nine
Sucks To Be You

It was two days before Thanksgiving. The day in Ajo began cool, crisp and severe clear. Luís stood in the backyard of Ben's house, drinking coffee and watching the sunrise.

Presently, Ben joined him.

"Mornin'. Another grand Arizona sunrise," Ben said.

"Yep. Ever since I was a kid I've tried to catch every sunrise and sunset that I could. I just never get tired of 'em." Then he sighed. "I sure hope this isn't the last one."

Ben put his hand on Luís shoulder. "We've got this, Pal. It may not seem like it. But we've got this."

Luís looked at Ben and gave him a confident nod.

"Sarah just started breakfast," Ben said, "Let's go give her a hand."

About an hour later they were just finishing eating.

"More coffee anyone?" Sarah asked.

"No thanks," Luís replied. "Sarah, that was delicious. I'll bet I've gained a pound a day since I've been staying here."

"Well, that's your own fault," Ben said. "There's no requirement that you eat at Marcella's too, you know. We just need to show up there because everybody knows that's probably where you'll be."

"I can't argue with that," Luís agreed.

"Speaking of which…" Ben reminded.

"Yep. I'll see you out front. See ya' Sarah. Thanks again for your wonderful hospitality."

She hugged him and said, "You know we love you. You're always welcome, Luís."

Sarah watched him leave the kitchen, then turned, leaned on the sink and looked down.

Ben took her hand, pulled her to him and held her tightly.

Then he looked into her eyes and said, "It'll be okay. You'll see. Just trust me?"

Sarah just nodded and then laid her head on his shoulder.

***

At the Sikes' residence in Cambridge, Biscuit, the big, jolly yellow Lab, was snoozing on his dog bed near the back door. Suddenly, he heard a scratching noise coming from the door and his ears perked up. He listened carefully, then got up and walked to the door, twisted his head slightly and watched the door knob intently. Uncharacteristically, he didn't bark, but just watched and listened for a moment, then he began a deep, low rumbling growl.

Suddenly, the hackles on his haunches raised and moved slowly up his spine toward his mane. About that time, the door came ajar slightly, and a man's hand appeared on the edge of the door as it slowly opened. Biscuit watched the man's hand until his wrist was in view. Then he lunged, wedging the wrist between his molars before he clamped down with the force of approximately 200 bone-crushing pounds per square inch. The man let out a bloody scream, the door flew open and then two shotgun blasts rang out.

"Good boy, Biscuit!" Ezzy said as he pushed the dog back inside as he entered and closed the door.

Just then Anna came running from the front of the house.

"Dad, why are you coming in the back door? And what was that awful noise?"

Then she saw the double-barrel shotgun in his hand.

"Have you been shooting in our back yard? You know that isn't allowed."

"It's all okay, Anna. I'll explain just as soon as Bill gets home. He should be here any minute."

Ezzy went to the front door and waited. Presently, Bill rushed in the door.

"Good you're already here. Ezekiel said that he called you. Just let me explain this to Anna and we'll all head to the campus. Is mother, here—?"

Then he saw the shotgun in his Ezzy's hand.

"Dad, you know that it isn't appropriate to take weapons on campus."

"Bill…"

"We have security that is perfectly capable of protecting us."

"Bill…"

"What?! I mean… sorry Dad. Sir?"

"I don't believe that we need to take refuge on campus any longer."

"And just why not? Are you planning to protect us from God

knows how many unknown assassins with that shotgun?"

"Just follow me."

"To where? This is urgent, Dad. We must get to the campus immediately!"

Ezzy put his hand on Bill's shoulder and repeated, "Just - follow - me."

Bill gave an exasperated sigh and replied, "Okay, Dad."

Then he followed his Ezzy toward the back door, complaining the entire way; "This is ridiculous. We have an emergency and you're leading me around my own house. If you have a point, you'd better make it soon because…"

Ezzy opened the back door.

"…every minute wasted is— Oh, my God! Are they dead?!"

Ezzy looked at his son and said, "Bill, for a brilliant professor at MIT, sometimes you can be really dumb."

Just then Anna came down the hallway with Biscuit walking beside her. When she saw the dead man near the back door she placed her hands over her mouth and screamed.

Then she said, "Oh, my God! Is he dead?!"

Ezzy sighed, rolled his eyes and said, "Anna, call the police. Bill come with me."

At Ezzy's house, he showed Bill the bodies of two more assassins lying in the back yard.

Bill didn't ask if they were dead.

***

As Luís stared into his coffee at Marcella's, one of the wait staff came up and asked, "Are you off your feed or something today, Luís?"

He looked up and said, "Oh, hi Lisa. Yeah, I'm just not that hungry today," and glanced at Ben.

She patted him on the shoulder and said, "Well, I hope you get to feeling better soon, sweetie."

"Thanks."

"It's about that time, Pal," Ben said.

Luís nodded and went to pay for the coffee.

As Luís approached the door, Ben was already standing there, and looked back at him. Two customers walked in. He waited a moment and then said, "They're here. Glance to your right as you walk out the door. The camper across 85. It's parked facing away from us. It probably has a hole cut somewhere in the back wall to shoot through. I'm going to get the scope and verify my theory. Wait here until I signal you. Then you know what to do."

Ben opened the driver's side door of his truck, which was backed into the parking spot along with Luís' truck, with the passenger side facing toward the highway and the camper. He sat up a mannequin dressed to look like himself that was lying on the seat, and positioned it at the steering wheel. Then he retrieved his spotter scope from underneath the seat, and positioned himself where he could inconspicuously observe the camper.

"Uh huh, just as I thought," he said to himself. The tip of a rifle barrel was sticking through a small hole in the wall just underneath the rear window. Ben signaled Luís and then positioned himself on the running board at the driver's door.

Before Luís left the restaurant, he quickly told the staff and patrons what was happening and asked them to take cover behind the counter.

As Luís went to his truck, which was blocked from the shooters view by Ben's truck, Ben said, "Don't run over yourself and prepare for flying glass."

"Ben, I'm tellin' you now, this is the last time I plan to be a live target!"

"If we make it, the beer's on me."

"Deal!"

Luís set up his mannequin, and then cranked his truck. He stood on the running board and reached in with his right foot, pressed the brake and put the shifter in drive. Then he carefully released the brake and allowed the truck to slowly roll forward. Just as his truck moved into the line of fire, a rifle round shattered the passenger's window, split open the head of his mannequin and shattered the driver's window as well. A split second later, Ben's truck and mannequin met a similar fate.

Ben pushed his mannequin over onto the seat and Luís let his truck roll into the empty lot across the street. Suddenly the camper accelerated away, heading north on Highway 85.

Luís walked back across the street to Ben's truck and said, "You look really good for a dead man."

"So do you," Ben replied, then he called the off-duty deputy guarding his house to let him know what was going on, and also called his wife.

After hanging up he said, "Looks like they got what they wanted. All clear at my house."

"Thank God," Luís sighed.

Ben also contacted the Com Center and the sheriff's department, advising them, as per previous agreement, to release false reports that two Border Patrol officers had been killed in Ajo.

Then he said, "Luís, you need to get out of here. I'm going home to my family. You need to go to yours. This will be a crime scene for a while, so a deputy is on the way to give us a lift to my place. From there you can take my Jeep."

"While we wait, I think I recall that the beer is on you," Luís reminded him.

"It is." Ben opened the door for Luís and said, "After you, fellow zombie."

Later that day Luís made his way to Payson. Bekah was anxiously waiting for him at his parents' house and gave him a very warm welcome when he finally arrived.

***

The day before Thanksgiving passed uneventfully at the Gonzales house in Payson, although the specter of assassins hung over everyone like a pall.

Thanksgiving Day in Payson dawned chilly and beautiful, with the tall and stately mountain pines and evergreens mixed with colorful maples, oaks and other hardwoods painting the multicolored splendor of autumn in the Arizona Rim Country.

Fortunately, Bernie had come up with an idea to advise his other kids and family that he and Mama had a last-minute change of plans and wouldn't be home for Thanksgiving. The family holiday gathering was changed to Christmas and, for the most part, everyone was okay with it.

Mama, Bekah, Abby and Zeke were working on various different food preparation tasks, and Javi was watching.

"Happy Thanksgiving family!" Luís said as he walked into the kitchen and gave all of the ladies a kiss on the cheek. "You favorite zombie is searching for sustenance."

"Fresh tortillas are on the stove, zombie son," Mama said as she slid the turkey into the oven.

"Ma, I'm not the only zombie son present you know."

"Yes, but my other zombie son is cutting veggies."

"Are you suggesting that I work for my food?"

"Yes!" Everyone replied at once.

Abby pointed to a pan of sweet potatoes on the counter and ordered, "Wash, coat with cooking oil and wrap with tinfoil."

Luís replied with a muffled, "Yes mam." as he held a folded tortilla in his mouth and poured himself a cup of coffee.

Just then Bernie came into the kitchen, said, "Happy Thanksgiving family!" and gave Mama a kiss on the cheek.

Then he pulled Zeke and Luís aside. "One of the floodlight zones was triggered around 4 a.m. I think they were testing our security."

"That means they'll probably try in daylight. One less security obstacle," Zeke suggested.

"So you think that one of us should keep watch outside?" Luís began.

But Mama interrupted. "What are you three in a huddle about over there?"

Zeke glanced at Abby and whispered, "Maybe we should talk in the living room. Abril has exceptionally good hearing."

"Yes, I do," She replied.

Bernie sighed. "Well, I might as well say it; I think we're being watched."

Abby gave Zeke a concerned look. He went to her and put his arm around her shoulders.

"Well, if they mess up my Thanksgiving dinner, they're in trouble," Mama said.

"Everyone, is your weapon ready?" Luís asked.

"You betcha," Abby replied.

"Yep," Bernie said.

"Mine too," Said Bekah.

"Oh, yeah," Zeke said. "Thanks for bringing my LAR-15 by the way."

"You're welcome," Luís replied. "I just hope that you don't need it."

"Me, too," Zeke sighed.

An hour later, two security sensors on opposite sides of the house went off simultaneously.

Zeke looked at Luís. "They don't know we're here. That gives us an advantage. You go out the front and go right. I'll do the same through the back. Bernie, lock the door after me. Kill anything that comes in this house. Abril, lock the door after Luís, then get in the master closet with Javi, Bekah and Mama."

Abby looked at Zeke, pointed at him and Luís and said, "You two be careful!"

"Yes, Mam," They replied.

Zeke eased out of the back door, turned right, went low and crept behind the hedges toward the corner of the house.

Abby locked the door behind Luís, drew her pistol and went with Mama, Bekah and Javi toward the master bedroom.

Mama looked at Abby's pink-handled pistol and asked, "Is that yours?"

"Yes, Mama, this is my Glock 26. Ezekiel bought it for me."

"Oooo, that's pretty!" Then Mama looked toward the kitchen and said, "If those pinche bastards cause me to burn my turkey, I'm going to shoot them with your pretty pistol!"

From the front and rear corners of the house, Luís and Zeke cautiously watched for movement in the woods on either side of the property. Suddenly, Luís saw a shadowy figure moving toward the shop at the back of the property and moved quietly along the wall, taking cover behind the HVAC outside unit near the corner of the house. The man crept along the shop building, paused and peeked around the corner to make certain no one was in front, then started to dart across the lawn toward the back door.

At that point he spotted Zeke behind a hedge at the back corner of the house and yelled a warning to his partner.

Luís stepped out from behind the outside unit and yelled, "Halt! Drop your weapon!"

The man froze. Just at that moment, his partner turned to head into the woods but Zeke stepped out and yelled, "Halt! Lower your weapon and turn around."

The man obeyed and walked passed Zeke toward his partner.

Luís commanded the man again, "I said drop your weapon!"

Instead, the man looked at Luís and said, "Hey man. You're dead. I saw your head explode."

"Yeah," Luís replied. "I was dead. I have a hole in the back of my head. You just can't see it. I'm a zombie now. You wanna join me?"

Zeke listened to the conversation and cracked a smile, but continued to train his pistol on the man in front of him.

Then the man looked at him and said, "Hey, you're supposed to be dead, too. You died in a plane crash."

"Yeah, I'm like my partner, I'm a zombie. And you're both going to drop your weapons. Just ease it on the ground. Now."

Neither man moved.

"This isn't going to end well for you, gentlemen," Luís said, "Just do as he says; drop your weapons."

Just then both men glanced at each other and made their move. Simultaneously, Luís put three rounds into his man's chest and Zeke put one round through his man's head. Then they each moved quickly to kick the weapons away from the downed men and checked for a pulse.

"Scratch two more wise guys," Luís said.

"Think so?"

"It's a good bet. Hired guns. That's who tried to kill Abby."

Then Luís looked at the man Zeke shot. "You like those head shots, don't you."

"Eh," Zeke shrugged.

"Well, that's how Abby dispatched one of her two bad guys; two out of three rounds, right through the skull."

"Really?" Zeke smiled. "That's my girl."

Just then Bernie peaked out of the back door.

"It's all clear, Papa," Zeke said.

"Good. The police are on the way."

In the distance, sirens could already be heard.

The following day at breakfast, Zeke was preoccupied.

Abby leaned over and whispered, "What's wrong, Honey?"

"I've not been able to reach Ray or Kathy. Something's wrong."

"You know what you've got to do," Luís said.

"Yeah."

Abby looked at Luís and then at Zeke. "I'm getting that sinking feeling again."

Zeke looked at Abby and sighed, then said, "Papa, I need a lift."

"Where to?"

"DC."

"Oh. Well, let's get it planned and get packed."

"We can't file a flight plan," Zeke said, "We'll have to avoid control zones and meet Grandpa Ezzy at a small strip near DC, but it's doable."

"If I can find 900 feet of flat, I'll put my toy on it," Bernie said, "Strip or not."

Bernie suggested that Zeke chart the course and determine the approximate flight time – "It's good practice studying for your pilot's written exam," He said.

Then Zeke called Ezzy, explained the plans and coordinated a rendezvous time and location.

After the call, Ezzy immediately met with his buddies and they began formulating a plan of action.

That evening in bed, after making love, Zeke and Abby cuddled together and talked.

Abby whispered, "What I said to you the day you went to Mexico still stands, Husband; just do your best to come back to me. That's all I can ask."

Zeke caressed her beautiful face and said, "You know I will Sweetheart, you know I will."

***

Luís and Abby dropped them off at the Payson airport. Abby kissed her dad goodbye and then she and Zeke held each other close in a long embrace. She looked into his eyes and said, "Be safe, Husband. I want to grow old with you."

After their last kiss goodbye she said, "Now climb in that plane before I throw you in the truck and make you stay here!"

Zeke smiled and replied, "Yes, Mam."

Just as Zeke climbed in the left seat, Luís placed his hand on his shoulder and said, "Doc, don't worry about things here, I've got this. Abby and Javi will be safe. You just concentrate on your mission. And come back alive, okay? You're having a baby!

Zeke grinned and said, "Yes, we are!"

In the pre-dawn hours of November 24th, Bernie's venerable Maule M-7 lifted off in route to Davis Airport, near Laytonsville, Maryland, 25 miles north of Washington DC.

As Abby watched the Maule disappear into the dark eastern sky, she closed her eyes and prayed, "God, please guide my husband's mission, and bring him and my Papa safely home to us. In Jesus' name I pray, amen."

Just over thirteen hours later Ezzy greeted Zeke and Bernie as the aircraft rolled to a stop at Davis Airport, Maryland.

"Welcome to God's Country!" Ezzy said as they climbed out of the cockpit.

"Good to be here," Zeke replied as he stretched. "That wasn't my first cross country, but it was certainly the longest. Seemed like we'd never get here."

Bernie patted the engine cowling and said, "She's not fast, but she's dependable."

"Amen to that!" Zeke replied.

"Well, Z," Ezzy said, "A lot has happened since we talked. My guys and I have made some interesting contacts and had some amazing conversations. It turns out that you and Ray are not alone after all; the DIA and INSCOM have been running ops on your mad Chinese general. We even have someone on the inside of his organization and the intel is very damning. Their findings, along with the results of your investigation makes this a slam dunk. Assuming that Ray is alive, and we can keep you alive until the armed services committee hearing on the 5th. That's nine days from now."

"And nine days in which to kill me," Zeke replied ominously.

"Yeah. There is that. But we're going to do our damnedest to see that you make it to that hearing."

Then he turned to Bernie, put his arm around his shoulders and said, "Thanks for bringing Z."

"Hey, we're in this together," Bernie replied.

"Yes, we are, my friend. We've arranged for your aircraft to be hangared while you're here, and you'll be staying with one of my guys." Then he addressed Zeke. "What is your plan for finding Ray?"

"My only hope is that he left a trail of breadcrumbs. I've been unsuccessful otherwise. He's dropped off the grid. Even our secure channels are useless. I'm also worried about Kathy, his admin assistant. I'd like to go to the office, but I need a convincing disguise, with proper ID. That will be difficult."

"Not necessarily, as long as you don't mind impersonating an Army captain," Ezzy replied.

Zeke looked at him directly and repeated, "An Army captain."

"Yep. Pentagon ID, the whole nine yards."

"So, even if I manage to avoid being killed by the bad guys, I could still be federally prosecuted for impersonating a U.S. military officer to gain access to DEA Headquarters that I'm already authorized to enter."

"Right," Ezzy said.

"Well, it'll make an interesting trial in federal court anyway. Who knows, I might not even be sentenced to hang."

Ezzy wrinkled his nose, nodded his head and said, "Probably

would."

"Thanks a lot; nothing like a confidence builder."

"I wouldn't want you to set out with false expectations."

Zeke gave him a sideways glance; "No chance of that…"

Ezzy's plan to make Zeke look like an Army captain worked perfectly. A bit of brilliant counterfeiting to produce a valid-appearing picture ID, and pair of dark-rimmed eyeglasses set off the disguise perfectly. So, on Monday morning, November 26th, Zeke was cleared through DEA security as a visitor for Senior DEA Agent Ray Alexander.

Zeke knocked on the door of Ray's office. The door opened and Zeke found himself looking into the chest of a very big guy wearing a dark three-piece business suit with a flashy pink silk tie.

The big guy looked down and said, "State your business."

Somewhat taken aback, Zeke slowly followed the broad chest upward until he found a stern, deadpan face, and then just stared for a moment thinking, this joker could very easily pinch my head off!

The big guy just waited.

Zeke cleared his throat, swallowed and said, "Ah… is this Senior Agent Ray Alexander's office?"

The big guy just pointed to the plaque on the wall beside the doorway with Ray's name on it and repeated, "State your business."

Zeke looked at the plaque and then back at the big guy and said, "Oh. Right… I'm, ah, Captain Wrightson to see Senior Agent Alexander."

The big guy reached to his right, picked up a clipboard, glanced at it and then said, "You're not on the visitor's list."

Zeke paused for a moment and then said, "Oh. Right. Yes, that's correct, I'm not. This is an unscheduled visit, ah, but I do need to see Senior Agent Alexander right away."

"Why?" The big guy blinked once, but otherwise had no expression.

"Well… I have some information for him that I believe he needs to see."

The big guy just stared expressionless back at Zeke, and blinked once more. Then he stepped back and closed the door in Zeke's face.

Just as the door was closing Zeke raised his finger and said, "I, ah…um…" then dropped his arm to his side and mumbled, "Unbelievable! He shut the door in my face!"

Just then the door opened, Kathy reached out, grabbed him by his lapel, pulled him inside and hastily shut the door.

"Are you crazy?!" she whispered. "What are you doing here?! I thought you were dead until you began trying to reach the office. At first I thought it might be an assassin using your phone and laptop, but then I realized that it had to be you. I was so relieved, but I couldn't answer…"

Then she looked at the nametag on his uniform. "Why are you impersonating Captain Wrightson? I know him! He's deployed to Kuwait right now. Are you out of your mind?!"

"Quite possibly. But I really need to see Ray."

"So do I, I'm worried sick about him."

"What about you?" Zeke asked, "Are you safe here?"

"Apparently I'm not suspected of having any relevant knowledge—although, that isn't necessarily true. But Ray—Agent Alexander, hired Ralph to protect me."

Then they both looked at the mountainous hulk standing nearby.

Ralph smiled, waved, and said, "Hi."

Ralph is a professional bodyguard," Kathy said, "He's a sweetheart, but he loves to intimidate people."

"Sorry," Ralph said.

"It's quite alright. You're actually quite good," Zeke replied, "I was very intimidated."

"Thanks. I try."

Zeke turned back to Kathy. "What happened with Ray?"

"The same morning of your crash, Ray—Agent…"

"It's okay, I know that you two are close."

She smiled and blushed. "Ray said that he was certain that he had been followed on his way to work. Then he said that it all fit. The bad guys wouldn't risk killing a DEA agent in DC unless they had no other choice, but that you and he were scheduled to testify that day."

"So they had no other choice," Zeke replied.

"Apparently. Then, when Agent Breen called him about your plane crash, we were both just devastated. Then he suddenly said, 'I'm going off the grid,' and made me promise to lock the office and stay here until Ralph showed up later that day. He also ordered me to attempt no contact of any type with him, you, Luís or Agent Breen;

that we were all in danger. I'm so worried about him, Zeke!"

Then she started to cry and hugged him.

"Awww," Ralph whispered, pulled out a pink hanky and wiped away a tear as he watched the scene unfold.

Zeke took Kathy by her shoulders, looked into her eyes and then wiped away her tears. "Look, we need to get out of here. I need a place to think. Can we go to your place? Maybe between us we can figure out where he is."

"Okay, that sounds good to me. Where are you parked?"

"In the visitor's lot."

"I'm in the parking garage. Come with us. We'll drop you at your car."

Just as Ralph opened the passenger door for Kathy, two men appeared from behind a nearby car and began walking toward them.

"Mam, get in the car now," Ralph said. "Zeke, you, too."

Just then one of the approaching men said to the other, "Hey! That's Sikes! Get 'em!"

Zeke ran and the other man ran after him. As the man ran by Kathy's car, Ralph stepped toward him and stuck out his foot. The man tripped and plowed headlong into a parked car, knocking himself out.

The man who recognized Zeke continued approaching, drew a .45 caliber pistol with a silencer from his coat, pointed it at Ralph and fired one shot, point blank, into his chest. The man stopped less than an arm's length from Ralph, looked bewildered as he stared at the bullet hole in Ralph's pink tie, then Ralph's face as he stood there, seemingly unaffected. Then he looked quizzically at his pistol.

Meanwhile, the man who had plowed into the car got up, staggered around a bit, then regained his bearings and ran off after Zeke.

Ralph suddenly grabbed the man's gun arm at his wrist with his left hand and lifted him off of his feet. The man tried to grab Ralph with his free hand as he emptied his pistol into the concrete ceiling of the parking garage, sending shards of cement and dust showering down on them.

While that was happening, Ralph lifted his tie and was looking at the smoking bullet hole. Then he looked at the man and said, "This was my new pink silk tie. It cost me two hundred bucks."

Ralph then grabbed the man's head, slammed it into the roof

of Kathy's car and released his grip on the man's wrist. He fell in a heap at Ralph's feet.

Just then Ralph looked up to find a lady looking at him as she was about to get into her car across the way. He simply pointed at his chest and said, "He ruined my silk tie."

The lady jumped into her car and sped away.

Kathy then climbed out and excitedly asked, "Ralph are you alright?!"

"My pink silk tie's ruined," he said as he looked down at it again. "I liked this tie."

"Ralph! You were just shot in your chest!"

"Oh, no Mam. I'm wearing one of those new-technology bullet-proof vests." He replied and then rubbed his chest, "Although, it did hurt a bit. Kinda like being hit with a baseball bat."

Kathy put her hands on his chest and sighed, "Ralph, you are totally unbelievable!"

"Mam, we need to go," Ralph said. "Just let me tie this guy up."

Ralph took the guy's pants off, tied his hands behind him with his own belt, then wrapped his pants around his neck and used the pant legs to tie his feet together. He stuck the guy's gun into his shorts, and then sent him down the elevator to the lobby.

While Ralph was doing that, Kathy called Zeke on her smart phone.

"Zeke? Where are you?"

"Are you okay?" Zeke asked.

"I'm fine, thanks to Ralph."

"Thank God."

"Yes, thank Him, too."

"Where are you?"

"Not heading toward your place, that's for certain. Apparently, they've decided that you need to be dead, too."

"I know. Where can we meet?"

"I'll have to get back to you. Right now I'm being followed. They picked me up just as I left the parking lot. I guess the guy that was chasing me tipped them off."

"Be careful!"

"That's my plan…"

Zeke watched his rearview mirror closely as he headed north out of Washington DC on surface streets trying to lose his tail. He managed to keep a good distance ahead of them for a few minutes, then the traffic slowed and they caught up.

As soon as they were in range, the passenger stuck a small sub-machine gun out of his window and sprayed the back of Zeke's car with bullets, shattering the rear window and peppering the seat, dash and windshield.

Zeke swerved into the on-coming lane and accelerated away again. Moments later, they caught up with him again and sprayed another burst of rounds, hitting his car. Directly ahead, he saw a delivery truck backing out of an alley to his left and across both lanes of traffic.

Realizing that he was about to be forced to stop, Zeke swerved across the on-coming lanes, onto the sidewalk, barely missing the front of the delivery truck, onto the adjacent sidewalk, across the on-coming lanes again and back on course.

Just then a car came down the alley and stopped in front of the delivery truck, blocking the path that Zeke had just taken. The pursuing driver stood on his horn until the delivery truck moved enough to allow them to get by, which delayed them enough that they lost sight of Zeke. They continued on driving in the same direction, counting on traffic to slow Zeke down again, allowing them to catch up.

As Zeke continued driving north he spotted several car dealerships and pulled into one of the lots.

He cruised slowly around the lot until he saw someone stop a car in front of the showroom, then the person got out and went inside. Zeke pulled up behind the car, stopped and got out. Then he walked up to the driver's side window, realized that the car was running, jumped in and slowly drove away.

Zeke then drove to the nearest exit and resumed his journey north. He had only gone about a mile when he glanced in the rear-view mirror and spotted his pursuers behind him.

"Dammit!" He yelled, and hit the accelerator pedal.

Just then he saw the Silver Springs, Maryland, sign pass by and called Ezzy.

"Grandpa, I thought I lost 'em, but they're on me again. I just passed the Silver Springs city limits sign."

"Good. We're in position. Make your way to Downtown Silver Springs. Turn right on Bondifant Street. That will put you heading northeast into a housing area. Turn left on Cedar and then take an immediate right on Dartmouth Avenue. Dartmouth is one way and you'll be going the wrong way. Watch for my signal there."

Zeke made his way toward Bondifant Street, weaving in and out of traffic. Trying his best to evade his pursuers. Concerned that they would be spotted by police, they changed their tactics and decided to just keep their quarry in sight until they had an excellent opportunity to take him out.

Finally Zeke spotted Bondifant Street, turned right and accelerated, but his pursuers hung with him. Then he spotted Cedar and turned left.

Just as he turned, a motorhome pulled across the lanes behind him, blocking his pursuer's path. The driver sat on the horn and tried to swing around the massive vehicle. Other cars were also stopped, and honking their horns as well, but the driver kept moving the camper slightly, each time cutting off Zeke's pursuer as he tried to go around. Finally the camper drove away. The pursuers looked in the direction that Zeke had gone, and spotted Zeke's car in the distance, on Dartmouth Avenue.

After Zeke turned left on Cedar, he had made an immediate right onto Dartmouth, going the wrong way. But seconds before, a pickup truck had pulled across Dartmouth, blocking traffic just before the intersection. As Zeke turned onto Dartmouth, Ezzy was standing on the opposite side of the street and signaled him to stop. Zeke stopped and waited. When Ezzy saw the camper pull away, he waited until Zeke's pursuers saw his car, and then signaled Zeke to make a U-turn and pull into a waiting enclosed car hauler trailer that Ezzy was standing beside.

Zeke quickly drove his car inside the trailer. Just then, his pursuers turned right onto Dartmouth, going the wrong way of course. A police cruiser, waiting behind the car hauler trailer, pulled out with lights flashing and gave chase. The driver tried to evade the police car, but, having no escape route, gave up and stopped the car. Shortly both men were on the ground in handcuffs.

Zeke climbed out of the trailer, helped Ezzy shut the door-ramp, then they climbed in the dually pickup towing the trailer and drove away. Zeke returned the stolen car to the dealership, apologized for the terrible misunderstanding, and they loaded into the trailer the shot up rental car that he had left behind.

That night, Kathy and Ralph met Zeke and the others at the house of one of Ezzy's buddies.

"Zeke," Kathy said in frustration, "I just can't imagine where he might have gone. I don't believe it would be far, but I just don't know. It's driving me crazy with worry!"

"There has to be somewhere that Ray would feel safe. Somewhere that no one else knows about but maybe you and him."

Kathy thought a bit, then said, "Appalachian Inn."

"Appalachian Inn?"

"Yes, it's a bed and breakfast near Greencastle, Pennsylvania. He and I have stayed there before to get away from it all. It's peaceful and so beautiful. We get a local pilot to fly us up to a grass strip about a mile from the Inn. It's called the Cumberland Valley Airstrip. We love to go there. It's wonderful."

"Papa?"

"Hang on, I'll look it up on your laptop."

Zeke looked over Bernie's shoulder as he completed his search and measured the distance.

"Fifty miles northwest of Davis Airport. I can have you there in fifteen minutes from wheels up."

"Let's do it. Kathy, you're coming, right?"

"Are you kidding me? Of course, I'm coming!"

"Me too?" Ralph asked.

Bernie looked at Ralph and said, "I don't see why not… how much do you weigh?"

"325."

"I'll need to check weight and balance. I can carry 847 pounds, but we don't need to fuel up, so we should be okay."

The following morning, Bernie touched the Maule down on the grass strip and taxied to parking. After the aircraft was tied down and secured, they set out toward the Appalachian Inn. When they arrived, Kathy went in to see the landlord.

"Oh, hi Kathy!" She said, "We didn't expect to see you this time. Ray said that he was by himself."

"It's a surprise. I've brought some friends to see him, too."

"How lovely! He's in number three. Just go on up."

Kathy knocked on the door. There was no answer. She knocked again and Ray answered the door.

"Yes? I—Kathy!" He pulled her inside, hugged her and said, "My love, what in the world are you doing here?"

"I've brought some friends."

"Oh? And who—." Then he looked outside and saw Zeke.

"Ezekiel! Oh my God, you're alive!" He said as he hugged Zeke. "I thought we'd lost you young man. Damn it's good to see you!"

"It's good to see you too, Boss. We've been worried about you, especially Kathy."

Ray turned to Kathy. "I'm so sorry Love. I didn't want you to worry, but I was afraid that you would get hurt when they tried to get to me. I had to go, and quickly. I'm so sorry to worry you."

"I understand honey. But they came after me anyway, and Ralph protected me."

Ray looked at Ralph. "Ralph, man I owe you more than my life. Kathy is my life." Then he tried to reach around him to give him a hug.

"It was my pleasure Ray. Besides, I haven't had this much fun since I played with the Packers. I got to sack some lowlife that shot a hole in my tie. I got to ride in a cool little plane. You guys are a blast."

"Ralph, I love you man!" Ray said and hugged him again.

Then Zeke said, "Ray, this is my father-in-law, Bernie Gonzales. He flew me to DC and also flew us out here."

"We finally meet," Ray said and shook Bernie's hand. "I feel that I already know you; we talked so much on the phone while we were making the honeymoon plans for Abril and Ezekiel."

"It's good to meet you, too, Ray. What you, Ezekiel, my son and Ben have accomplished is nothing short of historic."

"Well, it could be historic if we can pull it off. Right now we need to get back and try to get our ducks in a row before the hearing eight days from now."

Bernie looked at Kathy, winked and said, "I think we can wait one more day, don't you Kathy?"

Kathy smiled and took Ray's hand. "I think so."

"Good. We'll fly back to Davis this morning, and I'll pick you two up at Cumberland Valley tomorrow afternoon. That sound good?"

"That sounds wonderful!" Kathy said as she smiled and looked at Ray.

***

Back at Ezzy's buddie's house, he and his crew were feverishly working to organize a counteroffensive to the Senate Armed Services Subcommittee's agenda during the meeting set for December 5th. Anticipating the tone and intention of the agenda was very speculative. Little was being said about the upcoming meeting except that Ray's report would be the focus.

The general thinking among Ezzy's contacts was that the committee chairman, Senator Spade, would attempt to quash the report as unsubstantiated claims and put it on the back burner, effectively burying it in the bureaucratic morass of DC politics until time forced it into obscurity.

Zeke contacted Kathy on the morning of the day that Bernie had scheduled to fly in and bring her and Ray back to DC.

"Hi Kathy, are you and Ray having a pleasant time?"

"Oh, yes!" Kathy replied. "We've just had breakfast and was planning to go for a walk before Bernie arrives."

"Well, things are going great here. It looks like Grandpa and his buddies have worked out a doable plan. You won't believe who these guys know and what they've been up to. It's amazing. But the thing is, we're doing okay here, so why don't you and Ray stay a few more days. Chill, enjoy yourselves and don't worry. Things are looking up. Tell Ray not to worry. We have this."

"Thank you, Zeke. That's wonderful news! Thank you so much! We'll see you in a few days. Bye!"

"That sounded very positive," Ray commented.

"Oh, it was," Kathy replied.

"Well?"

"We'll have plenty of time for that walk." Then she took him by his hand and led him toward their room. "We have something else to do right now…"

On December 3rd Ray and Kathy were waiting as Bernie and Zeke landed at Cumberland Valley Airstrip, taxied in and swung the agile bird around, opened the door and motioned them into the plane.

"Have a good time?" Zeke asked.

They just smiled at one another and Ray replied, "Oh, yes. Simply marvelous."

"I think I mentioned that the plans for the meeting were amazing when we talked the other day."

"Yes, Kathy told me."

"The consensus is that Senator Spade has intentionally scheduled the hearing right before the Christmas recess, hoping to force the process to move more quickly. So, your report, on its own, didn't hold much water. But, we thought we were alone in this investigation. And we were wrong."

"Oh yeah? How so?"

"Well, you recall that you told me that you didn't have any reliable contacts with the DIA?"

"That's right."

"If you had, you might have been able to find out that they were also running an investigation on General Zhang."

"Oh, really. Well, I'll be damned."

"And something that none of us anticipated; Grandpa's old outfit, INSCOM was running one, too. We have some serious horsepower planned for the meeting. It should be interesting…"

"Well, I'll be damned!" Ray said to himself and looked at Kathy. She smiled and kissed him.

***

10:00 a.m., December 5th, United States Senate Chambers, Capitol Hill, Washington, D.C.

Within the chambers of the US Senate, Senator Jake Spade, chairman of the senate armed services committee, had just brought the meeting to order. Upstairs in the gallery, Zeke's parents and grandma, along with Abby, Luís, Bekah and Ben Breen intently watched the proceedings.

"Ladies and gentlemen, esteemed colleagues, I bring before you the main agenda item; the Senate Armed Services Subcommittee investigation into corruption allegations and collusion by the U.S. Consulate in Hermosillo Mexico with Chinese General Quan Ji Zhang.

"This investigation was launched after my esteemed colleague from Virginia, Senator Roland Martel, was handed a report made by a now-deceased senior agent of the U.S. Drug Enforcement Administration. Senator Martel brought it to my attention and I felt that, since the implications were a threat to the sovereignty of the United States, an investigation was in order. Unfortunately, during the investigation we learned that the senior agent and his associate were deceased. Our ensuing investigation found no corroborating evidence that any of these alleged facts and allegations are true.

"Therefore, at this juncture, Senator Martel and I feel that…"

Suddenly the Senate chamber doors opened and the Director of the Drug Enforcement Administration entered the chambers, walked down the aisle and stopped at the front row of seats typically used by those being interviewed by the senate, and remained standing.

Senator Spade watched him as he walked down the aisle and asked, "What is the meaning of this?"

"Senator, I'm Rockwell Susskind, Director of the Drug Enforcement Administration."

"I'm aware of who you are Mr. Susskind, what I wish to know is why you are interrupting this meeting."

"If you'll bear with me, sir, that will become apparent momentarily."

The chamber doors opened once again and Lt. Gen Wilberforce Stenson, Director of the Defense Intelligence Agency, Major General Winston Bradley, Commander of INSCOM (U.S. Army Intelligence and Security Command), and General Regis Abernathy, U.S. Marines, retired, all came down the aisle in single file and proceeded to stand in front of the row of seats where Susskind was standing.

"Mr. Susskind, I can tolerate no more of this disruption. Please explain why these gentlemen have now joined you."

While the generals were taking their seats, General Ashurst Kent, U.S. Army retired, and former commander of INSCOM, called the Deputy Sergeant at Arms aside and gave him some instructions, then he entered the chambers and joined the other generals.

"Mr. Susskind, you have one more minute before I call the Sergeant at Arms."

Just then the Deputy Sergeant at Arms opened the chamber door, stepped through and announced in a bold voice, "Mister Chairman, distinguished senators, Congressional Medal of Honor Recipient, Ezekiel J. Sikes; U.S. Army Retired!"

The generals immediately jumped to attention as Ezzy entered the chambers and walked down the aisle. When he got about half-way down the aisle, four more men entered the chamber behind him and Ezzy announced, "And his band of retired Army Intel miscreants."

Ezzy proceeded to the end of the aisle. At that point, all of the generals saluted. He turned, came to attention, returned their salute and said, "Thank you gentlemen."

Then his associates joined him and they all sat down.

"It is indeed an honor to have a Medal of Honor recipient in our midst, Mr. Sikes," Senator Spade said, "However, Mr. Susskind, I fail to see what any of this has to do with the present hearing, which is still in progress."

Just then, two Army officers quietly came into the chambers and took seats in the back.

"Senator, we are all here to either offer additional testimony, or support, to those who are prepared to testify today."

"I see no one on the docket who is scheduled to testify at this hearing. Who are these witnesses?"

"We were unable to get the witnesses on the docket in time for this meeting, Senator. However, we have an audio file to play first. After the recording is heard, it will become very apparent that this distinguished committee will want to hear all of the available testimony."

Senator Spade began, "This is all entirely out of order and is doing nothing more than making a mockery of these proceedings—."

"Senator Spade," Senator Roland Martel cut in, "While I agree that decorum has been violated, I'm certain that these honorable men have not come before this committee because they wish to make a mockery of this august body, or these proceedings. The director of the DIA, the commander of INSCOM, the director of the DEA, General Abernathy and General Kent all represent an unprecedented presence on the floor of this great and historic hall. The very least we should do is hear the testimony."

Senator Spade paused, drumming his fingers on the table, then said, "I concede to the Senator from Virginia. However, if I see an attempt to subvert justice within this unprecedented display, despite the importance of these men to our nation, I will call the Sergeant at Arms and have every one of them removed from the building."

"Very well," Senator Martel replied, "That is your prerogative. Mr. Susskind, present your evidence."

"Thank you, Senator," Susskind replied, and produced a small digital audio player from his coat pocket and asked, "Can I get a microphone over here please?"

An aide brought a microphone and handed it to Susskind. "This first digital recording, obtained by INSCOM in Red China, is of a telephone conversation between Chinese General Quan Ji Zhang and Alfred Chase, Deputy Chief of Mission, U.S. Consulate, Hermosillo, Mexico."

Susskind played the tape, which discussed the deposit by General Zhang of 55.8 billion pesos in the Banamex bank in Hermosillo. Then they went on to discuss Velazquez and his role in the upcoming construction project, and the percentage of cut of the contract amount to Chase and the ambassador for their cooperation.

After the recording ended, Senator Spade said, "Mr. Susskind, I must say that is very troubling, but also highly circumstantial. And

I must remind you again, unless you can substantiate the origin of these recordings, I must dismiss your evidence and move on."

"I understand, Sir. This next recording was obtained in Mexico by the DEA, under authority of the Foreign Intelligence Surveillance Act of 1978. It is a telephone conversation between Ambassador Samuels and another, high-level government official."

Susskind began playing the recording. Senator Spade's voice was readily recognizable and he objected immediately.

"This is fabricated nonsense! I will not stand for this in the Senate chambers. Sergeant at Arms!"

Senator Martel stood and yelled. "Belay that order! Mr. Chairman, you are out of order. Mr. Susskind has the floor. This committee has requested the audio files be played, and they will be heard. Mr. Susskind, please resume the audio."

At that point, Senator Spade attempted to leave the room.

"Sergeant at Arms; at once!" Senator Martel ordered, "You will keep Senator Spade in his seat."

Susskind resumed the playback. Spade squirmed in his seat as the conversation revealed, in no uncertain terms, that he was the one who ordered the assassinations of Ray, Zeke, Ben, Luís and their family members.

After the recording stopped, Mr. Susskind raised his arms, pointed to opposite sides of the chamber and called out, "Marshals!" and then pointed both fingers toward Senator Spade. "Assist the Sergeant at Arms, and arrest Senator Jake Spade on charges of murder, espionage, threatening the sovereignty of the United States of America, as well as corruption and collusion with the U.S. Consulate in Hermosillo Mexico and Chinese General Quan Ji Zhang."

Four U.S. Marshals approached the Senator, two from each side of the room. One began reading the senator his Maranda rights under the US Constitution. After that, the Sergeant at Arms instructed the Senator to stand up and go with him.

Just as the senator stood, Izzy left his seat and approached the podium. "Senator Martel, may I address Senator Spade?"

"Yes you may. And, on a personal note, it is an honor to have you here today, Sir. Please proceed."

"Thank you, Senator."

Ezzy looked at Senator Spade, standing there in stark humiliation, with the Sergeant at Arms behind him, and two US Marshals on either side. Yet Spade was obviously enraged as he glared down at Ezzy.

"Jake, you and I have been down a long, long road. We're old men, and we've seen a lot together. You stood with us and fought against those trying to cut funding that would have put the lives of my unit, and many other soldiers, in danger in Vietnam. We have worked together over the years on many such projects. You believed in America and fought for what you believed in. Why, Jake? Why have you done this?"

Spade looked away and said, "You wouldn't understand."

"Perhaps not. But as for me and my band of intelligence miscreants, who have just risked our lives yet again for our country, we are dismayed and saddened beyond comprehension by what you have done. And I believe that I can speak for these honorable men here with me today, and all true Americans, that they feel the same way. What you have done is beyond contempt. Beyond belief. But there are two more members of our entourage that you need to meet."

Ezzy turned around and motioned to the two military officers in the back of the room. As they came forward to join Ezzy he said, "We apologize for their uniforms. They are not military offices. The disguises were necessary due to the fact that several attempts have been made on their lives and they have been constantly hunted by assassins."

As the men approached, and the senator to recognize them, his eyes grew wide.

"This is impossible," Spade said, "You're supposed to be dead."

"No," Ray said, "You ordered our assassinations. But every command that you utter doesn't necessarily come to fruition. Agent Sikes and I are prepared to testify, not only corroborating the evidence that we gathered against you and your conspirators, but also to detail the many attempts to murder us and our families that you ordered. You are done, Senator. You are done."

"Ray, I don't believe that I could have said it better myself," Izzy commented, then continued, "I would just like to conclude by saying one more thing to Senator Spade if you'll permit me, Senator Martel."

"By all means."

"You know something, Jake? Right now I'll bet it sucks to be you."

In the gallery, everyone applauded.

Senator Martel glanced up toward the gallery briefly and then said, "Thank you, gentlemen. That was quite appropriate. I also have a brief statement for the record. In all the years of my participation within this great body; the United States Senate, an honor that has been faithfully entrusted to me by my constituents from the great state of Virginia, for the first time in my life, I'm ashamed for our nation. I'm ashamed for the United States Congress, and I'm infuriated at you, Senator Spade. Had I a weapon in my hand I would execute you where you stand.

"Sergeant at Arms, please remove Senator Spade from this building and deal with him appropriately. We will now call a short recess before we continue to hear evidence and testimony on this matter."

The evidence that was presented, combined with the testimony given to the committee that day, including intelligence gathered by the DIA in China on General Zhang, proved conclusively that Senator Spade, Ambassador Samuels, and Alfred Chase had conspired to commit murder. Also, Spade, some members of his staff, Ambassador Samuels, Alfred Chase, and several members of the US Consulate in Hermosillo, as well as Velazquez and General Zhang were implicated as being complicit in the planning of a clandestine military base built in the guise of a logistics and space port, with the sole purpose of facilitating a military attack on the United States.

Within days of this news hitting the media, Fox News announced, "Chinese billionaire General Zhang shot and killed during his arrest by government officials at his headquarters in Shanghai."

Other, Liberal Media headlines announced, "Hollywood elites stage push for more gun control."

Based on the laws established by the Espionage Act of 1917; "To convey information with intent to interfere with the operation or success of the armed forces of the United States or to promote the success of its enemies." The committee determined that colluding with General Zhang to build an enemy military base of operations in Mexico with the sole purpose of attacking the U.S. represented a clear and present danger to the security and sovereignty of the United States and charged all of the conspirators with espionage and treason. These crimes are punishable by death or by imprisonment for not more than 30 years or both. All participants were indicted for and eventually convicted of those crimes in federal court.

On January 5th, in the White House Oval Office, a ceremony was held to honor the actions of Ray, Zeke, Abby, Luís, and Ben during what had come to be called the Spade-Zhang Conspiracy.

"By now, all of America and the world is aware of the details of the Spade-Zhang Conspiracy." The president began, "But what has not been done, is to bring attention and accolades on the brave people who uncovered this conspiracy, and during October, November and December of last year, very likely saved the United States from being attacked and entering another terrible war, and for the first time, on our home soil. What they have done is no small feat, and now I am honored to present to our heroes these well-deserved awards. Our nation is in your debt and your heroic actions will never be forgotten."

For bravery above and beyond the call of duty, and exposing the Spade-Zhang Conspiracy, Senior Special DEA Agent Ray Alexander and Special Agent Ezekiel Sikes were awarded the Public Safety Officer Medal of Valor, and the Presidential Medal of Freedom.

For bravery above and beyond the call of duty, and exposing the Spade-Zhang Conspiracy, US Customs and Border Patrol Agent Luís Gonzales was awarded the Border Patrol Newton-Azrak Award, and for gunshot wounds received during a firefight with assassins from the Serpiente Drug Cartel, Luís was awarded the Border Patrol Purple Cross.

For bravery above and beyond the call of duty during a firefight with assassins from the Serpiente Drug Cartel, US Customs and Border Patrol Agent Jackie Williamson was awarded the Border Patrol Newton-Azrak Award.

For bravery above and beyond the call of duty by placing himself in an assassins line of fire for the sole purpose of fooling the assassin into believing that he had accomplished his task, U.S. Customs and Border Patrol Acting Patrol Agent in Charge, Ben Breen was also awarded the Border Patrol Newton-Azrak Award.

"And last but certainly not least," the President said, "Especially since she is carrying her and Agent Sikes' unborn child. For uncommon valor and bravery in simultaneously facing the overwhelming odds of, not one, but two hired assassins, and, while being attacked physically and fired upon, shooting and stopping those assassins, I am very proud to award Mrs Abril Esmeralda Gonzales Sikes with the Presidential Medal of Freedom."

Abby smiled and said, "Thank you Mr. President." And then reached up and gave him a kiss on the cheek.

The President smiled and said, "This entire ceremony was worth it, just for that kiss!"

After the ceremony, Rockwell Susskind, Director of the DEA greeted Ray, Kathy, Zeke and Abby, and congratulated them.

Then he said, "Ray, I'd like to see you in my office in the morning. I think we should talk about your promotion."

"Promotion, Sir?"

"Yes, I have several positions that I would like for you to consider."

"Well, Sir, no disrespect intended, but I'm happy right where I am." And then looked at Kathy, and added, "I believe that I can make the most contribution in my present position."

Susskind thought for a minute and said, "I value honesty, and I like your attitude. If you say you're most effective where you are, then that's fine with me. However, expect a full grade pay increase retroactive to the first of last year." Then he shook his hand and said, "And thanks again Ray, for all that you've done."

"Thank you Sir."

Kathy hugged Ray, and he kissed her.

Then Susskind turned to Zeke. "Special Agent Sikes, your future is wide open. We have great need for men like you. Where would you like to go?"

Zeke looked at Abby, gently stroked her cheek and said, "I've put myself in harm's way far too many times, Sir. I just can't bring myself to do that to Abril again. I want to kiss her goodbye every morning on my way to work, see her beautiful face greeting me when I return home, and sit down to dinner with her and our kids every evening."

"I can certainly understand your motive for wanting that. What about a position at the academy?"

"I certainly appreciate your offer, Sir, but I'd like to take an Intelligence Research Specialist position at the Phoenix Field Division. My wife and I would like to be close to our Arizona family."

"Well then, you've got it, Special Agent Sikes. I'm glad that you're staying with the DEA. And don't worry about your pay, you'll keep your pay grade and law enforcement entitlements. All I ask is, if you decide that you prefer to be a Special Agent, contact me first."

As Zeke offered his hand in parting he said, "Will do, Sir. And thank you."

"Thank you, Zeke and Abby, for everything."

As they stood watching Susskind walk away, Zeke leaned over to Abby and said, "He'll never see me again for the rest of our lives."

Abby grabbed him around his neck and gave him a long, wet kiss.

***

Ajo Station Acting Patrol Agent in Charge, Ben Breen was promoted to Agent in Charge, Ajo Station, later that same month.

After an in-depth analysis of the computer network at Ajo Station, the IT guy discovered that Ray Addison had hacked into Zeke's email in an attempt to intercept information that was intended for Ben. Addison was demoted and transferred.

Luís was promoted to Assistant Patrol Agent in Charge, Ajo Station.

Four months later, on May 6th 2019, a call came into Zeke's section at the DEA Intelligence Research Lab, Phoenix Field Division.

One of the techs answered. "Oh, hi Abby. Yes, Zeke's here. He's just down the hall… Wait, here he comes now. … Tell him what? Okay, hold on."

Zeke walked through the door and started to return to his desk as the tech called to him, "Zeke, Abby's on the phone, she says to tell you that it's time."

Then the tech glanced at the phone, and looked back toward Zeke. "Okay, I'll tell—. He's gone! He was right there, and now he's gone. … Yes, dear, I'm, sure he's already on his way. Good luck!"

The tech hung up the phone and yelled, "Abby's having her baby!"

Zeke dashed through the doorway of his house in a panic.

"Hi Honey, could you get the diaper bag?" Abby calmly asked.

"Diaper bag?! You're in labor! You have to get to the hospital!"

"I'm not on fire, I'm just in labor." She said as she kissed him. "We have time. Settle down. I'm fine."

"Well, you'll be a lot finer when you're in our truck and we're heading to the hospital."

Then Abby reached to pick up her overnight bag.

"What are you doing?! Don't lift that! I'll get it."

Abby giggled. "Honey, you are so cute when you're like this."

"Thank you, Sweetheart. Now can we please just go?"

"Okay, I'm ready."

Zeke sighed. "Thank God."

As they walked toward the truck Abby said, "Now, no speeding. Take your time."

"Yes, Mam." He replied as he opened the door and helped her get in and buckle up.

He climbed in, started the truck and revved it up.

Abby gave him one of her looks and asked, "What did I just say?"

"No speeding."

"Very good. Now let's go. And take your time."

About halfway there, Abby grabbed her belly and said, "Oh, oh."

"What?!"

"Forget what I said about taking your time; my water just broke."

Zeke floored it. Moments later he screeched into the emergency room driveway, ran around and opened Abby's door, then ran into the emergency room and yelled, "We're having a baby, now!"

Techs responded immediately with a gurney and Abby was rushed to the maternity ward.

Ten minutes later, Zeke reached out and helped deliver a very irritated, but perfect baby girl.

"Happy birthday, Little One," He said as he gently placed her into Abby's waiting arms, umbilical cord still attached, and then said, "Look who I found," And kissed Abby.

"Awww, she's so beautiful!" Abby said with a wide and tearful smile.

"Just like her mama," Zeke replied and smiled. "Just like her mama."

Anna Abigale Sikes weighed seven pounds and six ounces.

Mama and daughter are doing perfectly fine

Dad insists on doing the 2 a.m. feedings; "Go back to sleep, you need your rest," he tells Abby.

"Husband, I've only had a baby," She replies, "I'm not recovering from heart surgery!"

Then Zeke gives her a kiss on her forehead, tucks her in and whispers, "Shhhh, go back to sleep Sweetheart, our daughter is calling me…"

About the Author

James A Graves, Jr. was born in Pensacola, Florida, and grew up fishing, swimming and scuba diving in the crystal clear water of Morrison Spring, located in eastern Walton County Florida, and hunting and exploring the swamps of the Choctawhatchee (Choc-taw-hatchee) River that runs from Alabama, through the Florida Panhandle, to the Choctawhatchee Bay near Ft Walton Beach and Destin.

Music was the creative spark that began a lifetime journey as a writer, musician and songwriter. James began writing songs after learning to play guitar at age ten, formed a Rock band at age thirteen and continued playing music throughout high school, college and beyond.

Chasing a fascination with airplanes, he joined the U.S. Air Force and was selected for an assignment with the Quick Strike Reconnaissance Test Project, Tactical Air Warfare Center, Eglin AFB, Florida. While on active duty he earned a degree from Saint Leo College.

After the USAF, James toured with the Southern Rock band, Erik the Red, as second lead guitar. Unfortunately, bills must be paid, so he was forced to resign from ETR and fall back on his electronics skills, accepting a job in the US defense industry with Cubic Corporation as a field engineer on the US Air Force Air Combat Maneuvering Instrumentation (ACMI) System at Eglin AFB, FL, the Luke AFB ACMI in Ajo, Arizona & the US Navy NAS Oceana Tactical Air Combat Training System (TACTS) in Manteo, NC.

James also continued pursuing aviation and earned his pilot's wings in 1984 at Dare County Regional Airport (MQI) in Manteo, North Carolina.

In 1987 he accepted an electronics technician position with the Federal Aviation Administration Airways Facilities Navigation/Communication Unit at Tucson International Airport, Tucson, Arizona. While living there he wrote and published his first Action-Adventure Fiction Novel, Aftermath: The Fight For Survival. A short time later he wrote and published his second Action-Adventure Fiction Novel, *Aftermath: The Deadly Game.*

In 1998 he transferred to the PNS Technical Operations Systems Support Center's Nav/Com Unit at Pensacola International Airport, Pensacola, Florida. While living on Garcon Point, near Pensacola, he wrote and published an expose'; *Assembly Line Justice: The American Drug War,* which was later retitled and published as a 2nd edition *Assembly Line Justice: How The American War On Drugs Has Failed.*

James retired in 2014 and moved to Payson, Arizona. There he wrote his third Action-Adventure Fiction novel, *The Wrong War,* published by Global Authors Publications.

James now resides on his ancestral property in Ponce de Leon, Florida.

www.ingramcontent.com/pod-product-compliance
Lightning Source LLC
Chambersburg PA
CBHW020632180626
46816CB00003B/932